Christine-

THE MAD TATTER

Never give up
on your dreams!

xoxo

J.M. Darhower

This book is a work of fiction. Any references to historical events, real people, or real places are used fictitiously. Other names, characters, places, and events are products of the author's imagination, and any resemblance to actual events or places or persons, living or dead, is entirely coincidental.

ISBN-10: 1942206143
ISBN-13: 978-1-942206-14-9

Overture

"Drop it! *Now!*"

A flashlight shined behind him, illuminating the darkness of the building. He instinctively opened his hand, the metal canister slipping from his fingers, clattering to the broken asphalt and rolling to a stop right at his feet.

He looked down at it for a moment before slowly turning his head, glancing over his shoulder, making sure not to make any sudden movements. The light blinded him as it bounced around his face. Blinking rapidly, he vaguely made out the blurry forms of two police officers, blocking his only exit, guns drawn and aimed right at his head.

Shit.

"Turn around," an officer yelled, "and keep your hands where we can see them!"

It took a moment for him to follow that order, caught off guard by the situation. Slowly, he turned the whole way around, raising his hands in the air in front of him. Streaks of black paint splattered his palms, coating his fingertips and staining the edges of his hoodie sleeves. Caught red-handed.

Or black-handed, as it was.

Son of a bitch.

In a blink they were on him, slamming him against the wall as they forced his hands behind his back. Gritting his teeth, he closed his eyes, feeling the rough coldness against his cheek. Handcuffs were tightly secured around his wrists, cutting off circulation, before he was yanked back away, covered in the still-wet paint.

"It's been a long time coming," an officer said, standing in front of him as his partner clutched the handcuffs from behind. He shined the flashlight intentionally right in his eyes, making him flinch as it stung, blinding him. "I knew we'd catch you eventually."

One

"Oh God... Reece... oh, yes, like that... right there!"

Her voice echoes through the small bedroom, bouncing off the walls plastered with movie star posters and pink princess bullshit. I'm a *'lights on'* kind of guy, like watching as a woman comes apart beneath me, *because* of me, but I had to turn them off this time.

I'm in a vortex of Disney, and there's no way I can keep a hard-on looking at that *bippity-boppity-boo* shit.

She's eighteen, I remind myself, the words pounding through my head as I pound into her. *Morally questionable, maybe, but legally fuckable.*

"Uh, God, yes, please... more, Reece... yes... yes... *yes*!"

Her toned legs wrap around my neck, propped over my shoulders, as I push into her hard, again and again. Each thrust, each slam of my hips into hers as I fill her as deep as a cock can humanly go, makes her let out a high-pitched squeal. I savor the sweet sound, wearing it like a badge of honor.

I make her sing like the pretty little birdie she is.

Lark. I only remember her name because she had it tattooed on the small of her back on her eighteenth birthday... exactly fourteen days ago. I gave her two weeks to let her tattoo heal, two weeks of inane texting and ridiculous flirting, before throwing her down on a bed and fucking the daylights out of her. I'm a man, yeah, and I was tempted the second I met her, but I'm also a professional.

Business first, then pleasure.

"Oh God… I'm gonna… I'm gonna… *uh*!"

I feel it as she comes, her body convulsing with pleasure, pulsating around me as I thrust hard and deep, keeping my rhythm. As soon as she's satisfied, as soon as I feel her body start to relax back into the bed, I let loose my own release.

"Fuck," I grunt, intense pleasure exploding through me as I come. I thrust a few more times before stilling myself, dropping her legs to the bed as I collapse on top of her, exhausted.

I stay there for a moment, catching my breath, as her hands explore my sweaty back, nails gently scratching at the skin. The rhythmic sensation relaxes me, lulling me toward sleep, until I feel her warm breath against my ear. She places a soft kiss on my cheek, her lip-gloss sticky. The intimate gesture makes my skin prickle, like it's trying to fucking slink away.

Danger! Danger!

Red alert, asshole!

Before she can kiss me again, I roll over off of her, discarding the condom in a small trashcan beside the bed as our naked bodies tangle up in the satin sheets. She lays facing away from me, body mostly covered by the flowery blanket, but her back is left exposed. My eyes trail down her spine, to the vibrant patch of ink.

Stunning.

Unable to stop myself, I reach out, my fingertips tracing the lines of the tattoo. Two birds framing her name in fancy cursive. Girly as shit, sure, but still goddamn beautiful.

At least it has meaning to her.

I wait until Lark falls asleep, her soft snores filling the room, before I slip out of the twin bed and scrounge up my discarded clothes, nearly tripping over a gigantic stuffed toy on my way to the door. *Un-frickin'-believable.* I practically dance down the hallway, still putting on my shoes and trying to fix my pants, as I head straight for the front door of the quiet townhouse.

Cold air blasts me when I step out into the night… or morning, rather. *Whatever.* My watch reads a quarter after five when I glance at it in the glow of the streetlight. In a little over an hour, the sun will start to rise, the sky lightening, another day dawning over Manhattan.

By the time I finally get to sleep, my alarm will go off for work. *Lovely.*

Reaching into the pocket of my black hoodie, I snatch out my pack of Newports, pulling out the only cigarette left. *Shit.* I stick it between my lips as I step off the front steps, mentally cursing myself.

My *last* cigarette.

I'd just bought the pack, determined it would last me all week, and it hasn't even made it twenty-four hours. But this is it for me. I'm done. I have to be. No more scrounging up change for something that takes years off my life, when I have too much to live for.

I have *her* to live for... and I made a promise.

A promise I desperately need to keep.

Crumbling up the empty pack, I toss it in the trashcan along the curb as I stroll down the street, pulling my hood up over my head to block out the chill in the air. Glancing around, it takes a minute for me to recognize the neighborhood I'm in, just a few blocks away from my apartment in the Lower Eastside, close enough to walk home.

I light the cigarette, inhaling deeply, relishing the burn in my chest as the nicotine soothes my nerves one last time. Come sunrise I'll be an insufferable prick, there's no doubt about it in my mind, but here, right now, in this moment, I'm as content as can be.

Which, for me, still tends to be pretty fucking miserable. There are moments—hours, days, *weeks*—when I wonder what the point of it all is, wonder why I even bother getting my ass out of bed in the mornings. But then I see *her* face, and she smiles that smile, the one that stole my heart the first time I ever saw it, and I remember. I remember why I bust my ass, why I fight so hard to be a better man, why I struggle to make my way in the world. I remember why I get out of bed, why I still try, even though it feels like I can do nothing but fail.

I do it all for her.

Even if she's probably better off without me.

The Mad Tatter

Buzzing echoes through the back room of the shop, the constant drone melding with the music pouring from the old, beat-up Sony boombox.

Tupac today.

What the customer wants, the customer gets.

The bass vibrates the long wooden shelf above my head, the song washing through me as I unconsciously mouth the lyrics, listening but not really hearing anymore. No, I hear nothing, feel nothing, *see nothing*, except for the rendition of Van Gogh's *Starry Night* splayed out on the table before me. The guy walked in this morning, his back a blank canvas, but in a matter of minutes he's going to walk out a fucking masterpiece.

Or partially one, anyway.

There's really no helping a fucked-up face. And Jimmy? Jimmy has so many piercings he looks like someone slammed the ugly bastard face-first into a tackle box.

The buzzing dulls as I pull the needle back and wipe away the residual ink and small beads of blood that surface. The art will take more than one session to finish, but I've managed to get a good bit of it laid out in our first sitting. I absently smack on a piece of gum—the same piece I popped in my mouth when I started hours ago.

I feel like I'm chewing on a wad of rubber, the mint flavor long gone, leaving a nasty taste in my mouth.

"Alright, Jimmy, how about jumping up and having a look," I say, cutting the power to the tattoo machine. The humming fades away, the room suddenly feeling too damn quiet, despite the thumping music.

"Badass," Jimmy says, grinning like a mad man as he surveys the ink in the full-length mirror off to the side, affixed to the bright blue painted wall.

Standing up, I tear off my black latex gloves and toss them in the trashcan when someone steps into the doorway. Ellie, the curvy

8

receptionist at *Wonderland Ink*, leans against the doorframe, gnawing on the end of a cheap BIC pen as she stares down at the ragged appointment book. Her bright red hair is pulled up in childish pigtails, like Pipi Longstocking in the flesh.

"Your six o'clock just called," she says without even looking up. "They're not gonna make it. Family emergency or something."

My eyes drift to the clock above the door. Ten till. Hell of a notice. It's a memorial piece I've been sketching for a week that would've taken the rest of the night to knock out.

"I rescheduled them for next month, so you have nothing else now until morning," Ellie says, glancing at me, a twinkle in her unnaturally blue eyes, so bright they sparkle like the diamond studs pierced in her cheeks. "Unless..."

I cock an eyebrow at her. *Uh-oh.* "Unless?"

"Well, we have a walk-in waiting."

I blow out a deep breath as I take off my blue Yankees hat and toss it on the desk along the side of my workspace. I run my hands through my light hair, gripping the locks in contemplation, making some of the wayward strands stick straight up.

I hate walk-ins. They're usually quick, and simple, and often not thought out, the impulse buys from people wandering by with shit else to do but mark up their skin.

Tattoos are art—I pride myself on being an *artist*. Maybe I'll never be the next Picasso, but I lost interest in bullshit like coloring between the lines of somebody else's pre-made pictures when I was just a snotty-nosed kid with a bucket of broken crayons.

And even *then* I preferred drawing on the walls instead.

"One of the other guys can't do it?" I ask, spitting my gum straight in the trash. There are three of us at *Wonderland Ink* at the moment—Kevin runs the place, while Martin and myself pick up his leftovers, so to speak.

"They're both in sessions right now," Ellie says. "Martin will be done in about an hour and can probably squeeze it then, but Kevin has appointments lined up the rest of the night."

I run my tongue across my chapped lips before biting on the silver hoop piercing near the corner of my mouth, considering my options. *Not like I have any.* As much as I want to say no... and I *really* fucking want to... I know I shouldn't. I *can't.* Money is money, and being as how I never seem to have enough of that, I'm certainly in no position to turn down any.

Sometimes you have to just lie down and take one for the team, no matter how degrading it feels.

Just fuck me and get it over with.

"Fine," I mutter, motioning toward Jimmy, who is still surveying his fresh ink in the mirror. "Let me finish up here first."

"Great," Ellie says. "Her name's Bridgette."

I bandage up Jimmy's back and quickly go over aftercare. Pointless, really, since I've inked him before. Once he heads off to the receptionist's desk to pay and schedule his next appointment, I hit stop on the boombox and pull Tupac out of the cassette deck, tossing it in the box beneath the desk for next time.

Off in the distance, I can hear buzzing as the others in the shop steadily work away. *Wonderland* is laid out sort of like a clinic, with a main lobby and separate rooms surrounding it. All of us spend more time here than anywhere else, so we relish having our own workspace, something we can call our own and do with as we please. Kevin prefers his colorful and chaotic, while Martin's room is a geek's wet dream, murals painted on the walls with memorabilia cluttering every inch of free space. Mine? Well, mine's pretty vacant.

I never got around to doing anything with it.

All that surrounds me for a moment is irritating silence as I clean up my station before an animated voice carries through the shop, loud enough to reach my ears.

"Oh, what about this one?" a girl exclaims. "No, wait, *this* one! I like this one much better!"

I can faintly hear the clang of the hanging album as whoever it is shifts through the pre-drawn tattoo samples that decorate part of the lobby near the door, mockups that had been conceived in a warehouse somewhere and mass-produced, sent out to hundreds of studios in dozens of cities, so thousands of jackasses walking the street ended up with the same exact designs branded on their skin.

For fuck's sake, please don't be my walk-in.

10

"This is the one," she says. "This is definitely what I want."

Seriously, I silently plead to whatever God/Buddha/Fairy fucking Godmother that is willing to listen. *Don't make me do something off that goddamn wall today.*

I haven't had a cigarette in a little over twelve hours, the longest I've gone without one in twelve damn years. I feel like a live wire, my muscles taut as parts of me spark and twitch, in danger of electrocuting whoever dares cross me. I ache, my mind erratic, making focusing a struggle. It has been the longest day of my life, running on little sleep and no nicotine, and I have a sneaking suspicion it's about to get a hell of a lot longer in a moment.

After thoroughly cleaning up, making sure everything is sanitized, I step out of the room and cautiously glance around the lobby of the studio, spotting a few waiting guys but only two females, the girls eagerly looking through the generic tattoos. *Guess they're mine.* I clear my throat to get their attention and am about to speak when one of them turns around and catches my eye.

I freeze.

Mouth hanging open, words on the tip of my tongue forgotten the second I set eyes on her: long brown hair, insanely dark eyes, and the tightest pink dress hugging the curviest frame. She doesn't have much up top, but fuck if her hips don't just beg for a pair of hands to grasp them as she's pounded into from behind.

The girl is a *goddess*, Aphrodite in the flesh.

Thank you, whoever the hell is above, for answering a prayer I didn't even know I had.

There's something about her, something familiar on a peculiar level. I don't know her, but I oddly feel like I could. Like she has a face I've somehow seen before, one that stands out in a crowd.

Her skin is smooth, the color of cream, and I instantly want nothing more than to run my tongue along every inch of her and find out if she tastes as sweet as she looks. The thought of doing just that momentarily distracts me, every other craving fading away.

I'm still tense, but I know exactly how I can take the edge off.

Changed my mind. You can definitely be my walk-in. "Bridgette?"

11

The moment I speak the name, the girl beside the goddess stops looking through the drawings and turns around. "That's me!"

Damn.

I force my gaze to meet the other girls' as an equally strained smile touches my lips. I habitually bite the inside of my cheek. The goddess's friend is shorter, five-foot-nothing with dirty blonde hair and bright red lips. Usually I would find her attractive—she looks a bit like the pretty little Lark I made sing last night—but in comparison to her friend, she's barely a blip on my radar.

Shifting to thoughts of business, trying to focus, my eyes scan Bridgette, calculating. She looks like a cheery girl, the kind who pledges *Kai Beta Bullshit* and throws mixers on the weekend with the frat boys at *Alpha Kappa Douchebag.* I know the kind well. She'll want flowers, maybe, or else some hearts... something new school, frilly and feminine, with bright colors. Easy peasy, but boring as shit. "What can I do for you, sweetheart?"

"I want to get this," she declares, pointing at a picture on the wall beside her.

Slowly, I step forward and survey the drawing: a red heart with a banner across it, surrounded by pink and purple flowers.

Hearts *and* flowers.

"I want the name Johnny written on it," Bridgette says, smiling proudly. "In pretty cursive, of course."

"And Johnny is your…?"

Please be your kid… or your father… or Johnny Depp, for that matter. I don't care if it's Johnny goddamn Appleseed. Anything but your—

"Boyfriend," she squeals.

Boyfriend. I stand there for a moment, looking between Bridgette and the drawing on the wall, suddenly feeling the urge to burn down the fucking shop to get rid of everything—and *everyone*—inside of it. A conflicted sense of integrity pesters me. I try to have standards, and well… this breaks every personal rule I have.

I open—and close—my mouth a few times, on the verge of trying to talk her out of her choice, certain she will someday regret it, when amused snickering distracts me. My gaze shifts to the goddess on Bridgette's left as the girl fights, and fails, to restrain her laughter.

"What's so funny, A?" Bridgette asks, looking at her friend.

"Nothing," the girl says quickly, a slight flush overcoming her cheeks at the attention as she waves us away. "Was just thinking about… something. It doesn't matter. Don't mind me."

Bridgette shrugs it off and turns back to the drawing, launching into detail about how she wants it done and where and why, while I can't tear my eyes off of her friend. She fidgets at the attention, still trying to contain her smirk, her face only growing redder under my intense gaze. I can feel my cock stirring, hardening and straining the fabric of my ratty old jeans as my eyes scan her slowly, assessing like I always do when I meet somebody.

Working in this business taught me to be a pretty good judge of people, and this girl… this goddess… is a virgin. Probably not a sexual one, but she is undoubtedly a blank canvas, untainted, *uninked*, and I love nothing more than being first. Very little is more thrilling than conquering the unconquerable… attaining the unattainable… claiming the unclaimed.

Doing what everyone says I can't do.

Proving them all wrong finally.

Others may have touched the goddess, and maybe even marked her for a short time, but I want to be the one to leave the lasting mark.

I want my touch to be permanent.

"Sounds great," I say, reluctantly turning my focus back to Bridgette when she stops yammering. *Business first, then pleasure.* "I'll get it drawn up for you and then we'll get started."

Nodding politely at the girls, I grab the picture from the album and take it back to my workspace. Before I start, I pop a fresh piece of gum in my mouth.

It doesn't take me long to play copycat and sketch a rendering of the tattoo, grudgingly adding the name 'Johnny' in script and hoping like hell they'll be together for a long time after this. Shaking my head, knowing the odds aren't in their favor, I head back out to the lobby, my footsteps faltering when there is only one girl waiting now.

13

The goddess.

Christ, it's peculiar.

I can't put my finger on it, but for some reason she's striking.

"Is your friend...?" *Please tell me she came to her senses.*

"Bridgette just walked outside," she says, motioning toward the glass front door of the business. "She said she needed a quick cigarette."

The word is like a trigger on a gun, pulled carelessly, a bullet haphazardly striking me right in the gut. *Shots fired!* It feels like hot iron, the yearning burning my insides. And I know just one cigarette, one puff of the nicotine-laced smoke, will be all it takes to cure what ills me, to put out the fire raging inside.

Too bad I promised *her* I would kick the bad habit, no matter how miserable quitting makes me.

Fuck knows she's probably disappointed enough by everything else I've done.

"So, uh, have you worked here long?"

I raise an eyebrow when the goddess attempts small talk. "A few years now."

"Oh. Cool. You must be good, you know, to work here. Bridgette says this place is one of the best in the city."

I chuckle as she wrings her hands together in her lap. Nervous. "I like to think I know what I'm doing."

In more ways than one...

Before she can respond, the door to the shop opens and Bridgette steps back inside. The odor of smoke clings to her, calling to me, making my body twitch and my skin itch. I want to spray her with Lysol and send her right back out the door, far, far away from me.

Clearing my throat, blowing out a deep breath to try to shake it off, I motion for the girls to follow me to my room. Goddess takes a seat in a folding metal chair off to the side as Bridgette climbs up on the reclining tattoo table. Quietly, quickly, I tweak the drawing to her specifications before printing off the stencil and positioning it on her body... on her chest, over her heart.

"That's where he is," she says dramatically. "In my heart. He'll be there forever."

14

Unlikely. Give it a decade, and if she even remembers he exists, she'll probably want nothing more than to wring his fucking neck.

"Choose some music," I say, kicking the box out from under the desk. It's packed full of old tapes I've accumulated over the years, a little something for everyone.

"Cassettes?" Bridgette asks, shifting through them. "Do these things even still work?"

"They work perfectly fine," I say. "Pick your poison."

Bridgette settles on Bon Jovi. I shove it in the boombox and press play. After putting on a pair of black gloves, I flip on the tattoo machine and set to work, sighing exasperatedly when Bridgette cries out the second she feels the needle against her skin.

Low pain tolerance.

"You and Johnny been together long?" I ask curiously, trying to divert her attention off of the pain. The more she flinches, and writhes, and tries to slink away, the longer this session will take.

"Yes," she says. "We're going on six months now."

I try not to, but I cringe. Only six months? "You know tattoos are permanent, right? They're a bitch to have removed."

She laughs. "Of course, but I'm not worried. Johnny and I will be together forever."

"Good to know," I mutter, once more ignoring my common sense and continuing on with her tattoo. Again, what the customer wants, the customer gets.

I work diligently, trying to pour myself into the tattoo, but the tedium of the design doesn't interest me and the goddess in the corner keeps distracting me. My eyes shift her way whenever she speaks, or moves, or even fucking *breathes.* I want to block her out and focus on my work, but it's hard to disregard her presence. I can even smell her perfume every time she shifts around in her seat, slowly scooting closer to where I sit, the sweet scent sending shivers down my spine when I inhale deeply.

Fuck.

The girl has magic wafting from her, entrancing me, her body calling out to me in more ways than one. I'm not sure what's tempting me most at the moment. Cigarettes suddenly seem the least of my concerns.

The tape is flipped once before I finally finish my work. I shut off the machine, the humming dying as I move away from Bridgette. "Give it a look, sweetheart, and let me know what you think."

She jumps up, practically running to the mirror, and lets out a squeal of excitement. "Oh my God, it's perfect!"

I stand and tear off the gloves, throwing them in the trashcan. Bridgette continues to gaze in the mirror as I lean back against the table and turn to her friend. "Your turn?"

Her eyes widen slightly at the question as she shakes her head. "Oh, no… no way… not *me*."

I cross my arms over my chest. "Fear or repulsion?"

"What?"

"There are usually two reasons people snub tattoos—they're either afraid of the pain or they don't like the art. So which is it?"

She hesitates. "It's just that, well… it's like you said. They're permanent."

"So you're not a fan."

Goddess's eyes shift to her friend as she continues to admire her fresh ink in the mirror. "I am… sometimes. But other times, you know..."

Other times they're senseless pieces of shit, stupid mistakes you can never completely fix. You can cover a tattoo, or try to have it removed, but parts of the original always leave a mark on a person.

I understand that. I live it everyday.

"Tattoos are personal… or, well, they should be. What's good for someone won't be for everyone else. You just have to find something that's you."

"And I haven't," she says. "I haven't ever found anything. I don't know what that something could be."

I reach past her and snatch one of my business cards off of the desk. I hold it out to her. "Well, if you ever want to figure it out, you let me know."

Goddess takes the card, blush staining her cheeks. Her brow furrows momentarily as she reads it. I watch her mouth slowly move, silently reading the words, and nearly moan out loud, imagining those lips wrapped around my cock.

This girl is sin in disguise, lust embodied, unleashed on earth to taunt and tease me.

I surrender.

"Reece Hatfield," she says, glancing back at me. "That sounds familiar for some reason."

"I don't know why it would."

She ponders that for a moment before shrugging it off, pocketing the card. Kevin's name is the one everyone remembers. He's the moneymaker of the shop, the White Rabbit that draws the crowd into Wonderland. He's taken to calling me the *Mad Tatter* these days.

Bridgette swings around, excitedly raving about her tattoo as she pulls out some money, leaving a hefty tip. I smile politely, pocketing the extra cash, as Bridgette runs outside to call her boyfriend.

Goddess stands up then, smiling sheepishly as she smoothes some invisible wrinkles from her pink dress. "Nice to meet you, Reece."

"You, too…" I hesitate. "I don't know your name."

"Avery."

Avery… I don't think I've ever met an Avery. While I'm decent at remembering faces, I've always been terrible at names.

She starts to walk out when I reach over and grasp her wrist, stalling her. I don't even think about it when I do. It's instinct. I'm not ready for her to leave yet. Her gaze darts to my hand, startled, before she hesitantly meets my eyes.

"I mean it," I say, my voice low, earnest. "Let me know if you're ever interested in me, you know… exploring *you*. It would be my pleasure."

And most decidedly yours, too.

Two

The dark sky is spitting when I step out the front of *Wonderland Ink* at closing, sporadic raindrops falling, hitting the damp sidewalk around me. I hesitate right outside the door, fixing my hat so it's straight before pulling my hood up over my head. I shove my hands in the pockets of my black hoodie, lingering there for a moment as the door is locked up behind me.

"Night, Reece," Ellie says, elbowing me as she dodges past with Martin in tow. "Get some sleep, will you? You look like a dead man walking."

Silently, I nod, watching them head down the street, toward Ellie's beat up old Volkswagen Bug, as Kevin pauses beside me. He fishes around in his pockets, pulling out a pack of Marlboros, and holds it out toward me.

I stare in silence at the rumpled up red-and-white pack for a moment... and then another moment... and another fucking moment... trying to get my mouth to work to say no, but I know if I open it, all that will come out is a pathetic whimper.

Man, after the day I've had? I'd *kill* for one.

After another moment, I shake my head, using every ounce of my willpower to look away from him.

He shrugs, popping a cigarette between his lips before pocketing the rest of the pack. He blocks the raindrops as he lights it, taking a drag so deep that it makes even *my* chest ache. He exhales slowly through his nose, casting me a wary look. "You finally quitting?"

"Yeah," I grumble, running my fingers along the edges of the lighter still in my pocket. "I said I would, so… yeah."

Kevin regards me for a moment before smiling and taking a step away, keeping his eyes fixed on me. He points at me, his fingers clutching the lit cigarette. "I don't care what anybody says. You're a damn good kid."

Before those words are even completely from his lips, I'm rolling my eyes. *Kid.*

"I mean it," he says, ignoring my reaction to the word. Kevin is in his late forties, was tattooing roughnecks way back when I was still in diapers. To him, I'm still that troublemaker he met years ago, the kid with too much time on his hands and not enough sense in his head. "You might be a little rough around the edges, but I always saw the good in you. You wouldn't be working here if I didn't. And talent?" He lets out a low whistle. "I was admiring your work before I even knew who you were."

He salutes me before turning and strolling away.

"Ellie's right, though," he calls back. "You look like shit. Get some damn sleep."

I wait until Kevin is gone before lowering my head, glancing both ways as I quickly jaywalk across the street. I head straight for the small dive bar just down from the shop. *The Spare Room* is everything you'd expect from a hole-in-the-wall in the Lower Eastside: dim lighting and cheap booze, an outdated jukebox and the stale odor of old beer. The floors are stained, the stools are old, and the bartender doubles as an overworked therapist to the drunks he serves.

My kind of place.

People leave each other alone here. They don't judge each other here. We're all a little bit fucked up, broke as shit but needing to relax. Nobody looks at me like I don't belong here. I appreciate it.

I slide onto the wooden stool closest to the door… my usual stool… and rap my knuckles against the bar. The bartender shoots me a look, offering a nod in greeting, before sliding a can of Genesee my way. "Rough day?"

I pop the top on the beer and take a long drink before

responding. "You could say that."

He pours a single shot of whiskey and nudges it toward me, but I instantly motion for a second one before he can walk away. Bridgette left a decent tip, and I'm all too eager to spend it.

He pours another shot before moving on to someone else. I pick them up, downing the liquor quickly, and relax back in my seat. As I sip the beer, I pull out my lighter, gripping the cheap plastic as my thumb turns the metal flint wheel, creating a small spark, over and over and over again.

What am I doing here? I don't know. Out of habit, maybe... or maybe I just really don't want to go home.

I drink a beer, then another, all the while turning the wheel on the lighter, igniting the flame, cursing when I burn my thumb with it. *Idiot.* After tossing money on the bar to pay for all of my drinks, I walk back out.

I'm barely outside when my phone starts to ring. Something inside of me lurches, tightening at the sound. I reach for it, pulling it out, the face of the goddess from the tattoo shop still on my mind. *Avery.* I expect her to call eventually, but this soon?

I don't bother to even look at the screen. Hitting the button to answer, I bring the phone to my ear. "Yeah?"

"Reece!"

I cringe at the voice. *Lark.* "Uh, hey."

"You ducked out early this morning," she says. "I didn't get to say bye."

"Yeah, you know... work."

"I get it," she says. "What are you doing now? You want to come over? My parents are still out of town."

I pause on the street corner just down the block from the tattoo shop, my attention drifting toward a new construction site diagonal from where I stand. The entire corner is blocked off, the sidewalk extended out to divert foot traffic past the work area. The side of the abandoned building is covered with dark weatherproof tarps, including the concrete wall along the bottom, twenty feet tall, spanning over sixty feet long. It's little more than a box of black plastic, a far cry from the colorful onslaught that used to always greet me at this corner.

It's amazing how much shit changes when you're not looking.

The sight makes my muscles grow taut, a heavy sensation swelling inside of me, like I've swallowed lead weights.

It feels like I've been kicked in the gut.

The world is a little less bright today.

I'm exhausted, and it's starting to grow cold. The last thing I want at the moment is to be alone. "I'll be there in ten minutes."

Turning away from the construction site, I head in the opposite direction, back toward the townhouse I skipped out of at dawn this morning. I have a thing against repeat visits, especially this soon, but what harm can it do?

My world is already fucked up.

The damage is done.

The parts of me that aren't damaged, the part of my heart that still strongly beats, belongs entirely to somebody already... somebody who isn't good at sharing. Whatever's left—the broken, hardened parts of my soul—has no interest in ever being healed. I don't need God, or Dr. Oz, or Dr. Phil… I have all I need.

Fuck everything else.

Literally.

I live with a void most days, a bitter loneliness that a woman's touch eases, but it's only temporary. They satisfy the outside, caressing my skin, but no one ever gets further than that… and I prefer it that way.

So as wrong as I know it is, flirting and fucking my way through the female population, I have no intention of stopping, because very little ever feels right to me, anyway.

Lark is sitting on her front step when I make it there, sipping on something in a plastic cup, but she's not alone. Another young blonde sits beside her, the two of them dressed almost identically in jeans and boots and dark sweaters. I'd almost call them twins if I didn't know that Lark was an only kid.

I know, because she told me, along with every other damn thing about her, those two long weeks we texted.

"Reece!" Lark says excitedly, jumping up as a wide grin splits her face. She practically throws herself at me, wrapping her arms around my neck, and planting a kiss right on my lips. I dodge it the best I can, laughing under my breath, as I grasp her hips and push away.

"Hey," I say, glancing past her, at her friend, watching as the girl drinks what's left in her own cup before setting it down beside her. Lark turns around in front of me, leaning back against my chest, and starts to take a drink, but I steal her cup from her hand before she can. Bringing it up to my nose, I inhale, the concentration of alcohol nearly burning my fucking nostrils. I take a sip, grimacing. "Jesus, girl, what is this?"

"Banana Red."

"Banana Red *what*?"

"Mad Dog."

She giggles as she says it, while I just shake my head, taking another sip before tipping the cup over, spilling the rest out on the street behind me. The cheap bum wine is nothing to fuck with.

"What did you do that for?" she asks, eyes wide as she grabs the empty cup back from me.

"You shouldn't be drinking that shit," I tell her. "It's just one step away from drinking malt liquor from a brown paper bag. Who bought it for you, anyway?"

She rolls her eyes, crushing the cup, as she motions toward her friend. "Jenny."

I look at Jenny. "I'm guessing you're twenty-one, then?"

She smiles. "That's what my ID says."

Lark laughs. "I've seriously gotta get one of them. She's younger than me and they don't even question it."

Younger than me. "Eighteen?"

"Seventeen."

Jenny, oh Jenny… you're definitely too young for me.

"Well, if you'll excuse us, Jenny, your friend and I have some, uh, *business* to attend to," I say, tugging Lark toward her front door.

"Wait!" Lark says. "I thought she could join us."

I thought she could join us. The greatest words ever spoken, ones a man like me always yearns to hear. But while seventeen might be

23

the age of consent to the great state of New York, in my world, it's still too damn young to be playing these games.

"Sorry, pretty little birdie," I say, pulling Lark inside and slamming the front door, leaving her friend outside. "It's just you and me, baby."

She smiles… smiles like those words make her special, like she thinks I'm confessing she means something to me. I don't let her dwell on it, though. I can't.

I lead her right back to her bedroom, and fuck the memory of them right out of her head.

I fuck her until she's gasping, until the only word she seems to remember is my name. Fuck her until she convulses with pleasure, until she's exhausted and satiated, until she wants nothing more than to go the hell to sleep.

I fuck her until I forget… until I no longer feel anything… until my mind is a haze and I'm tricked into believing that's actually okay.

Because days always blur together in a collective stream of nothingness when I lose myself in familiar patterns, where nobody means anything and nothing really matters.

Nobody, and nothing, that is, except for my *little miss*.

"Seriously think about this," I say, sitting on the black leather stool in my workspace. It's Saturday, the shop's busiest day of the week, and my afternoon is fully reserved. Not with the usual clients, though. No, this is a special day. Two weekends a month and the occasional weekday, my schedule is blacked out for a VIP. *My* VIP. "It isn't a decision to make lightly."

"I know," she replies. "I already thought all about it."

"And you're absolutely positive?"

"Uh-huh."

She seems certain, eagerness in her expression telling me she isn't going to back down, no matter what I say. Sighing, I grasp my hat, turning it, cocking it on my head nearly backward. This shit is serious business. "Well, I guess if you're really sure..."

"I am," she says, matter-of-fact. "I want a dinosaur!"

Not flowers. Not hearts. Nobody's name.

Nothing feminine or frilly.

A fucking *dinosaur*.

I grin, reaching over and playfully nudging her under the chin with my tattooed fist. "That's my girl."

Lexie beams at my words, showing off the gap in her pearly-white chompers from her first missing tooth.

"You know the drill," I continue, waving her away. "Pick your tunes and we'll get this party started, Little Miss."

As Lexie noisily rifles through the cassette box, Ellie strolls to the doorway and pauses. She watches Lexie for a moment, smiling, before turning to me. "There's someone here to see you."

"Nobody should be on the books for me today."

"Nobody is," she says. "They just walked in."

I shake my head. *Hell no.* "Give them to someone else."

"They asked for you specifically," Ellie says.

"Nobody asks for me specifically," I say with a laugh. "They ask for Kevin and end up with me instead."

"Not this time. The girl's pretty adamant about seeing you. I asked why and she said… well, she said she wasn't sure."

My brow furrows. "She's not sure why she's here?"

"Nope."

My gaze drifts to Lexie momentarily, contemplating, before I sigh. *Please don't be somebody I fucked and forgot about the next day.* "Send whoever it is back here. I'll talk to them."

The music of the day is some boy band… the out-of-sync new kids on a backstreet or something. I feign annoyance, scrunching up my nose and dramatically groaning as I stick the tape in the boombox, earning an enthusiastic giggle. I knew she would pick it. It's the only damn reason I have a copy of it in my collection—for her.

I press play and reach into my desk drawer to pull out an array of sharpies, everything from plain black to the pinkest of pink. I spread them out on the desk for her to choose a color as my eyes drift to the doorway when the woman appears.

Goddess.

She's more subdued today, wearing a pink sweater and the darkest, skinniest skinny jeans, making her look curvier than ever. I scan her instinctively, exhaling slowly. Jesus, she manages to be even more tempting leaving so much to the imagination, like whatever is beneath those layers of clothes is possibly the eighth wonder of the world, and damn if I don't want to explore it.

Conquer it.

Check that shit right off my bucket list.

"What can I do for you today, Aphrodite?"

Her eyes widen, taken aback by the greeting. "It's Avery."

"I know," I say. "You change your mind about getting that tattoo?"

"Uh, no." Her brow furrows as she glances around the room with confusion, her eyes settling on Lexie. "I just came to… well, I don't know why I'm here, honestly."

"So I heard."

A few sharpies are ultimately chosen, of course… Lexie usually always wants a lot of color to match my tattoos. I have full sleeves, the whole way down to the faded words inked above my knuckles, and part of my back and chest done.

"Well, if it helps," I tell her, "I know why you're here."

"You do?"

"Yes."

Avery just stands there, not at all pressing me to elaborate, as I grab black and shove the rest of the sharpies aside. I lower the table, pushing the back of it up to form a chair for Lexie to climb up. She settles in, holding her arm on the armrest. I grab her gently, pinning her arm there with my left hand, as I start drawing on her bicep with my right. Lexie giggles, since it tickles, but she tries her best to stay still for me.

Good girl.

"What in the world…?" Avery trails off. "What are you doing?"

"What does it look like I'm doing?" I cut my eyes at her. "The

26

girl said she wanted a tattoo, so I'm giving her one."

"Her? You're giving *her* a tattoo?"

"Yeah, why not?" I ask. "Who am I to tell her no?"

"An adult," Avery says. "She's just a kid. It's your job to tell her no."

"Ah, well, I don't like to say no," I reply, "so I usually don't."

"But she's just a kid," Avery says again.

"So?" I cock an eyebrow as Avery takes a few steps into the room to get a better look. "It's not like I'm using the needle or anything."

"You should," Lexie says, chiming in excitedly. "I want a real one, like yours!"

"Not today," I say casually.

"Tomorrow?" Lexie asks.

"I don't work tomorrow."

"The next day?"

"You won't be with me."

"Next time I'm with you?"

"We'll see," I reply. "Ask me then."

Avery lets out a laugh of disbelief as she grabs the folding metal chair and drags it closer to take a seat beside me. I catch a whiff of her perfume and briefly close my eyes as the scent washes through me.

What the hell is she doing to me?

It only takes me about ten minutes to draw the outline of the T-Rex, then another five to color it in with shades of green and brown. As soon as it's finished, Lexie jumps onto my lap and wraps her arms around my neck, hugging me tightly, before running out. I can hear her screeching as she tears through the busy shop, growling and raising hell, showing her brand new tattoo to anyone who will look at it.

Chuckling to myself, I put the markers away and turn off the cheery pop music. My gaze shifts to Avery as she stares at the empty doorway, lightly biting her bottom lip.

"So you, uh…" She glances at me, raising her eyebrows as she seems to riddle it all out. "You have a daughter?"

"I do."

Avery smiles. "She kind of looks like you."

Understatement. Lexie is practically my clone, with her pale skin and wild hair and bright blue eyes that mischievously twinkle whenever she's up to something, which is pretty much *always*.

Instead of responding to that, I merely nod before changing the subject. "So you figure out why you're here yet?"

"No."

"It's out of curiosity," I say. "But the million dollar question is, what are you really curious about? Do you want to find something that's you, do you want to learn more about me, or...?"

"Or?"

I wheel my stool closer, gazing at her. "Or are you just curious what I can do to help you figure it all out?"

Avery is quiet for a moment, her breath hitching when I lean even closer in her direction, our knees touching. She's beautiful. I still can't put my finger on it. She's kind of like sunshine. She's bright. And warm. And yellow.

She's yellow.

I don't know how else to explain it.

"Maybe it's all three," she says eventually.

"Maybe," I agree, testing her as I reach out slowly, waiting to see how she'll react. I graze her cheek with my knuckles before tucking some hair behind her ear, grinning when she shivers from my barely-there touch. "I can't help you today, though. As you see, I've got the little miss, and well…" Standing up, I lean over and whisper in her ear. "The things I'd do to you aren't for the eyes of the innocent."

I pull away from her, turning toward the doorway when I hear the screeching tear through the shop, heading our way. Lexie bursts into the room, her hair all over the place, her eyes wild like an animal. "I wanna 'nother!"

"Another what?"

"Tattoo!" She points at her other arm. "I need a *try-terry-pops*!"

My brow furrows. "A what?"

Lexie growls, her eyes narrowed as she yells, "try-terry-pops!"

I stare at her, confused, as she holds her fingers up like devil horns. *What the fuck?*

Avery starts laughing. "A triceratops."

"Yes!" Lexie exclaims.

Five years into the fathering gig and I'm still not fluent in *kid-ese.* Her newfound toothless lisp doesn't help matters, either. I let out a chuckle as I shake my head, patting the tattoo table. "Let's do it."

Lexie picks out new music this time, but it isn't much better: the Spice Girls. I wheel my stool around to the other side of the table and flip up the other armrest, grabbing the sharpies and getting straight to work. Avery scoots her chair over even further to occupy the spot I had been in moments ago, and peeks over the table as I work.

"So you like dinosaurs?" Avery asks, glancing at Lexie, whose eyes light up with excitement at the question. The kid *loves* dinosaurs. It doesn't take her long to launch into it, rattling off facts and statistics, spitting out names I'm sure have to be made-up on the spot. What the fuck is a *Gasosaurus,* anyway? I remain quiet as Avery engages Lexie in conversation with ease, asking questions like she genuinely cares to know the answers.

It's nice, yeah, but weird for me.

I'm not sure how I feel about a woman I'm hoping to get naked talking to my kid like this. I try to keep those worlds separate for Lexie's sake.

Less messy that way.

I only do the head of the dinosaur, having no room on her skinny arm to fit its thick body. After shading it in, I set the markers aside and wheel my stool back against the wall. "There you go. One try-terry-pops."

"That's not what it's called," Lexie says defensively, looking at her arm. "It's a try-terry-pops!"

I grin. Exactly what I said.

Lexie jumps down, growling again as she bolts from the room back out into the shop for round two. I lean back against the wall, not bothering to shut off the obnoxious music, and glance across the table at Avery, noticing her mouthing along to the lyrics. She freezes when she catches me looking, her cheeks tingeing light pink.

It's a gorgeous shade.

Timidly, she ducks her head, refusing to meet my eyes. "I should probably get going."

I eye her intently as she stands up. "I work most days, so come by anytime."

"I wouldn't want to bother you," she says hesitantly. "I know you're probably really busy. So, I mean... I don't know... I shouldn't have even come today, but..."

"But you're curious." Her nervousness is endearing, but unwarranted. There isn't shit about me intimidating. "There's a bar just down the street. *The Spare Room.* I usually grab a drink after work. So if you don't want to see me here, you can probably find me there."

Her blush deepens as she nods. "I'll remember that."

Avery heads for the door the same time the growling once more tears through the shop. I glance over as Lexie bursts in, slamming right into Avery and nearly knocking them both to the floor. Avery startles, laughing, while Lexie barely misses a beat. She swings around to me, pulling her shirt up to point at her stomach. "Breaky-sores!"

"Brachiosaurus," Avery says quickly, translating.

I shake my head, reaching over to snatch Lexie's shirt back down, before tugging her into my arms. She giggles as I nuzzle into her neck, smothering her in kisses. "I don't think so. You know my rules. No more than two tats per session."

"But—"

"But nothing," I say, tickling her sides until she shoves away from me. "The long-necked brute can wait for next time."

"Next time," she echoes, her face lighting up. "It can be my real one! Right, Daddy?"

"We'll see."

Lexie is running off again before I can say anything else. I stand up, stepping toward the doorway as Avery walks out of the room. She lingers just outside my workspace, shooting me sly looks, like she doesn't *really* want to go. "Well... bye, I guess."

"I'll see you later, Aphrodite."

I watch her leave before cleaning up, putting the markers away and turning off the music. Shutting off the lights, I lock up my room and set off through the shop, greeting a few clients waiting to see the other artists. I can hear Lexie behind the receptionist's desk with Ellie, making all sorts of ruckus.

"Come on, Little Miss," I say, calling out to her. "Time to go."

Lexie shoots out from behind the desk, running for me. I hold my hand out, and grinning, Lexie slides her small hand into mine.

"I'm gone, guys," I shout, earning goodbyes from the others as I head for the door. Lexie skips along beside me, gripping my hand tightly.

"Where did she go?" Lexie asks when we step outside, her footsteps slowing as she looks around.

"Who?"

"The girl that visited you."

"Ah, she left."

I tug my daughter away from the shop as I glance down at her, my chest tightening at her expression. Suspicion clouds her eyes, like she isn't quite sure what to make of anything. Moments like this, she reminds me of her mother, and that isn't someone I like to think about more than necessary.

I raise an eyebrow at her. "What's wrong?"

"Is that girl your girlfriend?"

I let out a sharp laugh. "What? No. Of course not."

"Mommy says you have lots and lots of girlfriends."

I scoff. "I do not."

"Don't you like her?"

I blink a few times, taken aback. "Your mother?"

Wrong question to ask. I'll smile, for Lexie's sake, but I'm not sure I can lie about that with a straight face.

I'd be hard pressed to name someone I like *less.*

"No, that girl."

"Oh, uh… sure," I say. "She's nice, I guess. Why do you ask?"

Lexie shrugs. "If she's not your girlfriend, then you must not like her."

"I like Ellie and she's not my girlfriend," I say, unsure of how to explain it. "That means nothing."

"But that's different."

"How so?"

"Ellie doesn't give you goo-goo eyes, Daddy." Lexie laughs, dramatically rolling her eyes as if to prove her point. "Ellie says you have boy cooties."

"She does not."

"Uh-huh! She does."

"Did she really say that?" I ask, hesitating before shaking my head and backtracking. I'm seriously asking if someone thinks I have cooties? "Look, a guy can have friends that are girls without them being girlfriends."

"So she's your friend?"

"No… well, I don't know. We just met."

"Do you want her to be your friend?"

"Uh, sure." I shrug. "Why not?"

Lexie looks away from me and starts walking. Glancing down at her as we stroll, I contemplate her question, rolling her words around in my mind. Why did she just ask me that? "Lexie?"

Her eyes dart up to meet mine after a few minutes, the suspicion giving way to pure doubt. She's seriously questioning this shit.

"Do you want her to be *your* friend? Is that why you're asking?"

She hesitates before nodding slowly.

"You like her?"

Another nod.

"Why?"

Shrugging, she turns away again to look at her arms. "She likes my dinosaurs."

Three

I slide onto my usual wooden stool at The Spare Room. The bartender glances over, nodding once in greeting, before swiftly grabbing a can of Genesee and sliding it my way.

It's shortly before eleven at night on a Thursday, and I just finished up a grueling back tattoo of the solar system. My mind is still stuck back at the shop, continually critiquing my work, agonizing over mistakes and what I should've done differently, as I sip my beer, waiting for the alcohol to soothe my nerves. The bartender pours a shot of whiskey, forgoing asking about my day as he nudges it my way.

The high from my visit with my daughter has fully worn off, leaving me once more a frazzled, fucked-up mess of a man.

One who really wants a cigarette...

One who could use some company...

One who desperately needs to get laid.

It's getting to the point that I'm tempted to call Lark, even though I've been avoiding her all week.

The stool beside me shifts as I consider that, downing the shot of whiskey. I look over, doing a double take and nearly choking on the liquor when Avery casually slides into the seat. I stare at her, stunned, before a slow smile spreads across my face.

It's only fitting, I think, after spending all day sky-high in the solar system, that the goddess would appear before I fully crash back to the earth.

I say nothing for a moment, continuing to drink, as the bartender approaches for Avery's order.

"Uh, something fruity," she says. "Surprise me, I guess."

Hesitating, the bartender asks for her ID. She pulls out her license, and I peek over at it, like the nosey bastard I am.

Avery Nadine Moore. Twenty-one years old.

She's about as young as I suspected. I'm pushing the end of my twenties, thirty slowly creeping up on me. I feel a hell of a lot older some days as life tries to beat me down. But her? She has all the youth and innocence of someone not yet fucked over by the universe.

Lucky.

"Hey," she says shyly, peeking over at me when the bartender brings her a pink drink, something in a curvy glass that looks like it would come with a fruit wedge and a tiny umbrella in a classier place.

I nod in greeting as I cut my eyes her way, slowly scanning her. Her lips, a soft pink hue that matches the alcohol, wraps around the straw, her cheeks hollowing as she sips, her throat flexing as she swallows. I watch the motion, again and again, imagining her on her knees in front of me. I can feel my cock hardening eagerly, desperate to make that a reality.

"I'm glad you're here," I say. "It's nice to have some company."

"I'm sure you always have plenty of company."

"What makes you think that?"

"I know your kind."

I shift in my stool, turning slightly to face her as I finish off my beer and motion for another. "What *kind* would that be?"

"Oh, you know," she says. "Typical tattooed bad boy and his many admirers."

Huh. "You have much experience with that… *kind?*"

"Not personally, but I read."

"You read?"

"Yeah," she says. "You're starting to become somewhat of a cliché trope in romance novels, you know."

Surprised laughter escapes me. I should probably be offended by that, but I somehow feel a little lighter than I felt just moments ago. "You shouldn't believe the shit you read, Aphrodite. It's called fiction for a reason."

"So what *should* I believe?"

"Only what you know to be true."

She takes another sip of her drink before making a face and pushing it aside. "Okay, then… let's talk about what I know."

I nod for her to go on.

"I know you have a tattoo shop…"

"Work at one," I correct her. "I don't *have* anything… it's not mine… not even close. I'm just lucky enough to be employed."

"Okay, then… you work at a tattoo shop. I know you're there almost every day, and you have a daughter that I'm guessing few people actually know about. And... that's about it."

"So I'm an artist who works his ass off and tries to keep his private life private… what more do you need to know?"

"How about *why*?" she asks, gazing at me.

"Why is a dangerous question to ask," I reply. "The '*why*' is never as appealing as the '*what*'. It kills the fantasy, and all that's left is the reality, and trust me… that's not very pretty."

The reality? Classic case of fucked-up family spawning a degenerate son, then promptly disowning him when he proves he is, in fact, just as fucked-up as the rest of them.

"Well, maybe I don't like *pretty*." Avery shrugs a shoulder. "Maybe I like it ugly."

I chuckle. "That's good to know."

The bartender slings me a second beer, and I take a sip of it before turning to her again and changing the subject. "So tell me about you."

"I thought you were going to help me figure myself out."

"I'll help you with the why," I say. "But I want to know the what."

"There's not much to say, really. I'm a dancer."

A dancer. *Of course.* It's no wonder her body is so stunning. "That's cool. I've known a few dancers."

"Really?"

"Yeah, sure. Most were just trying to put themselves through college. We do what we have to do, you know? No shame in that."

"I, uh… what?" She gasps. "You think I… that I'm a *stripper?* Seriously? Do I look like one to you?"

My eyes scan her again. "You look like you'd make a good one."

She gasps again, playfully shoving me. "I'm a dancer. I *dance.* With my clothes *on.*"

"Ah," I say, laughing. "I guess there's no shame in that, either."

She rolls her eyes, the blush extending from her face down her neck.

"So where do you do this dancing?"

"At Juilliard, mostly," she says. "I'm in my fourth year."

"Bet that takes up a lot of your time."

"It does," she admits. "I practice every day, sometimes all night, depending on what we're rehearsing for. It doesn't leave much time for a life outside of it, although I try to keep one. It keeps me sane to have something else that's separate, away from all of that… something that's just mine, you know? That I can keep for just me."

"So in other words, you're an artist who works her ass off and tries to keep her private life private."

Avery hesitates, clutching her glass, her drink halfway to her lips as she considers that. "Yeah, I guess you could put it that way."

That's all I really need to know.

She finishes the rest of her drink, setting it down on the counter, as I motion for the bartender again. "Get her another one of these, and put it on my tab."

"You don't have to do that," Avery interjects.

"I know," I reply. "I want to."

Drinks flow, as does conversation, an easiness existing between us that unsettles me at moments, when she looks over at me, eyes half-lidded from a combination of the alcohol and a brewing desire. I can feel it oozing off of her, a familiar sensation I revel in, the feeling of pure, unadulterated lust making the air heady as it mixes with her sweet perfume. She knows what she's doing to me, with the way she gently bites down on her bottom lip as her gaze drifts to my mouth, like thoughts of kissing me consume her.

I'm not a big kisser, generally speaking, but damn if she doesn't make it tempting.

A few times she leans closer, and I follow her lead, but before our lips meet she pulls back away.

It's driving me fucking crazy.

I flirt, my voice low and smooth, and she absorbs every word, her body involuntarily reacting as she leans closer, our legs touching, my fingers occasionally trailing along hints of her exposed flushed skin. I've done this dance so much I could do it with my eyes closed, and it always ends the same way... naked and satisfied.

Time wears on, hours passing, before the bartender strolls by, slapping his hand against the bar to get our attention. "Last call, guys."

I glance at my watch. It's damn near four in the morning. I look at Avery, seeing the shock in her face as she realizes the time. "Crap! When did it get so late?"

Seeing as how the shop doesn't open until ten, and my first appointment isn't until noon, I have time to sleep off the alcohol. But based on her expression, I can tell she isn't so lucky. "What time do you have to be up?"

She laughs dryly. "I have a meeting at seven."

"You might be sober by then," I say, hesitating when she stands and stumbles over her own feet. "Or not."

I pay the tab, cringing when it takes nearly every penny in my pocket, and follow Avery outside, hesitating on the sidewalk in front of the bar as she stands along the curb.

I open my mouth, words forming in my mind that never make it past my lips. Before I can speak, Avery hails a cab and is gone without so much as even a "goodnight."

I stand there, staring at the taillights of the cab.

Blown off. *That's a first.*

Boom. Bang. Buzz.
  Blah, blah, blah.

My head pounds, magnifying the noises around the shop. I'm tense, my muscles taut as the remnants of a hangover linger in my system. I feel like one of Lexie's little wind-up toys, wound as far as it can go but never let loose. It's hard to relax, hard to unwind, without any kind of release. Everything is building up inside of me, needing to be purged, putting me further on edge as the hours slip away.

It's nearing ten o'clock at night, closing time, but the shop is still in utter chaos. I'm finishing my last job for the day, a touch up on a skeletal system I inked onto a guy's arms last summer, adding more detail and extending it to cover the top of his hands. I tried to talk him out of it, having a rule about hand tattoos, but the guy was insistent, despite knowing the risks.

I finish tattooing the last finger and pull the needle back, gently wiping the irritated skin. Surveying my work, I shut off the machine and sigh. "There you go."

I turn off the music, finding temporary relief to my headache without Metallica blaring above me, and head straight out of the room, not waiting on his visual assessment in the mirror. I go straight for the receptionist's desk, slipping in beside Ellie as she talks to a client, scheduling an appointment. I root around in her desk, ignoring the annoyed looks she shoots me, dodging an elbow jab as I steal a cigarette from her pack of Camels.

I'm lighting it before I even make it out the front door. I inhale deeply, the smoke infiltrating my lungs and soothing my nerves. Fuck, I haven't had one in damn near two weeks. Pocketing the lighter, I take another deep drag, savoring the harsh burn in my chest, when someone calls my name.

"Reece?"

I glance down the sidewalk at the sound of the voice, pausing when I see Avery. I exhale slowly, the smoke surrounding me in a cloud as she approaches. "Hey."

"Hey," she says, pausing in front of me, her brow furrowing slightly. "I didn't know you smoked."

There's something in her voice, something I know well. It's the same reaction I get from Lexie. *Disgust.*

I take another pull, holding the smoke in my lungs, before throwing the cigarette to the ground and tramping it out.

"I don't," I say, releasing the breath as a soft smile touches my lips. "I'm surprised to see you."

"Really?"

"Yeah, with the way you bailed out last night, I wasn't sure you cared to see me again," I reply, digging around in my pockets for a pack of gum. I pop a piece in my mouth to rid myself of the taste, to dull the still-lingering craving, and offer her a piece, but she declines.

"I'm sorry about that," she says. "I didn't mean to leave without saying goodbye, but... well..."

"No need to apologize. I get it."

"Do you?"

I nod. "You don't owe me anything."

She opens her mouth to respond to that when the door behind us opens, my client strolling out. He interrupts to tip me, thanking me profusely for the job, excitedly showing his hand tattoos to Avery. She laughs as the man struts off, turning to me as I pocket the cash. "Those look amazing."

"For now," I say. Give it a few months, I think, glancing at my own tattooed hands. They'll fade and blur and look like they were done in someone's kitchen with a cheap ink pen and a junkie's syringe. "So is that why you came by? To apologize?"

"Yes," she replies. "And I thought maybe we could pick up where we left off."

"Pick up where we left off," I echo, pausing before asking, "which was where, exactly?"

She laughs, motioning across the street. "The bar, I guess, and then wherever we go from there."

I cock an eyebrow at her. "What time do you have to be up tomorrow?"

"Not until afternoon."

"So no running away from me?"

"Not as long as you're done with me by morning." The

moment she says it, her eyes widen slightly. "I didn't mean it *that* way."

"Huh." I grin playfully. "That's too bad."

I tell Avery I'll meet her across the street as I go back inside the studio. I quickly clean up my workspace before locking my door and heading back to Ellie's desk. "Thanks for the smoke, El. I owe you one."

She eyes me suspiciously. "You're in a better mood."

"Yeah."

"You must've *really* needed that cigarette."

I offer only a shrug before heading out, going straight across the street. Avery is already sitting at the bar, a pink drink in front of her, with a can of Genesee to her left.

I slide onto the stool beside her, immediately picking up the beer. "You put this on my tab?"

"Yep."

"Yours too?"

"Yep," she says, taking a sip of her drink. "Picking up right where we left off, remember?"

I smile. "Good."

It comes easy for us once more, as we laugh and chat, flirting and drinking the night away. Our bodies are drawn together like magnets, slowly moving closer to one another as time wears on.

It's earlier tonight, not even two in the morning, when I can barely take it anymore. Avery sips on a drink—her third, forth, maybe even fifth. I watch her, reaching over and brushing my knuckles against her flushed cheek. I see her shiver from the touch. "You wanna get out of here?"

She nods, the corner of her lips tugging into a smile, as she continues to drink, quickly finishing what's left in her glass. I pick up my beer, chugging the rest of it, and stand up. I offer Avery my hand and she takes it without hesitation, linking her fingers with my strong, calloused ones. I stare down at them for a second as her thumb gently strokes my skin.

Is she doing that on purpose?

It's distracting.

"So, where are we going?" she asks when I lead her out into the cool night.

Her words slur. Definitely a lightweight. She's *drunk*.

I pause, turning to her. "Where do you wanna go?"

"Anywhere," she says, no hesitation.

I debate for a second. "Do you live on campus?"

Please say no.

"Yes."

Damn.

Her place is definitely out of the question.

My eyes dart across the street to the darkened tattoo shop, everyone gone for the night. We could certainly have privacy there, but it feels wrong. Mixing business with pleasure is a big ass no-no. I don't take girls to my place, though. Never that. I always go home with them, so I can slip out in the middle of the night and avoid the next morning awkwardness. Less messy.

I don't do messy.

Not anymore.

Fuck.

Hotel? No, that's just straight up demeaning, and not to mention expensive, unless I take her somewhere that charges by the hour. Jesus, I'm an asshole, but not *that* big of an asshole. Right?

"Well?" Avery says when I hesitate, sliding closer as she gazes up at me, practically wrapping herself around my arm. She's still stroking my skin with her thumb. "Where are we going?"

Fuck it.

"My place," I say, motioning down the street. "It's just a few blocks."

I hail a cab, much too impatient—much too drunk—to make the walk this time of night. Besides, if I put it off any longer, I'm liable to change my mind before we even get there. We make it to my building in a matter of minutes. Avery follows me inside and up the steps, to the second floor, fidgeting as I unlock the apartment door and motion for her to go inside. The moment I step in behind her, she practically throws herself at me, wrapping her arms around my neck and pressing her lips to mine.

I hesitate, startled by the feel of her kiss, before kicking the door shut behind me and kissing her back.

I don't bother turning on lights. Grasping her hips, I lead her through the darkened apartment and straight back to my bedroom, the last door on the right. We paw at clothes, fumbling with buttons and tugging on stubborn zippers, lips moving feverishly. She stumbles, barely able to stay on her own two feet as I lead her to my bed. She collapses into it, giggling, as I pull her shirt off and toss it aside. It's dark—too damn dark for me to see much of anything—but my lips explore her chest, caressing her soft skin.

"That feels so good," she moans, the words barely audible as she runs her hands through my hair. The drowsy tone of her voice slows my movements as I press barely-there kisses along her collarbones and up her neck. She loosens her hold on me and hums with contentment in my ear, the sound going straight to my cock.

Down boy.

Groaning, I pull back after a moment, knowing I have to stop. She's too damn drunk for this. She'll be passed out soon, and I know for a fact I'm not *that* much of an asshole. It takes a sick fuck to take advantage of a woman in this situation.

I gaze down at her, faintly making out her face in the darkness, watching as her eyes drift closed. I can only laugh at my shitty luck. We definitely picked up where we left off last night: unable to do anything.

Carefully, I move away and slip out of the bed.

She's fast asleep before I even make it out of the bedroom. I head across the hall to the bathroom and flick on the light, shielding my eyes from the bright glow. Shutting the door, I lean against it and let out an exasperated sigh.

I can't do it again.

I'm wound too tight.

I'm going to explode.

Reaching into my boxers, I palm my hard cock. It throbs, desperate for friction… desperate for the kind of attention it has been denied yet again. Closing my eyes, I start stroking myself. It isn't soft; I certainly don't savor it. I stroke rough, and fast, more about relief than pleasure, needing to release some steam or I'll be a miserable, short-tempered bastard come morning.

Even more so than usual.

"Fuck, fuck, fuck," I growl, banging my head against the door as I feel my orgasm building, pleasurable pain ripping through me. I clench my jaw to hold back the noises vibrating my chest. I come in my palm, shoulders sagging as some of the tension recedes from my body.

After cleaning up, I head back to my bedroom, hearing Avery loudly snoring as she snuggles up with my only pillow.

I don't know what to do.

There's a girl in my bed and she's fast asleep. She's *sleeping*.

Seriously, what the hell am I supposed to do?

Sighing, I carefully cover her half-naked body with a flimsy blanket and climb in beside her to try to get some sleep.

"Shit, shit, shit…"

My eyes pop open at the sound of the panicked voice. I blink a few times, disoriented, and roll over in bed, seeking out the source. The moment my gaze finds Avery, memories of last night come back to me, and I let out a sleepy chuckle.

Struck out two nights in a row.

Another first.

My laughter draws her attention. Her back stiffens as she snatches up her shirt and quickly pulls it on, eyes guarded when she finally turns to face me. Her cheeks are flushed, sleep lines still marring them, her hair in utter disarray. Anxiously, as if she can read my mind, she quickly runs her hands through the locks, trying to tame them.

"Good morning," I say, propping myself up on my elbows when she doesn't speak. It's definitely weird, waking up in my own room and seeing her here. "What are you doing?"

"I was, uh… well… you know, I was just…"

Brow furrowing, I sit straight up in bed when she slides on her shoes. "Are you *leaving*?"

"Yeah, I thought…"

"Are you late? Fuck, am *I* late?" I glance at the clock—only seven in the morning. No, not late. My gaze finds hers again, the answer in her flustered expression. *Son of a bitch.* "You were trying to sneak out on me, weren't you?"

"No," she says quickly. *Too* quickly. "I just thought…"

"You thought you'd slip out before I woke up, so you wouldn't have to face me, so you could avoid the awkward morning-after bullshit."

Avery stares at me, her body sagging after a moment. *Busted.* "Okay, I was."

I'm dumbfounded. That's my usual move… and she's using it on *me*?

"You gotta be much quieter to pull that off," I say, shaking my head. "You grab your clothes and change in another room, or even out in the hallway, so you don't wake anyone up while you're pulling yourself together. And you certainly don't talk while you get dressed. Hell, you try not to even breathe too loudly. But you… you sounded like you were doing a fucking rain dance with the way you were stomping around and chanting."

"Yeah, well, I've never done this before," she mutters, "so I didn't know."

"Well, now you know," I say, standing up, not bothering to put on any clothes. I head toward the bedroom door in my black boxers, stepping right past her. "You know, for the next time."

Yawning, still half-asleep, I stroll down the hallway toward the kitchen. Flicking on the light, I scour through the cabinets and start pulling stuff out. It only takes a minute before Avery appears in the doorway, fully dressed, all put together now and looking just as frazzled as she was moments ago.

"What are you doing?" she asks when I grab a pan and set it on the stove.

"Making breakfast," I reply, rubbing my stomach as it growls on cue. "You're welcome to stay, you know, or go. Choice is yours. I won't make it awkward for you."

"Too late," she mutters, hesitating before stepping into the tiny kitchen and taking a seat at the small table off to the side. "So you know how to cook?"

"Well... I can make pancakes," I offer. "I make them for the little miss whenever I have her."

"How often is that?"

"Every other weekend. Alternating holidays. Basic bullshit visitation schedule all fathers pretty much get."

"And the rest of the time she's with her mother?"

I nod as I start putting together the batter for the pancakes. "Or at school, or... you know... with her nanny."

"She has a nanny?"

"Yeah."

"But not one *you* hired?"

I shoot her a look of disbelief, almost offended by that question. Do I look like I can afford a nanny? Hell, even if I could, do I look like someone who *would* hire one? "You know, Aphrodite, for someone who tried to jet to avoid conversation, you sure have a lot to say this morning."

"Sorry, I was just trying to understand."

"It's okay," I say. "I'd love to have her more, but I take what I can get. Besides, she's probably better off elsewhere. I mean, what the fuck do *I* know about little girls?"

"You seemed to be doing good when I saw you."

"Thanks for the vote of confidence, but I live my life in a tattoo studio, you know? That's no place to raise a kid."

Nothing more is said about it as I make us breakfast, sitting down beside Avery at the bar with thick stacks of pancakes. I drown mine in maple syrup while she tops hers with just a tad of butter.

"I'm glad I didn't run out on you," Avery says after taking a small bite. "These pancakes are totally worth the morning-after humiliation."

I laugh. "They're better with stuff in the batter. Little Miss likes banana walnut."

45

Avery's mouth drops open. "Oh, that sounds good! What do I have to do to get some of those?"

"I don't know," I say. "Sleep with me, probably."

"I did." She blushes. "*We* did. Right?"

"Wrong… unless you mean the literal meaning of *sleep*, then yeah, we definitely slept. You were certainly snoring like a motherfucker, hogging my pillow."

Her eyes widen. "We didn't do more?"

"Nope."

"But we were… and you're, well… and I was…" She's speaking in tongues as she waves between us. "So I thought we…"

"Well, we didn't. Trust me, if we had, you'd know."

"How?"

"Because that's not something you'd ever forget."

She takes another bite of her pancakes. "Guess I tried to sneak out for nothing."

"Yeah," I say quietly. "Guess you did."

After I'm finished with breakfast, while Avery is still eating, I slip away to take a long, hot shower. I throw some clothes on, expecting her to depart without fanfare in my absence, but instead I find her still lurking in my living room. She's standing in front of my couch, her back to me as she surveys the lone work of art on the wall. My muscles grow taut, anxiety sweeping through me that I try to push back when she reaches out and swipes her fingers across the large canvas, examining it.

It feels like an intrusion.

Like an *invasion*.

"This is real," she whispers.

"It is."

She turns to me with surprise, raising an eyebrow. "Who painted it?"

"Nobody important," I say. "Just some pretentious asshole that thought himself an actual artist once upon a time."

"He *is* an artist, whoever he is," she says. "It's gorgeous."

The genuine tone of her voice softens the anger that stirs inside of me. "Thank you."

She gapes at me. "You?"

I nod.

"Seriously, *you* painted this?"

"Yes. It's a Hatfield original."

"You're an artist?" She blurts out the question, backtracking quickly. "I mean, I knew you were an artist, that you did art, like with tattoos, but I didn't know you were *this* kind of artist."

I glance up at the painting, an abstract watercolor dominated by shades of yellow. "I was in my last year at Columbia when I painted it."

"Columbia?" she asks incredulously. "You graduated from one of the best art schools in the country?"

"Never said I *graduated.*"

"You dropped out?"

"More like they kicked me out, but whatever... I would've dropped out eventually."

"Why would you do that?"

"Lexie."

Realization seems to dawn as her expression softens. "Oh."

"I was having a kid... I had to do something that would pay the bills. And as much as I loved art, I love my girl a hell of a lot more."

Avery smiles and glances back at the painting. "You're really good, though."

"Thanks."

"I mean it," she says. "Why'd they kick you out of school?"

"Long story," I say. "I guess you could say they weren't fans of mine. They didn't appreciate my technique, so to speak."

She looks at me with confusion but shakes it off. It's a good thing, too, because I'm not in the mood to explain.

"Well, their loss," she says. "And I know you have tattooing and all, but you shouldn't give up on *this* art."

"I haven't given up," I say. "It gave up on me."

Standing in front of a canvas, I feel nothing, see nothing, sense nothing. Years ago it came easily, but now there's just *nothing*. Tattooing is an extension of the other person, a commissioned work, whereas when I'm painting? There's only me.

And I've been drained dry.

I'm empty.

"I should really go," Avery says, glancing at her watch before timidly meeting my eyes. "I, uh… I mean…"

"It doesn't have to be awkward," I say as I motion toward the door. "Go, but just promise you'll be back for more pancakes."

"I will," she says, heading for the door and pausing there to look back at me. "Definitely the banana walnut next time."

I smile at her as she leaves.

After she's gone, I look back at the painting on my wall, my expression slowly falling. What the fuck am I doing? I invite her into my space, into my life, like there's any room for her here. I know better than that. And here I am, talking to her about my art, like she could ever understand my struggle.

Messy.

I don't like it.

What's wrong with me?

Four

"Think fast."

Those words hit me the second I step foot inside Wonderland. I glance over at Kevin, not having enough time to react before something strikes me right in the chest. I hear the distinct rattling as it hits the floor in front of me, the metal canister coming to a stop on the marble tile by my feet.

I stare down at it in silence.

A can of white spray paint... a cheap generic brand, the label decimated, making it unrecognizable.

Looking at it makes me cringe.

Wordlessly, I kick the canister, rolling it right back to him. It's way too early for this bullshit.

"Come on." He reaches down and picks it back up, shaking it toward me. The metal ball inside rattles against the sides as it stirs up the paint. The sound makes my hair stand on end. "Really?"

I ignore his question. His voice is light, almost joking, but it still feels a hell of a lot like an inquisition to me. My gaze flickers from him to the wall in the shop's lobby, eyes moving along the white mass he spray-painted. I'm not entirely sure what the hell it's supposed to be. Kevin's a great artist, yeah, but he's more technical, which means he sucks at free-handing graffiti. "You should probably leave that to the professionals."

He laughs, turning back to his project. "I just tried. You refused."

Sighing, I run a hand through my hair and start walking away, heading toward my workstation, as I mutter, "I'm retired. I don't do that shit anymore."

"Yeah, well, you ought to," he calls out, overhearing me. "Besides, no artist ever really retires. I mean, sometimes they go crazy as shit and cut their ears off and give them to prostitutes, but that doesn't stop them from painting, you know?"

I don't humor that with a response.

Sometimes, I feel like I'm just a step away from that, just one breakdown away from chopping my own dick off and slapping somebody with it. The only thing stopping me is that I happen to *like* my dick. It gives me some of the only pleasure I get out of this life I've been given. But tortured artist? Yeah, I feel that. I feel it and live it every single day. The need to create runs deep within me, but it's terrifying, the thought of not being able to perform.

I'm impotent.

A fucking impotent artist.

My dick has never betrayed me that way.

I'm distracted all day, hearing the sounds from the lobby, the rattling of canisters, the hissing sound the spray paint makes, loud enough that it overshadows the humming of my tattoo machine, audible over even the music, no matter how loud I crank the volume. The front door of the shop is propped open all afternoon, fans running for ventilation, but I can still smell the distinct fumes even holed up in my workspace. It makes my nose twitch, and I try to breathe through my mouth, but it makes little difference.

I'm an addict watching somebody else take a hit.

When I'm finished with my last client, I clean up quickly and make a beeline for the door, but Kevin intercepts me. He stands in front of the exit, halfway inside, halfway out, while casually puffing on a cigarette. He stares at me, making no move to get out of the way.

I pause a few feet from him. "You get off on torturing me, don't you?"

He laughs, a puff of smoke flying from his mouth and nose as he does. "I wouldn't call it torture."

"What would you call it then?"

"Making you reach your maximum potential," he says. "That's all I've ever tried to do, ever since the day you showed up here in your little orange vest to pressure wash the front of my building."

"You tortured me that day, too."

"Again, wouldn't call it that."

I shake my head, looking away from him as he takes a puff of his cigarette. He's annoying the piss out of me and he knows it, and no matter what he says, I know he enjoys it. I glance behind me, surveying the fresh graffiti in the lobby. It's a mass of color, like a rainbow spewed all over the walls, but I still don't know what the hell the white thing dead center is supposed to be. "Nice mural."

"It is, isn't it?" Kevin puts out his cigarette and tosses it in the trash before strolling back into the lobby, brushing past me. "Might be better if somebody would've helped me with it."

I don't stick around to continue the conversation. I'm in no mood for it. I'm so wound tight that the last thing I want at the moment is to have to interact with more people, so I bypass the bar, lowering my head as I make my way straight home. I walk slowly, in no hurry, breathing in the fresh air and taking a moment to let it clear my head.

The neighborhood gets worse the closer I get. Graffiti marks every flat surface, but not the kind that anyone could consider art. Monikers and gang signs scribbled in cheap spray paint, layer over layer of it, making everything indiscernible, like a mass of shapes that can't really mean a thing to anyone anymore. Sirens cut through the air and blue lights flash in the night sky, people shouting, others running, as loud music rattles from houses and cars backfire.

Or maybe it's gunshots.

It's New York.

Who really fucking knows?

As much as I love the city, I hate living in this neighborhood, but it won't be much longer. Soon enough I'll be able to afford to get the hell out of this place, maybe even get a townhouse like the one where the pretty little Lark lives. Little Miss will like it, having a bigger place, but for now she's still mostly oblivious.

She doesn't really know her father's a loser.

Even though her mother's not shy about telling everyone who will listen.

"Daddy."

My attention's focused on the tattoo before me: small red bows on the back of a pair of gorgeously sun-kissed, slim upper thighs. The design is just starting to come together when the word echoes through the room from the doorway, momentarily distracting me. "Uh, hold on."

"Daddy."

I only barely hear her over the hum of the tattoo machine, her small voice drowned out by the old Paula Abdul *Cold Hearted Snake* tune. I vaguely cut my eyes that way before looking back at my work. "One second."

"Daddy!"

She shouts that time, raising her screeching voice, demanding my attention. I don't flinch, unaffected by her outburst, but the girl on the table startles at the sound, nearly making me fuck up.

Pulling the needle away, I sit back and look over at my daughter. She stands in the doorway, hands on her hips, an angry scowl on her face.

"Yes, Lexie?"

"Is it my turn now?"

I shake my head. "Not yet."

"Soon?"

"Later."

"When later?"

I stare at her, not sure what answer will satisfy the girl. She isn't used to me being so busy whenever she's around. Usually I pick her up after work on Fridays and take the weekend off, but her mother unexpectedly dropped her off earlier this afternoon instead.

Without warning.

Not that I'm complaining.

I'll take all the time I can get with my girl.

But some fucking *warning* would've been nice.

Because Lexie isn't good at sharing my time. She wants my undivided attention and has no qualms being vocal about that whenever she feels even remotely ignored.

"Just... later," I say again. "Let me finish my work first, okay?"

I turn right back to my client without awaiting her response, barely having time to add a bit of red shading to the tattoo, when Lexie shrieks again.

"Daddy!"

Swiftly, I reach over and switch off the tattoo machine, the buzzing instantly dying. I force a smile for the pretty brunette lying on my table. Brenda? Belinda? "You mind if we take a break, sweetheart?"

"Not at all," she says, jumping up. "I've being dying for a smoke."

You and me both, lady.

Once she's gone, I pat the tattoo table. "Sit."

Lexie hesitates before dramatically stomping over and climbing up on it. She sits still, a pout on her lips as she glares at me. I wheel my stool as close as possible, staring at her.

Man, she looks pissed.

"Talk to me, Little Miss. What's bothering you?"

"I'm bored," she says, crossing her arms over her chest. "There's nothing to do here! I tried to play and Ellie yelled at me and Kevin said no running but I wasn't running, I swear! I was just walking, but it was fast walking, because I was playing! But then Ellie said no playing, 'cause tattoo shops aren't playgrounds, but we can't go to the playground, and I don't know what else to do!"

I stare at her as she rattles it off quickly before pausing to take a deep breath that sounds like a growl. I take that as my cue to chime in. "You want something to do, correct?"

"Yes!"

I glance around, grabbing my sharpies. "Draw a picture."

"On what?"

"On whatever you want."

Lexie doesn't look thrilled with my suggestion, but she doesn't argue, jumping down from the table and taking a seat in the folding chair off to the side. My client returns, retaking the spot on the table, as I set back to work on her tattoos.

Lexie remains quiet, drawing away, but every now and then I hear her dramatically huffing whenever the client starts flirting with me. I know I should admonish her, should put that attitude in check, but I just can't be mad.

We rarely get time together and fuck... I'd much rather spend it with her, too.

I finish in under an hour, discounting the session for the trouble Lexie caused. After the woman is gone, I look at the clock. Almost seven. I have another appointment at eight, a simple touch-up on an old back tattoo, but I know Lexie won't last through it without throwing another fit.

"I know you don't like being here when I'm busy, Lexie, but I have to work, and I need you to be on your best behavior when I do it."

She doesn't respond, her eyes glued to her work. She's drawing right on the blue-painted wall behind her.

"Do you hear me?"

She still says nothing.

"Lexie?"

"Hold on," she mutters. "I'm busy."

I shake my head, smirking with amusement as she tosses my dismissiveness right back at me. *Smart ass.* She's too clever for her own good.

"What are you drawing?" I ask curiously.

I step closer as Lexie halfheartedly moves out the way for me to see. A dinosaur, of course. A T-Rex. It's pretty good for her only being five years old. *Maybe looks aren't the only thing she inherited from me.*

"Looks good," I say as I pull my shirt up and point to a spot on my chest, to a section not yet inked. "I think it would look awesome right here. What do you think?"

Her expression shifts. She's beaming. "Really?"

"Yeah, really," I say, pulling my shirt back down. "Not today, though. How about we get out of here? I'm hungry, and tired, and I'm pretty sure there are some cartoons at the house just waiting to be watched."

"*Land Before Time*!" she declares. "Can we watch Ducky, Daddy?"

I grin at her. "Yep, yep, yep."

All evidence of her anger completely fades away. I clean up and apologetically ask Ellie to reschedule my next appointment before Little Miss and I jet out the door. She's bundled in her thick pink coat, shielding her from the cool air that seems to seep right through my hoodie as we walk. We are barely a block away when goose bumps coat my skin, a chill running through me, making me shiver. I pause at the corner, right across from the new construction site, and grab Lexie's hand as we wait to cross the street.

"What are they doing to that building, Daddy?"

I don't have to look at her to know what she's referring to. I eye the massive, drab tarps with distaste as they flap in the cold breeze. "Renovating it, probably... maybe tearing it down to rebuild."

"Why?"

"Because the building is old and has been abandoned for years. Guess they figure it's time to actually do something with the place."

"Like what?"

"I don't know."

"What was it before it got all abandoned?"

My gaze drifts to Lexie as I shake my head. "You're just full of questions, aren't you?"

Her expression is stoic. "Yes."

I'm quiet for a moment, leading her across the street, away from the construction area, before responding. "I'm not really sure what it was, honestly. It's been nothing but a shell for as long as I've been around. Always figured it would stay that way."

"I don't like it now," she says.

"Did you like it before?"

She nods. "It used to look like your tattoos."

I glance behind us, back at the building, my eyes gliding along the tarps... tarps that completely cover the once vibrant graffiti. Every inch of the place used to be coated in color, inside and out.

"Yeah," I say quietly. "It did."

"I wonder what's in this."

I glance over at Avery when she speaks, her lips wrapped around the cheap plastic straw, sipping her fruity drink... the same one she's drank every night she has shown up at *The Spare Room* to hang out with me. I'm still on a high from weekend visitation, so hanging with her is just icing on the cake.

I laugh, shaking my head as I take a drink of my beer. "Little of this, little of that... a lot of cheap liquor and a dash of pink shit. *Voila.*"

She shoots me a look as she playfully rolls her eyes. "I mean it. I don't even know what it's called."

"It's a cotton candy something-or-nother," I say, recalling people in the bar ordering them before. "Vodka, mostly, with some kind of, uh... pink shit."

I don't know how else to describe it.

She eyes her glass warily. "Does it really have cotton candy in it?"

"I'm sure it's supposed to," I say, "but here? Not a chance in hell."

Avery's eyes shift from her drink to me, before slowly scanning the bar around us, a look of concern on her face, like she's just now noticing how rundown the place is. "Why do you come here, anyway?"

I shrug. "Why not?"

"Well, it's just that there are plenty of places in the city where you could get a drink... *better* places."

I guzzle the rest of my beer before holding up the empty,

motioning for the bartender to bring me another. He slides the can of Genesee my way before pouring a shot of whiskey. I pick up the liquor, throwing it back and grimacing at the burn that runs through my chest.

Shaking the empty shot glass toward Avery, I say, "What's *better* than a beer and a shot of liquor for six bucks? Where else in the city can you get a cotton candy whatever-that-shit-is for five? Nowhere."

She glances back at her drink as she considered that.

"Besides," I continue, "it's right across the street from the shop and already on my way home, so it's cheap *and* convenient. I prefer when things are easy… the easier, the better."

"Like women?"

Her remark stalls me as I take a drink of the beer. I half-shrug, half-shake my head, but the fact of the matter is she hit the nail right on the head. I bust my ass, struggling to survive. I shouldn't have to work just as hard to get a bit of pleasure out of life.

But the way she says it, her tone quiet, almost hesitant, cuts deep. Real fucking deep. Maybe it isn't an accusation, but it damn sure feels like one.

And I'm guilty as sin.

Nothing hurts worse than the truth.

I don't respond right away, continually sipping my beer, as she finishes her pink drink. After it's empty, she shoves the glass aside, waving off the bartender when he tries to make her another. I glance her way as she wordlessly slides off the stool, putting on her jacket to leave.

She's been here for less than twenty minutes today.

"Not always," I say quietly, looking back away from her as I answer her question. "Depends on the woman. I'm sure good ones are worth the hassle. Problem is, in my world, they're few and far between."

"Then maybe you should step out of your world sometime," she says. "Because in *my* world, if you want something bad enough, you work your ass off until you get it."

Before I can respond, she leans over and presses a kiss to my cheek. The barely-there feel of her lips against my scruffy skin makes unsettling tingles run through me, my eyes damn near closing in response to the sensation. I don't react, don't say another word, my eyes focused on my beer sitting on the bar as she walks away, disappearing out the door.

I sigh exasperatedly. What the hell is the woman doing to me?

In a matter of seconds, another shot of whiskey is shoved in front of me. I glance up as the bartender pauses there.

"On the house," he says, motioning toward the liquor. "Looks like you could use it."

I laugh dryly, downing the shot without hesitation. "Could probably use the whole fucking bottle."

I don't wait for him to say anything else. I throw some money down on the bar before shoving my stool back and standing up. Keeping my head down, I head out the door, hesitating in front of the bar to look around. I spot her right away, just down the block, standing on the corner and hailing a cab already.

"Goddammit," I grumble to myself, shaking my head as I jog to catch up to her. "Hey, Avery! Wait!"

She turns at the sound of her name. Half a block and I'm already winded when I catch up to her. *Fucking cigarettes.*

"Look, I, uh…" I stand in front of her, my words accentuated by a cloud of foggy breath as the temperature out here dips below freezing. She's shivering slightly, obviously wanting out of the cold, but her undivided attention remains on me as I hesitate. "Look, I don't know what I'm doing. I don't know why I'm here or what we're doing, what *you're* doing… but I like you, and I get the feeling you like me, too. Maybe that feeling is wrong, I don't know. Fuck, I don't know anything. Except that maybe you're right, you know… maybe you're right."

I'm not sure if I'm making any damn sense. It all sounds so much better in my head, but the words don't seem right coming from my lips.

"Maybe I'm right," she whispers.

"Yeah," I say. "Maybe you are."

I don't know if she understands what I'm getting at, but her expression softens a bit. Taking a step toward me, she pauses, eyes studiously scanning every inch of my face, like she's searching for something. After a moment, she pushes up on her tiptoes, pressing a light kiss to my chapped lips as I stand still, having no idea what I'm supposed to do. It's a sweet kiss. The sweetest kiss that has ever touched my lips.

It gets under my skin.

I don't kiss like this.

She pulls back again before I can come to terms with it.

"Goodnight, Reece," she says, turning around to leave, hailing a cab and leaving me standing on the sidewalk, alone in the street.

Un-freakin'-believable.

Night after night, I habitually venture to the bar after work. Sometimes I sit there, alone, unwinding after a long day, but occasionally Avery stops by to keep me company. We share a drink and chat before she scurries away with an apology, saying her schedule is too busy for her to stay out late.

She never goes home with me, never hangs around long enough for it to get even remotely intimate, but I look forward to the moments. The easiness, the strange familiarity that surrounds us, does just as much to break the monotony in my life as the mindless flings used to do.

It has been a while—since that last night with Lark. I haven't touched a woman in weeks. I try to tell myself it's because Avery is a challenge, that I met my match, but deep down I know it's more. It isn't just about sex with her—although, Jesus, I certainly think about it enough. I want her, need her, *crave* her... but I'd give up a chance to take her to bed if only I could put my mark on the girl.

I'm heading across the street to the bar on Friday night, a few minutes past closing, when I spot the familiar face heading toward me. I pause along the curb, my hands in my pockets, and wait as Avery jogs to meet up with me. "Hey!"

I nod in greeting as my eyes scan her—knee-high boots, a matching sweater, and the tightest leggings known to man. She's wearing black from head to toe, like a thief in the night, and fuck if her outfit doesn't show off every curve. "You look nice."

"Uh, thank you," she says, glancing down at herself as if surprised by those words. "I kind of just threw this on."

"It works," I say. "It, uh... matches. Looks good on you."

What am I, a fucking fashion critic now?

She smiles timidly, motioning toward the bar. "We going in?"

I'm about to say yes when the door opens and some drunk staggers out. Casting him an annoyed look, my gaze drifts inside the open door, immediately catching the eye of a familiar person.

Lark.

Oh, Lark.

I wouldn't be surprised a bit if she was here looking for me. After all, I've continued to avoid her calls. I've ignored her texts. Never listened to her voicemails.

Awkward.

I turn back to Avery. "You wanna go somewhere else instead?"

"Where?"

"I don't know," I say. "We can grab something to eat, if you're hungry. I've got a few bucks on me. I'm pretty sure I can afford to buy you a Happy Meal."

"That'll be a first."

"What, never had a guy take you to McDonalds?"

"More like never been to a McDonalds, period."

I raise my eyebrows in surprise. "You're shitting me."

"Nope."

"Never?"

"Never."

"That's just... un-American."

Avery lets out a laugh. "My parents are kind of health nuts, so fast food was always out of the question."

"No fast food at all?" I stare at her incredulously. "No Burger King, Wendy's, Taco Bell, KFC? Fuck, no Popeye's Chicken?"

"Nope."

"Jesus, girl, what *do* you eat?"

"Lots. Grilled chicken, veggie burgers, bulgur, yogurt... I eat a lot of salad and grains, and things like flaxseed and chia seeds..."

"*Seeds.* Seriously? What are you, a fucking bird?"

She laughs, playfully flapping her arms like a bird. "Maybe."

Shaking my head, I throw my arm over her shoulders and pull her toward me, the two of us starting down the block, away from the bar. Avery easily slips under my arm, tucking herself against my side. "So, where are we going?"

"To live a little."

I was just joking about buying her McDonalds, but damn if I don't feel compelled to seriously take her there now. It's only a few blocks away on a strip of fast food joints in the Lower Eastside. I open the door for her when we arrive, letting her walk in before me, and step in behind her. She stalls right inside, her eyes studiously scanning the chaotic restaurant. People swarm the registers and pack the tables, laughing and shouting. Half past ten on a Friday night, so most of them are so fucked up they can barely stand.

It's like stepping into a jungle.

I stride toward the register, waiting in line, as Avery once more tucks herself in at my side. I scan the menu needlessly... I always order off the damn dollar menu, anyway. "What do you want?"

"What's good here?"

"Nothing."

Avery laughs. "Well, that sounds promising."

"Nah, the fries are good," I say. "And Little Miss likes the nuggets."

"Is the chicken all white meat?"

"Uh... sure."

"You don't sound very sure."

"First rule of fast food is you don't question what you're eating," I say. "Chances are, you don't want to know. So if you want it to be all white meat, than yeah... sure... all white meat."

"Okay," she says, shrugging. "I'll have whatever Lexie gets."

Two chicken nugget Happy Meals later, we're sitting at a tiny table in the far corner, knees brushing together as I sit across from her, shifting around in the hard plastic chair. Avery pops open her little red box while I sip my tiny ass Coke—three swallows and the fucking thing is about empty already.

"Oh, a toy!" Avery squeals, pulling out the little clear plastic bag. "I got some kind of pink journal thingy. What did you get?"

I glance in my box, snatching out the toy. "I got a truck."

Avery scowls, looking between our toys. "How stereotypical."

"Would you rather have the truck?"

"Yep." Before I can say anything else, Avery snatches the truck toy right out of my hand, tossing the pink journal on the table in front of me. "Enjoy!"

Grinning, she pulls out her food to eat, sniffing a nugget before nibbling the corner. She shrugs after a second, taking a larger bite.

"So?" I drown a fry in ketchup before popping it in my mouth. "Verdict?"

"It's edible." She dips her nugget in a tub of bar-b-q sauce, while I use sweet & sour. After a while, she reaches over, blocking me when I try to dunk, and dips hers into my sauce to try it. "Huh, that's even better."

Wordlessly, I push it toward her as I pop my last nugget in my mouth and glance in my box... nothing left except the apple slices. I pull the package out and toss it to Avery. "Here's some more rabbit food for you."

She laughs loudly, picking up the apples. "How thoughtful."

"Yeah, well, *thoughtful* is my middle name."

She eyes me peculiarly. "What *is* your middle name?"

"Trouble."

"I'm serious," she says, gently kicking me under the table. "What is it?"

"I don't want to talk about it."

"Oh, come on..."

"Nope."

"Please?"

I hesitate. Damn her saying please. "It's Trystan."

"Trystan?"

"And Alan. And Lloyd."

"What?"

"I have three middle names."

"Reece Trystan Alan Lloyd Hatfield?"

I nod. "The fourth."

"The fourth?"

"And it's spelled R-H-Y-S, technically. Rhys."

She gapes at me, like she thinks I'm just fucking with her, but I'm not. Rhys Trystan Allen Lloyd Hatfield IV is proudly displayed on my birth certificate, courtesy of my parents, the type of people who come from the kind of society where the more names they give you, the more morally righteous they are. "What kind of name is *that*?"

"The kind of name given to a kid with expectations. Rhys the Fourth was destined to be a great painter, like da Vinci or Michelangelo. But Reece?" I laugh dryly. "He's what my mother calls a *coloring book crook*... meaning my art looks like I ripped off a five year old."

Her brow furrows a bit. "Your mother said that?"

I nod.

"That's just..." She shakes her head. "I, uh..."

There's a commotion then, a drunken argument at the registers, shouting echoing through the restaurant that makes me feel a hell of a lot like I've been saved by the bell. I stand up before she can finish whatever it is she planned to say, leaving the tray with our trash right where it is, and tug Avery toward to exit. She clutches her drink and snatches up our toys before leaving the table, slipping the pink journal in my back pants pocket when we head outside. Her hand lingers there for a moment, over my ass, before she pulls away. "So dinner was, uh... interesting."

"Tell me about it," I say. "Next time I'll take you to Burger King. They like to throw punches over there."

"I'll hold you to that."

We stroll along quietly, neither saying much of anything. Avery tears her toy truck out of the packaging, playfully driving it up my arm as we walk. My thoughts drift, my mind going elsewhere as I get lost in the silence, a dangerous scenario for me.

I could use a drink.

Maybe even a cigarette.

Some pussy would be beautiful, now that I think of it.

Something to soothe these frazzled nerves of mine, to take my mind off of the shit I don't like to think about. Like my parents. My art. My failure of a life.

I was supposed to be somebody.

Now look at me.

"I get it," Avery says after a moment.

I glance at her curiously, wondering if she knows what I'm thinking. "You get it?"

"Yeah," she says. "My parents are kind of the same way. To them, the only thing that matters is traditional ballet. They think every other form of dance is a waste of time... a waste of *talent*. My mom, she's a little more understanding, but my father's set in his ways. So I get it, you know... I know what it's like to have those expectations."

"Do you know what it's like to be cut off because of it?"

My tone is harsher than I mean for it to be, harsh enough that her footsteps falter briefly. She falls a step behind me, and I slow, glancing at her curiously.

"They cut you off?"

I nod, turning back away. "Haven't spoken to them in five years."

"But... what about Lexie?"

I shrug. "What about her?"

"Don't they want to see her?"

"Not when seeing her means seeing me."

"That's just... that's *nuts*."

"It's life," I say. "My life, anyway."

"I don't get it. I don't get how people... how parents... how *anybody* can just cut someone they love out of their life..."

I chime in before she can continue with that thought. "You ever make a mistake, Aphrodite?"

"Of course."

"Yeah, well, you ever fuck up so bad that it derails your life? Makes your parents give up on you, damn near everyone you know turn their backs on you... ever do something that haunts you every day for years, all because you thought you were invincible and didn't have to play by the rules? Because I have. I've done it. I *did* it. And some mistakes, maybe they're harmless, but they have a way of messing up lives, anyway. And when people make those kind of mistakes, even if you love them, sometimes you gotta walk away. It's called *tough love.*"

She hesitates. "What did you do?"

Sighing, I shake my head. "What I did was think I was an artist when I was nothing more than a stupid kid."

Before Avery can respond to that, I pull her into a small store on the corner and stroll up to the counter. "I need a pack of Camels in the box."

I still owe Ellie some smokes.

The cashier grabs the cigarettes and tosses them down on the counter. I turn to leave after paying but hesitate as I approach the door. Reaching into my pocket, I feel around, pulling out a handful of loose change. Beside the door, a cluster of coin-operated machines covers the wall.

"Lexie loves these things," I say, stopping in front of them. I slide two quarters in the slots of one of the machines and shove the lever in, a cardboard sleeve popping out when I pull on it. I grab the cardboard, opening it, and pull out the glittery temporary tattoo. It's some bullshit heart design, something I'm pretty damn sure I've tattooed on someone for real before.

I wave it in front of Avery. "For you."

"Fast food *and* body art in one night? I'm beginning to think you might be a bad influence."

"Beginning to think? I must be doing a shitty job if you're just now catching on to my plan."

"And what exactly *is* your plan?"

"You don't know?"

"No. I mean, I can guess, I guess, but I don't *know,* you know?"

I laugh as I lead her back out of the store, the two of us lingering on the sidewalk beneath the streetlight. Without answering her question, I peel the plastic sheet off the tattoo and push her sleeve up, pressing it to her forearm. I steal a piece of ice from her McDonalds cup to wet it, pressing it on tightly for a minute before peeling the back off.

"Huh," Avery says, staring at it affixed to her skin. "Good job."

I wink playfully. "They don't call me the *Mad Tatter* for nothing."

She glances at me. "That's what they call you?"

"Yeah."

Her eyes narrow slightly. "Curious."

I grasp her chin, leaning toward her, lightly kissing her, as I whisper, "curiouser and curiouser," against her lips.

Six

"Hey!"

I glance up from my can of Genesee as Avery slides onto the stool beside me. I look at her, doing a double take when I see the sweat along her brow, her skin flushed and hair pulled back into a bun. She has on a black tank top and a pair of tiny shorts. Doesn't she know it's *cold*? Instinctively, my eyes glide along her bare legs, wondering how they'll feel wrapped around me when I plow into her.

If I ever plow into her.

It's been damn near a month and nothing.

I'm starting to question my skills because of her. "Hello."

The bartender strolls over, asking if she wants her usual, but she shakes her head. "Just water tonight, please."

I cock an eyebrow at her. "Water?"

"Yeah, I'm parched," she says, grasping her throat as if to emphasize her point. "We were in rehearsals all night. We've been working on this new choreography but it's been a bitch to nail down. People keep messing up so the choreographer had us doing it over and over and over and..." She trails off, gulping down her water when it arrives, before shooting me a sheepish smile. "Sorry, I'm just going on and on and... well, you know... *on*."

"Doesn't bother me," I say, shrugging. "My other girl does it, too. You've got *nothing* on Lexie when it comes to rambling."

Avery sets her water down, eyes widening slightly as she gazes at me. "What did you just say?"

"I said you've got nothing on Lexie."

"No, before that."

"I said it doesn't bother me."

She stares at me for a moment, blinking a few times.

"What?" I ask, confused by her expression. "What's wrong?"

She shakes her head, smiling softly. "Never mind. It's nothing."

I shrug it off. "So you just finished rehearsing?"

She hums in confirmation. "Just a few minutes ago, actually. I came straight here. I probably look like crap."

"Hardly," I say, my gaze scanning her again. "You look good all hot and sweaty."

She lets out a laugh. "You're trying your best to charm the pants off of me tonight, aren't you?"

My brow furrows as I reluctantly pull my gaze from her legs to meet her eyes. "I'm not *trying* to charm you. It just comes naturally. Besides, not sure if you're aware, but you're not wearing any pants."

She rolls her eyes. "I'm wearing shorts."

"If that's what you wanna call them," I say, my attention once more drifting downward. I can't keep my eyes off of her. "Jesus, they're indecent. I've seen underwear that covered up more."

"If it bothers you, I'll leave."

"No way in hell you're leaving," I say. "Not without me, anyway."

"You know, you're awfully possessive for a man who hasn't even seen me naked yet."

Yet. I smirk at the word. It's a beautiful goddamn word, one of the most beautiful to come from those gorgeous lips of hers. "I saw parts of you."

"But not all."

"Yeah, well, it's not from a lack of trying."

"I haven't seen you try very hard lately," she says. "And I certainly don't see you trying right now."

I cut my eyes at her. Those words sound eerily like a challenge. I stare at her, my gaze so intense I can see her flushing from the attention as she fights to keep from grinning. I finish my beer in silence, sipping it, each passing second as I keep my eyes trained on her making her fidget more and more.

I get under her skin. Good. *At least it's fucking mutual.*

Once my beer is empty, I set it down on the bar and stand up to leave, still watching her. "You coming, Aphrodite?"

"I guess that's up to you."

"If it's up to me," I say, leaning close to whisper in her ear, "you'll be coming the second I get you alone."

I need not say another word. Avery is up out of her seat and heading for the door. I shove my hands in my pockets and stroll out behind her, nodding my goodbye to the bartender. As soon as we're outside, Avery slips her hand into mine. "Your place?"

I don't even hesitate this time. "Absolutely."

We walk the few blocks, neither in any hurry, but once we step inside my apartment, there seems to be a shift in the air. Avery wraps her arms around my neck, standing on her tiptoes, pressing her mouth to mine. My tongue darts out, gliding across her bottom lip, and she willingly opens herself to me. I kiss her deeply, passionately, my hands moving from her hips to her ass as I pull her flush against me. She moans, her fingers running through the hair on the back of my head, when I press myself into her.

I lead her down the hallway to my bedroom, flicking the light switch when we make it inside, but Avery quickly reaches over and turns the lights right back off. Chuckling, I keep them off for her.

I take my time as I strip her out of her scant clothing, leaving every scrap of it in a small pile on my wooden floor. I stare down at her, pulling back from her lips between pecks, desperate to see whatever I can of her body in the soft glow of the moonlight from the bedroom window.

She can't say I haven't seen her naked anymore.

Avery climbs back on the bed as I hover over her. My lips leave her mouth and trail down her jaw, caressing her neck, and exploring her chest. A hint of sweat already lingers on her skin. I tear my own clothes off, haphazardly discarding them, before rolling on a condom and climbing between her thighs.

The first thrust, slow and deep, elicits a strangled gasp from

Avery. I groan at the sensation, savoring the warmth as I fill her for the first time.

I pause, deep inside of her, giving her a moment to adjust. She's tight, so fucking tight, that I can hardly contain myself. It's Heaven, pure goddamn beauty, and it's Hell, the most delicious torture, wrapped together in a storm of feeling... shit that I can't even begin to name.

Sex is good.

No, sex is *great*.

But sex when you haven't had sex in a while? It's fucking *everything*.

"You feel so good," I groan, pulling nearly the whole way out before filling her again, my lips finding their way back to her neck. Never before have I wanted inside of a woman so much in my life, never wanted to taste a pussy, or ravish a body, as much as I do in this moment, with her, and I'm going to take full advantage of every second I have her in my bed.

Avery wraps her arms around me and cocks her head to the side as she spreads her legs further, eagerly welcoming me in.

It's an invitation I take with pleasure.

I increase my pace, thrusting hard and deep, giving her every bit of myself that I can possibly give. I nip and suck at her skin, drinking in every gasp and moan and curse and cry that echoes from her, a shiver tearing down my spine the first time she whimpers my name.

"Reece," she cries, her muscles taut as she clings to me, nails digging into the skin of my upper back. "Oh, God... Reece..."

I trace my tongue along her jaw before kissing the shell of her ear. "What is it, Aphrodite?"

"I'm gonna..." She gasps, swallowing back the rest of the words when I reach between us and stroke her clit. Within a matter of seconds her body seizes up before exploding. She tilts her head, arching her back up off the bed, as orgasm sweeps through her.

Beautiful.

My eyes fight to close, the pleasure intense, when I feel her convulsing around me. I force them to stay open, though, watching in awe in the moonlight as Avery trembles, her hands impulsively grasping her own breasts and kneading her nipples between her fingers.

I nearly come from that alone.

As soon as her pleasure subsides, Avery relaxes, panting, her eyes wild, as she looks up at me in the darkness. I smirk, grasping her hips and yanking her toward me, pulling her onto my lap. She sinks down on me, moaning, as I lay back on the bed, giving her the control.

I want to watch her.

She rides me, grinding her hips. I suspected it, the first time I saw her... she knows what she's doing. I stroke her thighs, my fingertips trailing along her stomach before caressing her breasts, pinching her nipples just like she'd done to herself.

I feel her body grow taut the moment I do it.

I smirk. I love a woman that knows how she likes it and isn't afraid to show it.

Avery covers my hands with her own, her fingers grazing over the old tattoos before she links hers with mine, holding my hands. She leans down, softly kissing me, her tongue lingering at the piercing near the corner of my mouth.

It won't take me long. I know it. I can *feel* it, building inside of me. I force it down, not wanting her to stop, too captivated with watching the way she moves her hips, rolling them, shifting them, like we're dancing to music nobody can hear, but the pressure eventually mounts to the point where I can't control it anymore. I grab her hips, closing my eyes and gritting my teeth. I hold her in spot, just off the bed, and thrust hard up into her a few times. I come, losing myself in the sensation, vaguely hearing her cry out as my thrusts drive her over the brink.

Panting, Avery lays down on top of me afterward, resting her head on my chest. "Holy shit... that was... wow."

I push her hair out of the way, my knuckles grazing her cheek. "It was."

Wow.

Avery quickly drifts off, but sleep evades me all night long.

When morning comes, the sun just rising outside and lightening the room, I stare up at the ceiling as I casually stroke Avery's back, feeling every breath as she lies soundly against me. It's about the time when I usually slip out, disappearing to avoid any semblance of a relationship.

But there's no escaping whatever this is.

Sighing, I pull away from Avery and climb out of bed, throwing on a pair of sweat pants before making my way to the kitchen. Quietly, so silent my footsteps against the wooden floor sound magnified in the apartment, I put together the batter for pancakes and start cooking. I lean against the counter by the stove, tapping my spatula against the marble countertop, my mind drifting as flashes of last night infiltrate my thoughts.

"Smells good."

Her soft voice surprises me. I smile at the sound of it before straightening my expression out and turning to face her. Grabbing a stack of pancakes, I set the plate on the table. "Help yourself."

She steps that way, sliding up on the stool. "Banana walnut?"

"Of course."

Smiling, she grabs a fork and takes a bite, letting out an exaggerated moan. "Okay, this is amazing."

"Thanks."

"No, thank *you*," she says, her gaze wholly on the pancakes as she eagerly takes another bite. "I thought I would never experience a moment more satisfying than last night, but wow... these pancakes. Best ever."

"I'm not sure whether to be flattered or offended."

"Definitely flattered," she says, nodding assuredly. "No wonder these are your special occasion pancakes. They're like a secret weapon. You've probably built a legacy on these things and have a slew of women constantly coming back for more. Your own little pancake brigade. The banana walnut whores or something."

I open my mouth to respond but have no idea what the hell to say to that. Instead, I let out an awkward laugh, not having the heart to tell her the truth—the only lady I've ever made breakfast for is three feet tall with a love of dinosaurs.

I shower, standing under the scalding spray for only a few minutes, but when I resurface this time, Avery is long gone. She vanished from the apartment, leaving an empty plate in the sink and a note on the counter with a lone word scribbled on it: *Thanks.*

I stare at it for a moment before balling it up and tossing it right in the trash. *Thanks.* What does that even mean? Thanks for the breakfast? Thanks for the sex? Thanks for nothing, you crooked-dick motherfucker? I'm out of my element, in unchartered waters, and I don't like that familiar territory seems to be getting further and further away.

I'm catching feelings, I realize. Real feelings.

I'd rather catch the bubonic plague.

Days pass, days where I don't see the goddess, days where I feel all twisted and unsure of how I'm supposed to proceed.

It's karma, I think.

Now I'm the one being fucked and forgotten.

The past is catching up to me.

It's a week later when I'm sitting at the studio, finishing up a second session with Jimmy, the man with *Starry Night* adorning his back. I'm adding some shading, blending the blue in with the black, when Ellie strolls to the doorway. "Someone's asking to talk to you."

"Take a message."

"They're here in the shop."

"Take a message."

Ellie laughs. "You sure?"

I nod. "Take a message."

Shrugging, Ellie walks away, leaving me to my work. I finish some last minute touch-ups on the design before switching the machine off. "All done."

"Yeah?" Jimmy jumps up excitedly and looks in the mirror, grinning. "Awesome!"

I bandage him up and pocket the money, having no time to

dick around tonight. After Jimmy leaves, I clean up my workspace and glance at the clock: a quarter till ten. Locking up the room, I stroll over to the receptionist's desk.

"You and Lexie got any plans this weekend?" Ellie asks casually when I approach.

"Just the usual," I reply. "Might go to the museum. I'll stop by tomorrow to finish up my paperwork."

"Sounds great," Ellie says, scribbling a note in the appointment book. I'm about to leave when Ellie holds up a piece of notebook paper. "Oh, here."

I grab it. "What's this?"

"You told me to take a message."

Ah. I unfold the paper, seeing the vaguely recognizable scribble.

See you across the street?

~A

Avery. I sigh, bidding everyone goodnight, before heading out of the shop. I pause on the sidewalk, looking at my watch, although I already know the time. I'm supposed to pick up Lexie in a few minutes.

Hesitating, I shove Avery's note in my pocket before jogging across the street.

Avery is sitting on her usual stool, chatting with the bartender, laughing at something the man says. I feel a flare of something inside of me, possessiveness I don't like feeling. I shove it back as I approach, nodding at the man before looking at Avery. I don't sit, make no move to order a drink. "I can't stay."

Her brow furrows briefly at my standoffishness before realization seems to dawn on her. "Oh, crap… it's your weekend, isn't it?"

I nod. "It is."

"I'm sorry," she says quickly. "I was so excited tonight that it slipped my mind. I just came straight here without thinking."

"Excited? About?"

Her cheeks flush. "It's nothing, really."

"Tell me."

"Well, you know how we've been rehearsing for our big spring performances? Well, the seniors also have the chance to put on their own show, and I got chosen. I get to choreograph a dance for the production!" She smiles sheepishly, trying to contain her excitement. "I mean, it's not *that* big of a deal, not really… not nearly as big of a deal as the *real* performances…"

"It's great," I say, reaching over and cupping her chin when she ducks her head shyly. Her smile is radiant, tempting me toward her lips, but I don't make a move to kiss her, even though I really fucking want to. "I remember what it felt like whenever I saw *my* work on display. It's different. It's original. It's a piece of you out in the world for everyone to see. It's… great."

Man, I miss those days… it doesn't happen anymore. Hell, I can't even remember the last time it did. Everyone knows exactly what they want from me now. It takes an implicit trust to let someone permanently mark you, but there isn't enough trust in the world to let that someone dictate the art, too.

So to be given that kind of opportunity, to be entrusted with complete control of your passion?

Yeah, I understand… and it *is* a big deal.

"Thank you," she whispers, reaching out and grasping my arm.

I slowly pull away from her, letting go of her chin, her hand slipping from my skin. "I should get going."

"Oh, yeah, of course." She looks away, biting down on her bottom lip as she picks up her drink. "Have a good weekend. I guess I'll see you next week."

Nodding, I turn to leave, but hesitate after a few steps and glance back. "Aphrodite?"

She cuts her eyes at me, half-amused, half-confused, that I still call her that name. "Huh?"

"You busy tomorrow?"

"Uh, no," she says, shaking her head. "We have no rehearsals this weekend."

"I'm taking Little Miss to the natural history museum in the morning," I say. "We'll probably leave around ten o'clock. So if you have nothing else to do, you know…"

Avery stares at me, her mouth open but no words come out.

77

I've rendered her speechless. *Nice.* I don't stick around for a response. I give her a small smile, nodding my goodbye again, before walking out of the bar.

It takes me about twenty minutes to get to Lexie. I inhale deeply as I jog up the stone steps leading to the front door of the upscale brownstone in the Upper Westside. I knock before shoving my hands in my pockets and rocking on my heels, anxiously waiting.

It's like being on a roller coaster, these moments, knowing nothing bad will happen to you, but still not being able to steady your heartbeat every time you climb that first hill. I can hear the footsteps in the house, the methodic clicking of high heels toward the door, each one setting me further on edge.

I hate this shit… hate these moments. They lead to the best times of my life, my days with Lexie, but the lead-up is a bitch.

Literally.

The locks clang, the door tugging open, the blonde woman appearing in the doorway. I stare down at her blood-red high heels before my gaze shifts to meet her icy-blue eyes… eyes that never hold an ounce of warmth for me. "Rebecca."

"Rhys." Her voice is stony. "You're late."

"Only about ten minutes."

"You didn't call," she says. "Thought you weren't coming."

"Well, I'm here."

Those judgmental eyes scan me with disapproval. Rebecca lets out a deep sigh, her nose scrunching with disgust, before she turns away. "Alexis! Your father decided to show up, after all."

I hate how she words shit, like there's actually a chance in hell I won't come when I'm supposed to. In five years, I've never once missed a visit I've been granted… *never*. Neither rain, nor hail, nor blizzard, nor plague, nor bitch with a grudge will keep me from my little miss, regardless of how Rebecca feels about it.

I try not to hold it against the woman. After all, the man I've turned out to be is a far cry from the brilliant artist she screwed at a party back at Columbia. We're practically strangers, and that's the point. She doesn't fucking know me… she's never tried to get to know who I really am. She sees the tattered cover of the book she thought was a classic and never asks what the real story is about.

She fought hard to keep me away, blew tens of thousands of dollars on the best lawyers to fight her case, but I'm not easy to get rid of, and she hates that. She hates that her perfect little life is interrupted by someone like me.

Little feet scamper through the house as Lexie runs straight for the door. She doesn't pause, doesn't hesitate, merely slipping right past her mother. I crouch down, holding my arms open, as she launches herself right at me. "Daddy!"

"Hey, Little Miss."

Rebecca snatches up a little pink backpack and holds it out to me. "I packed her some toys, you know, so she has something to do."

I take it, even as I shake my head. "She has plenty to do at my place."

"I'm sure." Rebecca's bitter voice negates her words. "You prove that every time you bring her back home with her skin all drawn on, telling stories about those troublemakers at that shop of yours. That's—"

"No place for a kid," I say, cutting her off. "Got it."

I hear the argument over and over again.

"You ready?" I ask, looking at Lexie. "Let's get out of here."

Lexie barely gives her mother a glance as she drags me down the steps. I clutch her hand, swinging her pink backpack onto my shoulder, as the two of us stroll down the sidewalk.

"You were late, Daddy," Lexie says.

"I know," I say. "I'm sorry."

"It's okay." She shrugs. "Mommy said you got at the shop and would stay there all night."

"Sounds like your mother."

"She said that's all you ever do."

"Sounds like your mother again."

"She said you didn't wanna leave your friends for me."

I abruptly stop walking, tugging her hand to make her halt at the sound of that bullshit. "You know that's not true, right? Nobody's more important to me than you, Lexie. *Nobody.*"

"I know, Daddy," she says. "But Mommy says—"

"I know what your mother says," I reply. I know it all, have heard it all, and none of it is pleasant. "But what does Daddy say? Huh? What did I tell you about people's opinions?"

"Not to listen to what they say and to form my own 'pinions."

"Except for…?"

"'Cept for strangers with candy, and the weatherman on TV, and police that won't show you their badges, and people who don't like music, 'cause we can't trust those people."

I laugh. "You forgot boys who want to date you. You should always trust your daddy's opinion on *them*."

I stand in front of the sink in the kitchen, scrubbing syrup off our plates from breakfast. Near me, just out in the hall, Lexie lays on her stomach on the floor, playing with a bucket of old toys—little dinosaurs, plastic army men, and hot wheels are spread out as she acts out her own little version of Jurassic Park. Her backpack lays discarded somewhere in the living room, the Barbie dolls inside of it untouched.

I watch her as I clean up. I've just finished and am drying my hands with a towel when there's a timid knock. Sighing, I walk out of the kitchen, stepping over my daughter and being sure not to knock over any of her toys as I head for the apartment door. I glance through the peep hole, seeing Avery standing out in the hall.

I'll be damned… she actually came.

"Lexie, you know how I said we'd go to the museum today?"

She glances up, pausing what she's doing. "Yeah."

"Well, Daddy invited a friend to go along with us."

Lexie's eyes narrow, her fist tightly clutching the metal car in her hand. For a second, I almost think she's going to throw it at me.

"So I need you to be a good girl, okay? Can you do that for me?"

Lexie says nothing, turning back to her toys and picking up right where she left off playing.

Avery knocks again. Sighing, I open the door, startling her mid-knock, her fist still raised. She drops it quickly, smiling. "Hey."

"Hey," I say, motioning past me. "Come on in."

She steps inside, her eyes nervously darting around the apartment, her gaze settling on Lexie in the hallway.

"Lexie, you remember Avery?"

Lexie regards Avery carefully, nodding, before her eyes suspiciously seek me out. I've never brought a woman home like this before, have never invited them on outings with the two of us. I don't blame her for being skeptical. Hell, I'm just as surprised by it all.

Avery slowly approaches her. "Hey there."

Lexie clenches her fist around the car again. I tense. *Oh, fuck, please don't throw it at her.*

It takes a moment for Lexie to respond, finally letting go of the toy. Her voice is timid, more reserved than I've ever heard from my little spitfire before. "Hi."

Avery crouches down in front of her and glances around. "What are you doing?"

"Playing," Lexie replies, holding up an orange dinosaur. "The people are trying to go home but the dinosaurs keep eating everyone in all the cars."

"Oh no!" Avery gasps with mock horror. "What are they gonna do?"

A hint of a smile touches Lexie's lips before forcing itself into an unstoppable full-blown grin. "It's okay, though, because the army will stop them!"

"Whew." Avery relaxes. "You had me scared there for a minute."

Lexie giggles. "You don't have to be scared. They won't eat us, 'cause my daddy won't let them. Right, Daddy?"

"Right," I say. "You can count on me."

"Well," Avery says, reaching over and picking up one of the green toy soldiers. "Good thing he's around then, huh?"

Chuckling, I stroll past them, reaching down and ruffling Lexie's hair as I navigate the maze of toys. "I'll get ready and we'll head out."

"Hurry up," Lexie says, smacking my hand away. "I've *been* ready all day!"

"Yeah," Avery says playfully. "Hurry it up, slow poke."

Despite their orders, I take my time, leaving the bedroom door cracked open so I can listen to the two of them in the hallway, letting Lexie get accustomed to Avery's presence before we venture out in public anywhere. Twenty minutes later, I'm slipping on my shoes and finally rejoining them.

"You brush your teeth, Little Miss?"

"Yes."

"And your hair?"

"Yes."

"I can't tell it."

Lexie rolls her eyes as I grab a brush and take a seat on the couch, waving her over to me. I run the brush through her hair, sloppily pulling it back. Avery stands just inside the living room, eyeing us warily. "What are you doing to her head?"

"Fixing her hair."

"It looks like you're torturing the kid."

Before I can come back with anything, Avery takes over, sitting down beside me and pulling Lexie between her legs. Lexie doesn't resist, standing still as Avery runs her fingers through the messy locks. "What do you like? Ponytail? Pigtails? Bun? French braid?"

"You can braid?" Lexie asks, excited. "Daddy can't braid."

"Not surprised," Avery jokes as she starts braiding. "Look at *his* hair."

I instinctively run my hand through my hair. "What's wrong with it?"

Lexie giggles. "It looks all crazy!"

Avery swiftly whips up a French braid, securing the end of it with a black hair tie. "There you go."

Lexie immediately runs off, stumbling over her discarded toys as she scampers to the bathroom to look in the mirror. I grab my

Yankees hat and put it on before picking up my keys. I glance over at Avery as she watches me, offering her a small smile in thanks as Lexie runs back out of the bathroom. "Let's go... let's go... let's *go!*"

"We're going," I say, motioning toward the door. "Ladies first."

I have been to the American Museum of Natural History so many times the employees recognize us and greet Lexie by name when we arrive. As soon as we're inside, we bypass nearly everything and head straight up to the fourth floor.

Dinosaurs.

I stroll along behind, letting Lexie take the lead and drag Avery with her straight toward the orientation hall.

We take seats in the very front of the theater, and Lexie quotes along with the video, knowing every word. Despite having seen it over and over again, she looks just as captivated as she had the first time, her eyes wide. Avery looks just as enthralled, while I can't keep my eyes off the two of them.

Fascinating.

We spend most of the morning exploring the fossil halls, repeatedly visiting the same ones, as Lexie rambles on and on, spewing facts and telling Avery everything she has ever heard about dinosaurs before.

Do you know dinosaur means terrible lizard?

Do you know the Stegosaurus had a brain the size of a walnut?

Do you know the Velociraptor was the size of a turkey?

Gobble fucking gobble...

I'm always amazed she remembers all that shit.

We stroll through the vertebrae hall, not dwelling like we did with the others, but Avery pauses near the doorway.

"Oh, look!" she says, pointing toward the ceiling. "A pterodactyl!"

"It's called a pterosaurs," Lexie corrects her, and I keep my lips sealed, not correcting her for pronouncing the silent 'p'.

"Is it?" Avery asks. "Huh, I never knew, and it's my favorite dinosaur."

Lexie giggles. "It's not a dinosaur!"

"It's not?"

"No," Lexie says, shaking her head exaggeratedly. "You're silly!"

Lexie walks off ahead as Avery turns to me, her brow furrowed. "It's really not a dinosaur?"

"It's apparently a flying reptile," I explain. "Don't worry... I made the same mistake."

The afternoon wears on as we make our way down to the other floors, checking out a few exhibits, before heading to the food court to grab lunch. Lexie chows down on dinosaur-shaped nuggets while Avery and I share a small pizza. The atmosphere is relaxed as we eat in a quiet comfort until Lexie shatters it with a blurted out question.

"Is she your girlfriend *now*, Daddy?"

I choke on a pepperoni and take a drink of my soda as I cough. I delay responding, not sure what to say.

"Well, I'm a girl," Avery chimes in, "and we're friends."

"Right," I agree. "Friends."

Lexie's eyes shift between us skeptically, but she doesn't question it any more.

The girl is too smart for her own good.

Seven

Lexie has her own room at my apartment. There's not much in it—a bed and a dresser, a toy box with some toys. Pictures cover every inch of the walls, though, sloppily taped there, mostly drawings of dinosaurs.

Across from her room is another, not much bigger than a walk-in closet, but it doesn't matter. Nobody ever goes in there. I haven't been into the room in a long time, but stepping inside again feels as natural, as easy, as breathing.

A broken canvas remains perched on the wooden easel, an array of paints and brushes strewn out along the small adjacent desk. Gobs of dried, cracked paint cake a white palette, hastily abandoned. I can still remember the last time I stood in here. I tried to paint but came up empty, so empty, *always empty*, an artistic block keeping my mind as blank as the canvas. I stared at it... and stared at it... and stared at it some more... before punching the fucking thing and walking away.

I haven't tried since.

That was a long time ago.

It used to be I could lock myself in this room for hours, sometimes even days, crashing on the futon along the side of the room whenever exhaustion drained me of creativity, but now? Now those days are nothing but a memory. It had been my sanctuary, and it shows, the floor streaked with old paint, the white walls splattered and stained.

Sure as fuck never getting my security deposit back on this place.

Dust tickles my nostrils when I inhale, making my nose twitch. I glance around, taking in the familiar sight of the room that once felt more like home than anywhere ever had before. Sighing, I shake the black trash bag open and start tossing things into it—dried paints, ruined brushes, damaged canvases... everything I discarded and destroyed, ridding the room of the memory. After it's cleaned out, leaving only the bare essentials, a shell of what it used to be, I shut off the light and walk back out.

Not today. No, not tonight.

But someday, I think.

Someday it will come back to me.

"You... you have an art studio?"

Avery stands in the center of the room, nervously wringing her hands together in front of her. The lighting is dim, casting only a subtle, shadowy glow upon her. I haven't turned the light on, remembering she preferred the dark for whatever reason.

"I do," I reply. "Or I *did*, anyway."

I pause in front of her, eyes slowly scanning her. She's wearing the same pink dress she had on the night I first laid eyes on her at the shop. The sight of it does something to me, stirring up something deep inside of me.

Reaching over, I grasp the bottom of the dress, about to do what I wanted to do that very first day—take the motherfucker *off*. "Can I?"

Avery appears confused, eyeing me with caution, but slowly nods her approval. We skipped the bar—skipped the drinks—and headed straight to my place when I found out she didn't have to be up early for anything in the morning.

I pull the dress over her head when she willingly raises her arms in the air. I toss it aside, leaving her standing in front of me wearing nothing but a strapless black bra and a matching pair of panties. The dark garments make her skin look pale, a stark white in the moonlight, like a brand new blank canvas.

Perfect.

Slowly, I lean toward her, whispering, "don't move" before strolling over to the side of the room. I glance around at my old leftover art supplies and grab an empty palette, squirting an array of colors around it, before turning back toward her.

She hasn't moved. Not even an inch.

The scent of the paint washes through me. Man, it has been awhile since I've smelled that. I can't even explain it... it's like trying to describe the taste of water or the feel of air. They are subtle notes that most noses can barely detect, but it's like an aphrodisiac to me, a far cry from the tattoo ink I deal with every day, the sterilized odor making me feel like I exist in a giant bottle of hand sanitizer.

"I have some rules when it comes to tattoos," I say, pausing in front of Avery. "I bend them sometimes, for the right people, but not often. They call me a snob for it, because I don't just give people whatever they want, but I can't. Because tattoos are art... they're *my* art... the only art I have anymore... and I don't want to release a piece of work out into the public that I'm not proud of."

"Like Bridgette's," Avery says quietly.

"Exactly," I reply. "I broke a lot of my rules on that monstrosity."

"Why?"

Why? I've thought about that a lot since that day all those weeks ago, and I can only come to one logical conclusion: Bridgette doesn't fight fair. "She came into the shop armed, and I was no match for her secret weapon."

"What's that?"

"Not what... *who*. And that who, Aphrodite, is you."

"Me?" Avery's voice trembles. "How?"

"Your guess is as good as mine," I say. "But you walked in, and every rule I ever had was instantly broken because of it."

Avery blushes as she ducks her head, staring at me through her long lashes.

"Regardless, rules are rules for a reason," I continue. "There are some things I just won't do, places I'd rather not tattoo."

I swipe my pointer finger into the red paint before gently running it across her cheek, leaving a smear of wet paint. "Like faces." I trail it down her neck. "And necks."

Wordlessly, I dip it again in the red paint, making a similar mark on her other cheek. Avery swallows harshly when I swipe my fingertips along her neck. Slowly, I lean forward, kissing the dip in her throat. "Throats."

I grasp her hands, holding them in one of mine, as I dip my finger into the green paint. I swipe an x on the back of each hand before turning them over and painting her palms. "Hands are another no-no."

"Your hands are tattooed," she points out.

I glance down at mine instinctively. The words 'rise' and 'fall' are inked along my knuckles, faded and in desperate need of yet another touch up. "They are."

"What does it mean?" she asks. "Why those words?"

"It reminds me that whatever goes up always comes back down," I reply, "and when I'm down, the only place left to go is up. It puts things into perspective for me."

"That's brilliant."

"It's stupid," I correct her. "Hands, necks, faces… they heal terribly, and the ink can fade, and blur, and what you're left with usually isn't what you signed up for."

"Is that it?"

"No," I say, laughing. "Not even close."

I dip my fingers in the orange paint, swirling colors together, and kneel down in front of her. She grasps my shoulders, steadying herself, as I swipe paint along her feet. "I hate doing feet, but especially the soles. Definitely a no-no."

She curls her toes, shifting her feet, like she's trying to slink away from me. "Who in the world would tattoo the bottom of their foot?"

"You'd be surprised, but I won't do it," I reply, my hands trailing her legs as I stand back up, startling her when I cup my hand around her pussy. "I won't do there, either."

She gasps when my thumb strokes her clit through the flimsy fabric, a moan escaping that I silence with a deep kiss.

"Or the lips," I whisper against her mouth. "That's probably the stupidest fucking tattoo I get asked for."

I kiss her again, and again, a series of sweet pecks, before pulling away.

I dip my fingers into the blue paint.

"There are other places I personally prefer not to do," I say, letting a few drops of paint drip from my fingertips onto her skin. "But they're popular tattoos."

"Where else?" she asks, her voice breathy. "Show me."

I continually paint, smearing streaks of color along her body as I point out the places that hurt the worst, painting her ankles, hips, elbows, knees, and underarms, trailing paint along her ribs and all around the collarbones before stepping behind her. She shivers as I leisurely finger-paint a rainbow down her spine, my hand stalling at the small of her back when I lean down to kiss her shoulder.

I step around her again, eyes surveying her, as I reach down and smear some leftover paint along her upper thighs, my fingertips grazing her panty line. "I'll do it, of course, but it isn't pleasant. I've had people cry on my table, grown men pass out from the pain. And it's always fucking beautiful, when I'm done, but it has to be worth the agony to see it though."

"How do you know?" Avery asks. "How do you know if it's worth the pain?"

"You just feel it," I reply, smearing paint along her skin, adding color wherever it calls to me. "You know it's right, that it's worth it, when you can't imagine not having it. People get tattoos because they're cool, because they're sexy, and fuck... they *are*... but they have to mean something. It doesn't matter what others think, or how others feel about it... *you're* the one who has to live with it. I don't give a shit if a guy walks into my shop and wants a Chihuahua tattooed on his left ass-cheek. I guarantee I won't like it, but I'll do it, happily, as long as I know it's special to him. As long as it has *meaning*. Because art is supposed to."

The Mad Tatter

I paint a red squiggly line down Avery's stomach, swirling my finger around her navel. "People ask for names, and all I think is, how are you going to feel about that person in five, ten, fifteen years? What are you going to think in thirty, forty years, when their name is still tattooed over your heart? People change, they grow up and fuck up, and sometimes they walk away for no damn reason. They decide you're not good enough, not smart enough… they judge you for how you look, what you do… the only guarantee in your life is yourself, but few people ever want their own name tattooed on their body. They want Joey, and Vinnie, and fucking *Johnny*."

Avery snorts with laughter, shifting a step, making me mess up, accidently merging a blue line with red and yellow, causing an ugly brownish streak.

"First rule of tattooing," I say, cocking an eyebrow at her. "Don't move."

She smiles sheepishly.

I take a step back, my eyes slowly scanning her body, my makeshift canvas of skin and bone, curves and angles, the sleekest muscles and softest flesh, the pieces that make up the infallible woman. Unlike me, she has no holes. She hasn't been broken and sloppily glued back together. I have, though.

My cracks still show.

"Perfect," I say, my gaze settling on the smudge she caused. "Almost."

"Sorry."

"Don't be."

I pull my shirt off and toss it on the floor beside where Avery's dress lies. My hands find her hips, pulling her flush to me, as my lips meet hers. I kiss her passionately, grasping her thighs and pulling her up. She wraps her legs around my waist, letting out a playful squeal, as I carry her over to the small futon in the corner.

"We're going to make a mess," Avery says, wrapping her arms around my neck, transferring wet paint from her skin to mine.

I nip at her bottom lip with my teeth. "That's how you like it, isn't it? Filthy? Ugly?"

"Nasty," she whispers playfully. "Rough."

90

"Rough?"

"Oh God yes," she says. "*Definitely* rough."

This woman… this woman is trying to kill me.

I'm convinced.

She's my punishment. My Hail Mary's. My restitution.

In a heartbeat, we're a jumble of bare skin and slick paint, coated with sweat and sin, as I give Avery exactly what she asks for from me. Pulling my last condom from my wallet, I quickly roll it on. I slide into her, hard and rough, hips crashing together damn near painfully as I pound her again and again. Cries fill the darkness, ecstasy building to the point of agony and merging into something that I can only vocalize with strained grunts and strangled curses.

Fuck. Fuck. *Fuck.*

Avery wraps her strong legs around me, twisting her sleek, flexible body in ways I never knew a woman could bend. We push and pull, giving and taking, surrendering to the other before commanding control, over and over until neither can take anymore. I come hard, nearly losing my breath at the intensity. I suppress a scream with her lips, lying beneath her as she rides me, my hand roughly grasping the back of her neck as I kiss her.

Avery stills as I loosen my hold on her. Her body sags against me, her chest moving rapidly as she fights to catch her breath. I just lay there for a while, silently staring up at the ceiling.

"Reece?" Avery whispers eventually.

"Yeah?"

"I feel gross."

I laugh, slipping out from beneath her and standing up. My legs wobble, my knees weak. *Damn, I'm out of shape.*

"Come on," I say, offering her my hand. "Let's get it washed off."

I lead her through the quiet apartment and to the bathroom. I turn on the water, adjusting it to warm, before turning to Avery. It's the first time tonight I'm seeing her clearly, the first time, ever, seeing her naked with all the lights on.

My eyes instinctively scan her, her body covered in gray-streaked smudges, flaky patches of color from the paint that had already dried. She fidgets under my gaze, wrapping her arms around her chest as she turns sideway, shying away from the attention.

"Ah, don't be like that," I say, pulling her hands away when she shields her breasts. "You're beautiful."

"You trying to charm me again?"

"No," I say. "I just compliment beauty when I see it."

She has a gorgeous body, albeit a banged-up one. Her feet are particularly rough, and she seems to shift them away when I look down again. It's from dancing, though, battle wounds from fighting through her art, so if anything, it makes her more beautiful to me.

She's a fucking warrior.

A badass, tippy-toed, dancing warrior.

I pull her into the shower with me, taking my time as I wash the paint from her skin. She melts at my touch, relaxing, her eyes fluttering closed, the sight of her skin flushing making my chest constrict. The sex vixen in the darkness is a blushing angel in the light, a walking contradiction that has me twisted. I want to know everything there is to know about her, see everything there is to see, dig deep down into her soul and understand what makes her tick... tick... tick.

Because, I think, it might just be the same damn thing that claws around inside of me.

The pressure against my back alternates between feather-light tickles and downright uncomfortable burrowing. I sit as still as humanly possible, grimacing, my eyes peeled to my desk as I try to sort through paperwork for inventory.

"Daddy, I don't like these songs," Lexie whines, the pressure on my back pausing.

"I'm the one getting the tattoo here," I say, shifting through the stacks of paper. "I pick the tunes, remember?"

"But there's no words!"

"If I can work through your *MMMMBop* crap, you can survive some instrumental music."

"Ugh, it's so boring!"

"Hey, now, I don't judge your choices."

"But you told me to get my own 'pinion!"

"And your opinion is that my music sucks?"

"Yes!"

She screeches it, digging painfully into my bare back with the marker as she goes back to tattooing me. Cringing, I close my eyes and grit my teeth. I prefer the damn needle to this. I can't imagine what she's even drawing. With my girl, and the mood she's in? There's no telling.

Sharp feminine laughter echoes through the room from Ellie in the doorway. I open my eyes when she strolls over, sensing her pause behind me.

"You almost done filling out those supply sheets, Reece?"

I glance down at them, scribbling my signature on the last two, before holding them out to her. She snatches them away, laughing again.

"That tattoo's banging, Lexie-girl," Ellie says. "I might need to schedule me an appointment with you."

I laugh dryly. "I'm sure you can get her to do your face."

Nearly every inch of Ellie is covered in tattoos, all except for the areas I refuse to touch. She's been begging me to tattoo a series of stars on her temples, but I've been refusing. I told her to ask Kevin, or Martin, but she won't.

She knows they won't do it either.

"I will!" Lexie says excitedly. "I'll do it!"

"I'll pass," Ellie says, "for now."

"I like tattoos," Lexie exclaims. "Daddy, can I tattoo Avery?"

"Not before I do," I mutter, turning my attention to the rest of the paperwork, making sure everything is squared away.

"Avery?" Ellie asks, still lingering in the room. "Who's that?"

Lexie is quick to chime in. "She's Daddy's friend that's a girl."

"Wait, a *girlfriend*?" Ellie asks, raising her voice slightly. "You're seeing somebody, Reece?"

I don't respond, but I don't have to. Lexie has it covered for me. "She's not Daddy's girlfriend, silly! She's his friend, but she's a girl! We see her sometimes. She went to the museum with us, and she likes dinosaurs, too, but she doesn't know anything about them like I do."

"Ah," Ellie says, that word laced with so many damn questions that I know she won't contain for long.

"Hey, Little Miss," I say, holding a piece of paper out to her, a contract one of the other guys needs to sign. "Go tell Kevin I need his John Hancock."

Lexie grabs the paper, dropping the marker on the floor, before bolting through the shop. I push my stool back and stand up, walking to the mirror to look at my back. I can hardly make out whatever it is supposed to be, just big black shapes pieced together. Shaking my head, I tug on my shirt and turn to Ellie just as she speaks up.

"Seriously, Reece? You're bringing your bimbos around your daughter now?"

"*A*," I say, holding up one finger, "I don't need you to tell me how to raise my kid. Other people do that enough. And *B*, Avery's not a bimbo."

"So she's your girlfriend?"

"I don't know," I say honestly. "Why does everyone have to try to label everything?"

"Because that's life," Ellie says. "Everything's a label, even a non-label. If she's not your girlfriend, she's what? Your fuck buddy?"

"She's my friend."

"That you're fucking, correct?" Ellie asks. "Because I've never known Reece Hatfield to have a female friend he didn't fuck."

"You," I say. "Never fucked you."

"That's because I'm gay, you dumb twat, but I distinctly remember a time years ago when you tried any-damn-way."

I laugh lightly. "So maybe Avery and I are, you know, but that doesn't make her my fuck buddy."

"Then what does it make her?"

"A special friend."

"Oh, Jesus Christ, Reece, do you hear yourself? That's what I told my mother I had before I came out. I had a *special friend*."

"So?"

"So it's what you call a girl when you're too damn chicken shit to admit she's your girlfriend."

"C," I say, holding up three fingers. "I'm not now nor have I *ever* been chicken shit. And D, I don't remember asking you for relationship advice, so keep it to yourself, *Dear Abby*."

Lexie comes running back to the room just as Ellie starts walking out. "Yeah, well, how about E, Reece... *eat me*."

"F," I holler out at her as Lexie screeches to a stop in front of me. "*Eff you*."

"Oh, I wanna play!" Lexie says excitedly. "G. Garfield!"

I shake my head. "Uh, H. Hatfield."

"J," Lexie shouts. "Juice!"

"Next letter is I," I correct her. "Not J."

"Oh. I." Her forehead scrunches up before her expression brightens and she points at her eye. "Eye!"

I chuckle. *Close enough.*

"How about *I*," I say, pointing to myself, "take you to the park instead of hanging around this place all day?"

"K," Lexie says, clapping her hands like we're still playing the game. "'Kay? Can Avery come, too?"

"Uh, not this time."

"Why not?"

"Because I don't know how to get a hold of her."

"Call her!"

"I don't have her number," I say. "Besides, she's probably too busy with dance rehearsals to go to the park today."

"Can we go see her dance?" Lexie asks. "I wanna dance, too!"

"Afraid not, Little Miss," I say, frowning. "Maybe some other time, but today it's just you and me."

"It's okay, Daddy," Lexie says, smiling as she reaches over and pats the back of my hand. "Don't be sad. I still like playing with you, too."

Eight

An artist on vacation... a receptionist with a hangover... two cancellations back-to-back.

Monday at the shop is shaping up to be Hell.

I casually lounge in a chair in the lobby, my feet propped up on the corner of the receptionist's desk. Ellie flips through the tattered appointment book, the phone tucked in the crook of her neck. She looks like shit. "Uh, we have a short opening next Wednesday with Kevin, and Martin could maybe squeeze you in for a consultation when he gets back from his vacation Monday, but Hatfield could probably see you within the next few days."

I glance at the clock. It's only half past ten, and thanks to my cancellations, I have nothing to do until two in the afternoon. I nearly point that out to Ellie when she chimes back in on the phone call, her words silencing me.

"You said this was for a vine of flowers down your spine, correct? And you have a picture you found online? Right... your consultation would only take a few minutes, since you're set on the design, and then Kevin could probably do the tattoo the same day... the 30th."

Please go with Kevin.

"Martin, I believe, could get to it then, too."

Or Martin.

"Hatfield's schedule has a full opening on the twenty-second, if you don't want to wait."

Not me.

"Great," Ellie says, jotting something down on the twenty-second. *Fuck.* "We'll see you then."

She hangs up the phone, eyeing me intently as I let out an exaggerated sigh. My reaction makes her laugh as she flips back through the appointment book to the right day.

"She's a total Barbie doll, isn't she?" Ellie asks.

"Nope."

We've been going back and forth since the shop opened thirty minutes ago, Ellie trying to figure out Avery while I dismiss her absurd conclusions.

"She's probably a librarian," she says. "You guys get off on those prudes wearing reading glasses and pencil skirts."

"Sounds hot," I say, "but no."

"I bet she's a total cougar, though."

I laugh. "Cougars go for the young guys, Ellie. I'm pushing thirty here."

"So she's not an old broad?"

"No, she's young."

"Oh God, she's not, like, *high school* young, is she?" Ellie looks at me with horror. "Please tell me she's not a teenager."

"She's not," I reply. "Although, she is a student."

Ellie stares at me for a moment. "Huh."

"What?"

"She almost sounds normal," Ellie says. "What's wrong with her?"

"Nothing." I drop my feet to the floor. "Absolutely nothing."

Ellie regards me cautiously. "Where'd you meet her?"

"Here at the shop," I say. "She came in with a friend."

"Ha, I bet it's that chick that got her septum done. Oh, or that one with the bows on her thighs! She was all over you.... no, wait... Lexie didn't like her, right? Uh... damn, who does Lexie like?" Ellie's eyes widen. "No way, pink dress girl? The one who showed up here and said she didn't know what she wanted from you?"

I merely smirk.

"You fucker! It is!" Ellie balls up a piece of paper and launches it at me. "How did *you* pull *that*?"

I clutch my chest in mock offense. "I'm hurt."

"And I'm shocked," she replies. "I mean, you're you, and she... well... let's be real here. Miss Pretty in Pink? No offense, Reece, but she's totally out of your league."

My expression falls. This time I *am* kind of hurt.

The phone rings, garnering Ellie's attention once more. Sighing, I stand up and swipe a cigarette from Ellie's desk before walking away.

I light it as soon as I step outside, inhaling deeply, the smoke scorching my lungs. I exhale slowly, glancing around the busy neighborhood, and freeze when I see her standing damn near right behind me. "We've really gotta stop meeting this way, Aphrodite."

"Tell me about it." Avery waves the air as she steps closer, her nose scrunched up. "Thought you didn't smoke."

"I don't," I say, taking another puff, the smoke soothing my nerves. "Thought you had class in the mornings."

"I do," she admits, "but midterm recess started today."

"Ah, like spring break?"

"Sort of, but it lasts two weeks."

Two weeks? "You going anywhere?"

"Nope," she says. "Well, not unless *here* counts. I'm sticking around town to work on my choreography for the show, so I thought I'd come here and maybe, you know… watch."

"You want to watch?"

"Yes," she says, shrugging.

Smirking, I take a drag of the cigarette. "Sounds kinky."

"It could be," she says playfully. "I'll show you mine if you show me yours."

Looking over at her, I slowly exhale. "Not fair. You've already seen me tattoo. I haven't seen you dance."

"No, but you saw me, uh, twirling, and bending, and gliding, and bouncing…"

"Doesn't count. The lights were off."

She rolls her eyes, blushing, before immediately breaking out into a lazy dance, twirling around as she shakes her ass.

I laugh, taking one last short puff before tossing the cigarette down and stomping it out. "Nice try, but that's not going to work. I need to see some pointy toes and pirouettes and *nobody puts baby in the corner* kind of shit."

"With or without clothes on?"

"Huh." That question stumps me. "Let me get back to you on that one."

The door behind me opens, the jingling sound drawing my attention that way. Ellie appears, scowling, clutching the appointment book. "Reece, your two o'clock called and—" Ellie glances up, stalling mid-sentence when she sees Avery standing there, a smile creeping up on her lips. "Hey there."

Avery smiles politely. "Hello."

"My two o'clock called?" I raise an eyebrow at her, snapping my fingers in her face to get her attention. "And? Please tell me they didn't cancel."

"Nah, they asked if you could squeeze them in any earlier," she replies, straightening her expression out as she jots something down in the book. "I told them to go ahead and come in, you know, since you're not doing anything right now, but if you want me to call them back…"

"No, it's fine," I say, turning to Avery. "Guess you're in luck, voyeur. You get to watch, after all."

Jay Brandon, six feet tall and built like a bear, burly and hairy and a downright fucking brute, is a living billboard of what *never* to do. Ink and piercings cover him, from the top of his shaved head to the tips of his toes, a walking disaster of mistakes.

I've been working on him for a while, gradually covering his old homemade jailhouse tattoos with something the man can be proud of. It isn't easy, but if there's anything I love, it's a challenge.

I think the girl across the room proves that.

Avery sits in a chair out of the way, visibly recoiling when Jay ambles in. I greet the man with a nod as I finish working on the stencil. I get right down to business preparing the area, hiding my abhorrence at having to shave part of the man's brawny chest, and carefully position the hooded grim reaper silhouette over a trio of faded blue dollar signs.

"You know the deal," I say as I get my ink ready, kicking the cassette box. "Pick your poison."

Literally. *Poison.* I stick the tape in the boombox and pressed play, Brett Michael's voice instantly wailing through the speakers. I settle in on my stool, moving closer to the table as Jay stretches out, and set right to work. The buzzing of the machine melds with the loud rock music, surrounding me, sending me into a trance as I focus on the tattoo. I damn near forget Avery is even there, perched quietly in the corner, until Jay clears his throat. "So, who's the broad?"

I glance over when Jay motions that way, seeing Avery grimace at the term. "That *broad* would be Miss Avery Moore."

"Pretty little thing, huh?"

"Oh, most definitely," I agree. *Gorgeous.*

"Never seen her around here before."

"Yeah, she's sort of a new development."

Avery waves her hands in front of her face to garner our attention. "I'm sitting right here, fellas."

I smirk, while Jay lets out a hearty laugh, somehow managing to remain still despite his amusement. "I know, sweetheart, and don't worry… I ain't got a bad thing to say about you. You working with him now?" Jay's attention darts to me. "You get an apprentice?"

Before I can respond, a sharp laugh rings out from the doorway as Ellie approaches. She pauses there, leaning against the doorframe, clearly eavesdropping. *Nosey fuck.* "Definitely not. She's more partner than trainee, if you catch my drift. Less work and more play."

I pull the needle back as my eyes shoot straight to the receptionist, scowling.

"Ah!" Jay says, turning back to me. "Didn't realize you had a girlfriend, man."

Ellie grins with satisfaction, staring right at me, as she echoes that word. "Girlfriend."

"Uh, guys, again… *right here.*" There's a hint of urgency in Avery's voice as it raises an octave. "I can hear every word you say, you know."

I can't turn to her, can't look at her, as I feel my face heating. *Jesus Christ, I'm blushing like a little bitch.* I shoot Ellie a stern look instead. "Do you need something, Eleanor?"

"Nope."

"Then go away."

Ellie narrows her eyes at me, sticking out her tongue, before turning around and walking away. I let out a deep sigh, shaking my head, as I turn back to the tattoo.

"So," Jay said. "How long the two of you been—?"

"How about we take a quick break?" I suggest, cutting him off before he can finish that question. I switch the power off to the machine and wheel my stool back. We aren't even a quarter of the way into the session, not nearly long enough to need a break, but I need a moment to clear my head so I can focus.

Jay doesn't argue, lugging himself down off the table and strolling out of the room.

"Sorry about that," I mutter once we're alone. "I swear it's like a fucking high school cafeteria around here with the way these people gossip."

"It's okay," she says. "I didn't know you told them about us."

"I didn't." I turn around, looking at her, taking in her questioning expression. "They just assume things and have no idea what they're talking about." I step closer to her, smiling softly. "Well, except Jay. He was definitely right."

"About?"

"About you being beautiful."

I pause in front of her, one hand grasping the corner of the table while I tilt her chin with the other and lean down to softly kiss her mouth. I like kissing her.

"That's not what he said," she murmurs against my lips. "He said I was a pretty little thing."

102

I kiss her again. "You are."

"He called me a broad."

Another kiss. "He did."

"He said I was your girlfriend."

I kiss her once more, this time deeper. "I heard."

I start to stand back up straight but Avery grasps my arm, halting me. "Am I?"

I stare at her for a moment. "Do you want to be?"

She doesn't answer right away, her stare burning through me, as the question lingers in the air around us. I don't know what else to say, so I don't say shit. Within moments, Jay comes strolling back in, a sly smile twisting Avery's lips when the man takes his spot back on the table.

"Huh," she says, her voice low as she lets go of me, her hand slipping from my skin. "How about I get back to you on that one?"

I laugh when she turns my words back around on me.

The day wears on, the hours flying by. I immerse myself in my work, forgetting Avery is even in the room until she moves, hovering and watching, the scent of her perfume filling the air around me. Those moments, time seems to stop, each second an eternity as I inhale deeply, suddenly hyper-aware of every movement, every sound, every *breath*, until she backs away again. I work on my outlines with precise detail, expertly shading what needs to be shaded, coloring between the pre-made lines, but not feeling even a stitch of what I feel emanating off of her.

Intrigue. Passion. *Lust.*

I miss those sensations.

Painting used to stir them up inside of me.

Clients come and go, a monotonous schedule... after the chest reaper is an upper thigh revolver tucked into a tattooed garter belt, a flowery tramp stamp, and a second session on a massive snake winding around a bulging bicep, strangling the arm, venom dripping from its fangs. In between sessions I grab a few moments for myself, ordering pizza so Avery has something to eat, grabbing slices on the go while I work.

Night has fallen, closing time slowly descending upon us, when

I switch off the machine for the last time. My fingers ache as I flex them, a pain in my back from being hunched over all day. After the man pays me and departs, I hit stop on the boombox, silencing the sound of some heavy metal band just as it starts giving me a dull headache.

"Thank God," Avery mutters, lounging in the chair, her feet stretching out in front of her. "I don't know how you work with so much noise."

"It's not so bad," I say, shrugging as I discard my gloves. "You can learn a lot about a person by paying attention to what music they listen to."

"Is that why you let them pick?"

I nod. "Most of the time, I've only met them once, if even that, before I tattoo them, so it's hard to get a grasp on their personality. But music, you know... music tells me what they don't. They choose loud, angry music, and it makes for a loud, angry tattoo. It influences the work I give them."

"In that case, shouldn't *you* pick, since you're the one doing the work?"

"No. It's not *my* art. It's theirs."

"Do you ever get to do yours, though? You know, just given free reign to do whatever you want?"

I slowly shake my head as I gaze at her. "Not all of us are as lucky as you, Aphrodite. I've had some in the past give me some leeway, but they always have an opinion, or suggestions, and ideas, little things they want... and that's the way it should be, I guess. It's their body. They want something specific commissioned... they don't come in asking for originals."

Avery is quiet as she gazes at me, a frown tugging her lips. I turn away from her, realizing how pathetic I must sound, whining. Glancing around my workspace, I let out a deep sigh. "Let me clean up and we'll get out of here. You must be bored as shit from sitting here all day."

"Bored?" She scoffs as she stands up. "Hardly. I could sit here all day, every day."

Nine

Avery doesn't stay all day after that, but she wasn't exaggerating about every day. Over the next week, I no sooner get into work and set up for the day when Avery appears, quietly taking a seat in the folding chair. She hangs around the shop all morning, watching as I tattoo, before we have lunch brought in. We eat, chatting for a while, just stealing a few minutes in the middle of the afternoon. She hangs around for a bit afterward, until I start my next tattoo, and then she jets to work on her choreography.

After closing, as usual, I meet her across the street for drinks before heading to my place for sex.

A lot of fucking sex.

Day after day; night after night. We fall into a comfortable routine. She seems to always be there, burrowing her way under my skin as she infuses herself into my life, filling a void, like there has always been a place in it for her.

Friday morning, I'm sitting in my room at the shop, working on a tattoo design for a client as I wait on my first appointment. I glance at the clock—a few minutes until opening—when my phone rings. I pick it up, my eyes drifting to the screen, and tense.

Lexie.

Not Lexie, per se, but close enough. Rebecca never calls me unless it's about our daughter. I answer it quickly, on edge as I bring it to my ear. "What's up?"

"You need to keep Alexis this weekend."

"Uh, what?" My brow furrows. "Why?"

"Richard unexpectedly got called out of town."

Richard, her perpetual boyfriend-slash-boss, the head of the firm where Rebecca is a secretary. Lexie calls him Rich, but I can think of a more fitting nickname for the asshole. "What does that have to do with anything?"

"It's for work," she says. "I'm going with him."

"Why? He can't answer his own phone?"

"I do more than answer his phone, Rhys."

"I know." *You blow him, too.* "But you're not the only one with a job here."

"Oh, give me a break," she says. "You piss around at that little shop all week long while I take care of her. You can't give your daughter a day? You're too busy? What kind of father doesn't want his kid?"

"Of course I *want* her," I bite back, turning around on my stool, startled to see Avery standing in the doorway, listening. "It would just be nice to have a little notice."

"Yeah, well, here's your notice," Rebecca says. "I'll drop her off at three o'clock."

The phone beeps as the line goes dead. She hung up on me. Groaning, I toss my phone down on the desk and run my hands down my face in frustration. *Fuck.*

"Problem?" Avery asks, stepping into the room.

"Yes." I hesitate. "Well, no. Nothing I can't deal with, anyway."

Avery takes her usual seat as Ellie strolls to the doorway to give me my morning report, chewing on the cap of her BIC pen and staring down at the appointment book. "So you're booked solid all day, Reece. Four consultations and three back-to-back sessions. Plus there's a guy who just walked in that—"

"No walk-ins."

Ellie continues as if I hadn't interrupted. "That wants to talk to you about covering up an old tattoo."

"I'll talk to him, but he'll have to schedule an appointment like everyone else," I say. "And I need you to try to shift my appointments around tomorrow, reschedule as many of them as you can for another day."

Ellie grimaces, scanning the appointment book. "That's gonna be tricky."

"Yeah, well, I'll have Lexie this weekend now, so I don't really have a choice. She barely survived one session last time she was here. There's no way she'll sit through an entire Saturday at the shop with me working without tearing the fucking place to pieces."

Ellie taps her pen against the book before jotting something down.

Avery clears her throat. "I could watch her."

Ellie and I skeptically turn to her.

"What?" I say.

"I could watch her," Avery says again, shrugging. "I don't mind."

"I, uh…" I don't know what to say. "I don't know."

"We could just hang out here, you know, if you'd rather us, or we could go to the museum, or do whatever she wants to do, so that way you can get your work done."

"Are you sure about that?" I ask.

"Yeah, no problem," she says, smiling, but her expression falls quickly. "I mean, unless you'd rather me not… you know, if you don't trust me to…"

I don't usually trust *anyone* with my kid, am suspicious of everyone, but most of it is out of my control. I can't pick Lexie's teachers, or her nannies, or whoever the hell Rebecca gallivants through her home, and I fucking hate it… but I've trusted Avery enough to bring her to my place, to introduce her to my girl. I trust her, yeah, but that isn't really the problem here.

"She's not gonna like it," Ellie mumbles, still searching through the appointment book, her thoughts going the same way as mine. "She'll probably raise hell."

"She will," I agree.

"I can handle her," Avery says. "We'll have fun."

I stare at her for a moment. She looks genuine, and I most definitely can't afford to cancel my sessions. I need the money now more than ever, especially if I hope to get the hell out of the neighborhood I've been living in when my lease is up at the end of the year.

Sighing, I nod, waving toward Ellie. *Fuck it.* If ever there's a test for whether Avery and I have any sort of future, it'll be how long she can survive dealing with my little spitfire alone. "Keep my schedule as it is, then. We'll work it out."

Ellie shoots me a surprised look, letting out a laugh as she mock salutes me. "Whatever you say."

She walks away, to consult with the others, as I turn around in my stool to face Avery. "You don't have to do this."

"I want to," she says. "She's your daughter, she's important to you, and well… you're important to me."

Those words are spoken casually, just flowing from the tongue naturally, but they strike a deep part of me. When was the last time somebody said something like that to me? I can hardly remember.

Maybe never.

My first client of the day arrives, the woman's presence effectively ending our conversation. She's undoubtedly attractive— no man can deny that, even one *important* to another beautiful girl, and Avery seems to agree with the sentiment. She sits back in the chair, crossing her arms over her chest, her gaze piercing, as I greet the woman warmly.

"So you want this quote," I say, glancing at the sentences written out on a piece of paper at my desk, some quote about loving and living that I've tatted on half a dozen others before. "And we're putting it on your side?"

"Yes," she confirms, "but I want it up high, and kind of sideways… you know, to like curve up?"

She motions around the area, running her fingers along her ribcage and up toward her armpit, around the curvature of her breast.

"You'll have to take your shirt off," I say, hesitating before adding, "and your bra."

The metal chair immediately shifts, scratching at the floor as Avery abruptly stands up. "I'm, uh… I'll be back later."

108

I watch her hasty retreating form before focusing back to my client. I have work to do. I tweak the stencil, curving the script to the client's specifications, before standing up. Hesitantly, I close the door for privacy as I motion toward her. "You can take your top off now."

There's no sense of modesty as she tears her shirt off, tossing it onto the chair Avery was just sitting in. Without awaiting any instruction, she unhooks her bra and lets it slide down her arms. She flings it across the room, the bra haphazardly landing on the floor beside the metal chair. She grasps her breasts, lifting them slightly as I press the stencil against her skin, making sure it's on firmly, before slowly peeling the paper away. My eyes drift to hers as I take a step back. "Take a look in the mirror and let me know if it's okay."

She steps toward the mirror, eyeing the position, and nods. "Perfect."

I swallow thickly, turning away from her. *Fuck.* I used to not mind these sessions, a perk of the job, but it feels uncomfortable today. It's never sexual—business is business—but damn if it isn't intimate, regardless. The woman settles on the table, laying flat on her back, raising her arms above her head to expose the tattoo area to me.

"Do you want something to cover up?" I offer as I prepare my ink. "We have some of those pasties... you know, those nipple stickers... or you can drape your shirt..."

"No," she says. "I'm fine."

I shrug it off and set straight to work, focusing all of my attention on the words, making sure every curve of the tattoo is smooth, every line ruler-straight. A few times she flinches when I work around her ribs, jarring the lines, making me have to improvise to smooth it back out. It takes about an hour—a strained hour of her obviously flirting and me trying not to think about the fact that a half naked woman lays on my table—before I shut the machine off and shove my stool back.

"All done." I'm on my feet, my back to her, before she can even sit up. "Have a look and let me know what you think."

She jumps down from the table and heads to the mirror,

admiring the work. I peel my gloves off and toss them in the trash as I chant in my head. *Don't look at her tits. Don't look at her tits. Don't look at her tits.*

I turn around, my gaze going straight to her tits. *Fuck.*

She smiles radiantly, seemingly satisfied, and that's a good enough answer for me. I take a deep breath, quickly going over aftercare and getting the spot bandaged up, before grabbing her shirt and tossing it at her.

"I'll give you some privacy," I say, heading straight for the door, slipping out of the room and shutting it behind me, so nobody can wander by and look in while she's still exposed. Running my hand through my hair, I stroll through the shop, my footsteps faltering when I see Avery sitting on a leather couch in the lobby. I pause a few feet away, watching her flip through a magazine, turning pages hastily, her eyes glued to it but clearly not paying a bit of attention to anything on the pages.

I hear my room door open again, my client strolling through. I turn that way as she approaches me, the smile still on her lips. She holds out a rolled up wad of cash, and I reach for it, but she ducks beneath my arm instead, slipping it in my pocket.

"Call me," she says, winking, before strolling toward the door.

My brow furrows as I watch her. Reaching into my pocket, I pull out the cash, skimming through it. A hundred dollar tip and her phone number. *Huh.*

I pull out the slip of paper that holds her number and ball it up, rolling it around in my palm as I turn back to Avery. She still isn't looking at me, her gaze painstakingly on the magazine, but she clearly watched the exchange. The pages turn with such force I'm surprised she doesn't rip the fuckers right out, her foot moving with the intensity of a propeller on a helicopter about the take the hell off.

Smirking, I stroll toward her, her annoyance only growing at my leisurely approach. I sit down on the arm of the couch away from her, propping my feet up on the cushion as I gaze at her.

"You're cute when you're jealous," I say, flicking the ball of paper at her. It hits her chest, right between her tits, and lands on the magazine just as she turns the page again.

Her eyes cut my way as she flips back, grabbing the ball of paper. She smoothes it out, glancing at it, and dramatically rolls her eyes at the digits surrounded by hearts. She crinkles it right back up, clutching it in her fist. "I'm not jealous."

"You're cute when you lie, too."

Avery shuts the magazine, letting out an exaggerated sigh as she tosses it down on the table beside her. She tucks her leg beneath her as she turns her body to face me on the couch. Her eyes bore into me inquisitively. "Do you do a lot of women like that?"

"Like what?"

"Like *naked*."

"She wasn't naked."

"Fine. Topless."

"Occasionally."

"Do you, you know... *do* them, too?"

"I imagine it's kind of hard to tattoo and fuck at the same time, but I'm game if you want to try it."

She narrows her eyes, throwing the balled up paper back at me. "I'm serious. You know what I mean."

I stare at her, grasping the paper and rolling it around in my palm again. I want to lie to her. Fuck, it would be easiest to. I like easy. But the way she's looking at me with such vulnerability, such honesty, I can't. I can't do that to her. "Occasionally."

She looks from me to the door of the shop, where the girl disappeared outside just minutes earlier, before her gaze shifts back to me. "Do you still do it?"

"Do what?"

She groans. "Sleep with your clients, Reece."

"I haven't, not in a while, but I can't really say I never would again," I say, her expression twisting with hurt at my response. Before she can respond, I climb across the couch, startling her as I hover over top of her, pushing her back against it, my lips just inches from her skin. "Because the second I finally get *you* on my table, Avery? I plan to fuck the daylights out of you."

I kiss her hard, pressing myself against her and letting out a low groan at the feel of her body warmth. Avery gasps from surprise, and kisses me back briefly, before pushing against me. I sit up as she laughs, her cheeks flushing. "Not *here*."

"Yeah," Ellie chimes in, shuffling past us as she strides through the lobby. "We're not running a brothel here."

A voice chimes in from a back room. "Can we start?"

Kevin.

I chuckle, climbing to my feet. "We'd probably make a hell of a lot more money."

I offer Avery my hand and pull her to her feet before leading her back to my room so I can get ready for my next client. I start cleaning up, sanitizing my station, when Avery plops down on the chair and lets out a groan. "Oh, gross, she left her bra!"

I glance that way as she reaches down, carefully grasping the black garment by the strap, trying not to touch it. She holds it up, waving it toward me.

"Oh and of course," Avery says, glaring at it. "*Victoria's Secret.*"

Huh. Hundred-dollar tip, phone number, *and* a souvenir? "Guess you scored a free bra."

Avery grimaces, visibly gagging. "You're kidding, right? That's disgusting! I'd never wear that skeeze's bra. Besides, I've practically got mosquito bites over here and she's like, a freaking Double-D."

"She was more of a C."

Avery slings the bra at me, smacking me in the chest before it hits the floor. "Not helping."

I shrug. I'm just being honest. I toe the garment, picking it up, and toss it in a drawer of my desk.

Avery watches, still scowling. "You're *keeping* it?"

"It's the lost and found," I say with a laugh, motioning toward the drawer. "I can't just throw other people's shit out."

She scoffs. "Like she'll come back for it. Actually, you know what? Let me know if she does come back for it. It would take a lot of balls, you know… I wanna know if she's the kind of girl with balls."

"A girl with balls," I say with amusement. "I'm pretty sure she was all female."

"Again, Reece, not helping."

My next appointment shows up a few minutes early, just as I finish sanitizing my station. I sit down on my stool, working on the stencil, as Avery shifts around in her chair. "Please tell me your next appointment is a guy."

"It's not."

"Another woman?"

"Yes." I hesitate, running through my schedule in my mind. "They're all female today."

"All of them?"

"Yes."

"Are they at least going to keep their clothes on?"

I smile, not answering that question. I finish the stencil, eyeing the design, as my client waits in the lobby. She's young, barely eighteen, and nervous as hell. I remember her from her consultation weeks earlier… her first tattoo.

I love these.

The design isn't a favorite of mine. In fact, it isn't much different from the one they plucked off the wall and I slapped on Bridgette. Hearts, and flowers, a banner, and a name—but I meticulously drew this one from scratch based on my client's wishes. Violets, not roses… a keyhole on the heart with the key incorporated in the name on the banner. *Connor.*

Once it's ready, I call for my client to join me. I smile, greeting her warmly, walking her through everything and spelling out every move I make to set her at ease as I apply the stencil to her upper arm. I introduce her to Avery, not wanting any negativity building in the room.

"Pick out some music and we'll get started," I say, sliding the cassette box toward her. She plucks through it, pulling out a few, before settling on some cheery pop that Lexie would've picked. I put it in the boombox and press play before settling in to start her tattoo.

Conversation is relaxed. I remain attentive to my work, taking cues from her as to when to back off. She twitches more than most, slowing the process down, but I keep my patience, grateful when she starts to relax. The tattoo comes together smoothly, flawlessly, as the women chitchat about shit like shoes and movies.

It takes nearly an hour with the detail, but I only charge her for half a session. When it's finished, she steps over to the mirror and stares at it, tears welling in her eyes. "It's beautiful. Thank you."

"Thank you," I say, "for letting me do it."

She smiles brightly, wiping her eyes as she pays me. I fix her up, surprised when she wraps her arms around me in a hug. "Thanks again."

"My pleasure," I say, showing her out.

After she's gone, I hit stop on the music and start cleaning up. My next client is already waiting, hanging out in the lobby.

"You seemed awfully happy to be doing that tattoo," Avery points out. "You know, considering it looked a hell of a lot like Bridgette's."

"Yeah, but looks are deceiving," I say. "I told you—I don't give a shit what it is as long as it means something. And that? It probably meant more than every other tattoo I've done this month."

"Why? Who's Conner?"

"He was her boyfriend," I reply. "He passed away. And yeah, I hate tattooing names on people, because feelings change, but like I said before… I make exceptions. She's young, and will probably move on someday, and get married, and maybe that dude will hate it, but her? Her feelings won't ever change. Because people we love die, but the love? It never does. It became eternal the moment he stopped breathing. She'll always love his memory."

"That's deep," Avery says. "And really beautiful."

"It's just the way it goes," I say, shrugging.

The next session is short, a twenty minute consultation. She tells me what she wants—a dragon design twisting along the top of her foot to around her ankle—and I give her every warning under the sun about everything that could go wrong with a foot tattoo, but her mind has been made up. I concede, jotting down notes of what she wants, and have her head to the receptionist's desk to schedule the tattoo.

I sigh, stretching my back as I hunch over the design on my

desk for my next client. I tense, feeling the hands clamping down on my shoulders, the scent of Avery's perfume washing over me. She wordlessly rubs my shoulders, kneading the muscles, her hands stronger than I expect. My eyes drift closed briefly, tingles shooting down my spine. "Fuck, that feels good."

"I get banged up a lot," she says. "I know how to work tension from the body."

"I know how to work out tension, too," I reply. "But it mostly just involves banging you."

Avery laughs, playfully kneeing me in the back. "Maybe later."

"Drop the 'maybe' part and we have a deal."

"Reece!" Ellie's voice rings through the shop, loud and grating. Before I can holler back, to yell at her for fucking yelling and not walking to my door, the front door of the shop faintly dings, and an excited voice screeches.

I spin around, Avery's hands dropping from my shoulders as I spring to my feet. My eyes dart straight to the time. Three o'clock already.

"Fuck."

Lexie.

I stride out, meeting her in the hallway as she runs straight for my room. I scoop her up in my arms, kissing her cheek and nuzzling in her neck as she squirms, giggling and frantically trying to break free.

"Daddy, stop! It's tickles! Let me down! Please, Daddy?"

I carry her to the lobby, seeing Rebecca standing there, clutching the little pink backpack. I set Lexie on her feet in front of her mother. She tries to slip past me, to get away, but I pin her there. "Rebecca."

"Rhys." Rebecca glares at me, turning her nose up as she looks around at the shop, before her eyes settle on me again. She thrusts her arm out, nearly punching me in the chest with the backpack. "She has plenty to play with in there, and she's old enough to entertain herself, so she doesn't have to be involved in your things."

"In my things," I echo, taking the backpack. "What things are those?"

"You know what things," she says. "I wouldn't have brought her here if I had any other choice. You know how I feel about this place."

"Yeah, you've made your opinion known."

"Just… take care of her. And she's your daughter, for Christ's sake, not a coloring book, so stop coloring on her. You hear me?"

"Loud and clear." I motion toward the door. "I'm sure Dick's waiting for you."

"His name's Richard," she says, narrowing her eyes at me, before leaning down and kissing Lexie on the forehead. "Be good, Alexis. Mommy will be back Sunday night."

"Bye!" Lexie finally manages to escape my grasp, slipping through my legs when I loosen my hold. Her feet pound against the floor for a few steps before stopping abruptly, her voice cutting through the air. "Avery!"

Rebecca's footsteps falter momentarily, but she doesn't turn around, heading straight out the door. Sighing, I turn around, spotting Avery standing right near the lobby, smiling brightly at Lexie. The little girl slips by her, bolting through the hallway toward the room, as I start strolling that way.

"That's Lexie's mom?" Avery asks with surprise.

"Yep."

"Not very nice, is she?"

I let out a laugh. "That's putting it mildly."

I head into the room, catching Lexie just as she's climbing on top of the tattoo table. "Can I have a tattoo, daddy?"

"Of course you can," I say, "just not right now."

"Why not?"

"It's somebody else's turn."

Her expression hardens. She doesn't like that answer. "After their turn?"

"Sorry." I shake my head. "I have appointments all night."

Her eyes widen. "I have to wait 'til tomorrow?"

"I have appointments tomorrow, too."

That she *definitely* doesn't like. Her forehead scrunches up, her eyes piercing through me angrily. "But this is *my* weekend!"

"No, next weekend is your weekend," I point out. "This is an extra weekend, and Daddy has to work."

"That's not fair!" she exclaims. "I want this to be my weekend!"

"I know. And I do, too. But—"

"But it's okay," Avery chimes in, "because you and I are going to do stuff together while your daddy works."

Lexie's attention turns to Avery. She still doesn't look happy. "Do what?"

"Whatever you want."

"I want Daddy," Lexie says, frowning as she points at her arm. "I want my tattoo."

Her expression is like a stab right to the heart.

"Well, I know I'm not your daddy, but maybe *I* could give you a tattoo."

Lexie eyes her warily. "Do you draw like Daddy?"

"Well, not as good as him, but—"

"Nobody's gooder than daddy," Lexie says. "But he draws dinosaurs, and not everybody can draw them."

"I can," Avery says. "Well, I can *try*..."

Lexie jumps down and pushes me out of the way to scour through my desk, pulling out a marker and a crinkled piece of paper. She gives it to Avery and pulls her toward the chair. "Try!"

Avery seems startled. "Huh?"

"You offered to tattoo her," I chime in, shaking my head. "You never let someone ink you until you've checked out their work. Isn't that right, Little Miss?"

"Right!"

Avery starts drawing a dinosaur while I take my seat and start back on tweaking the design for my next client. The room is dead silent for a few minutes as we immerse ourselves in work until Avery lets out a sigh. "Okay. Done."

I spin around to look, my brow furrowing at the oblong-shaped something taking up half the piece of paper.

It looks like a fucking wiener dog.

Lexie just stares at it in silence.

"So?" Avery asks. "What do you think?"

117

"It's okay," Lexie says hesitantly.

"It's okay? So I can tattoo you?"

"No, it's okay that you can't draw good."

I try to hold back my laugh, but Avery quickly takes notice of my amused expression. She narrows her eyes, playfully sticking out her tongue as she balls up the paper and tosses it at me.

"Okay, so I suck at drawing, but I'm good at other things," she says, standing up. "Like hopscotch, and the monkey bars, and jump rope..."

"Oh!" Lexie jumps up and down. "Can we go to the park?"

Avery starts to say yes but cuts off mid-word, her expression serious. "We'll have to ask your daddy."

Lexie turns to me excitedly. "Please, Daddy? Can we?"

I wave them away. "By all means, go have fun without me."

Lexie doesn't hesitate, bolting from the room as she screeches excitedly. Avery stands up, smiling sheepishly. "Sorry, I should've asked you before..."

"It's alright," I say, pulling out my keys and tossing them to her. "You guys can go back to my place afterward. I'll be home as soon as I finish up here tonight."

Avery clutches them, the keys jingling in her hand, before slipping them in the pocket of her jeans. Popping the cap off the marker, she grabs my hand and turns it over, scribbling something down on it. "My cell number."

"Huh." I stare at the numbers on my palm. "I suddenly feel twelve years old again."

"I got you beat," she says. "I'm about to go experience recess for the first time in a decade."

I chuckle. "Yeah, well, that's every other weekend in my world."

They jet from the shop just as my next appointment shows up. All evening long I try to focus on work, to block out everything except for the tattoos, but thoughts of Avery and Lexie keep infiltrating my mind. What are they doing? Are they okay? Is Lexie giving her a fit? Does Avery know what the hell she's gotten into?

My eyes keep drifting to the clock, time moving at a snail's pace. Finally ten o'clock rolls around when I finish my last session, grateful to be done for the day. I quickly clean my station before locking up and heading straight for the door, not even bothering to bid anyone goodnight.

I call the number written on my palm as soon as I'm outside, but it rings and rings. No answer. I make the trek home quickly, bounding up the steps to my apartment fifteen minutes later. The door is unlocked, the place quiet and dark, except for the soft hum of the television in the living room. I step that way, pausing right inside when I see them both lying on the couch, their heads on opposite ends, their feet tangled somewhere in the middle. Avery is curled almost in a ball, her head resting on her hands, her expression serene, while Lexie looks like a wild animal, spread eagle on her back with her mouth wide open, snoring away.

Something about it stalls me right where I stand, my chest constricting. Fuck, it's beautiful. My girl.

My *girls*.

Slowly, I walk over, carefully picking Lexie up and carrying her to her bedroom. She doesn't wake as I tuck her in, kissing her forehead before heading back out. I sit down on the couch where my daughter had been laying and grab the remote, relaxing as I flip through the channels.

Avery stirs eventually, stretching as she shifts position, her foot kicking me hard in the thigh. I wince as her eyes shoot open, and she sits straight up, panicked. Her gaze settles on me, her expression softening with relief. "I thought I kicked Lexie."

"No, just me."

"Thank God," she murmurs sleepily, rubbing her eyes. "What time is it?"

"A little after ten. I just got home and put Little Miss to bed. She was crashed. Hell, you both were."

"Yeah, well, she wore me out," Avery says. "That girl has more energy than anyone I've ever met before."

Chuckling, I relax back on the couch and put my arm around Avery, pulling her to me. "We Hatfields are blessed with stamina. I can work a twelve hour shift with no break and still fuck you silly until dawn."

"Is that right?"

"Absolutely."

"I'm not sure I believe you," she says, shifting out of my arms to climb onto my lap, straddling me. "You willing to back up that claim?"

My hands migrate to her hips before slipping beneath her skirt and grasping her ass, pulling her tighter against me. I can feel the warmth through the flimsy fabric separating us, the heat making me grow hard. "For you? Any time."

Her hands grasp the back of my head, her fingers running through the hair at the nape of my neck as she leans over for a kiss. Tingles creep along my skin as her tongue swirls around my piercing, her teeth nipping at my bottom lip. I kiss her feverishly, wrapping my arms around her tightly, smothering her small frame in my grasp as she shifts her hips, grinding against me.

She unbuckles my pants, releasing me from my boxers, her soft hand wrapping around my cock. She strokes me a few times, her thumb teasing the tip, as she kisses along my jawline. My eyes drift closed as I loosen my hold on her. Swiftly, before I even realize what she's doing, she slips out of my lap and settles on her knees on the floor in front of me.

The moment I feel her lips wrap around me, taking my cock into her mouth, I nearly come. The feel of her tongue gliding along the shaft, the slick warmth, the graze of her teeth, drives me toward the brink almost instantly. She strokes firmly, taking me in as deep as she can.

"Fuck," I pant, my hands settling on the back of her head. My fingers run through her hair before I grip ahold of it, fisting the long locks. I remain still, not yanking, not thrusting, trying my best not to fuck her throat. Eyes peeking open, I watch her in the glow of the television, marveling in the hollow of her cheeks as she sucks.

It's just as beautiful as I imagined it would be.

It goes on for a few minutes before I can't take it anymore. Tingles engulf my lower half, as my body seems to grow taut like a coil. Instead of letting go, instead of letting loose and spilling down her throat, I pull her away from me. Her eyes dart to me with surprise as my hand wraps around hers tightly on my cock, stroking it a few times. With my other hand I grab her arm, motioning for her to stand up.

She obliges, and I don't have to say a word—whether she sees it in my eyes or if she just wants the same thing I do means little. She pulls her panties off and climbs back onto my lap just as I reach for my wallet, opening it. "Shit." *Shit, shit, shit...* "I'm out of condoms."

"It's okay," she says, sinking down on my cock without hesitation. " I'm on the pill."

I hiss as I slide inside her warm pussy, tossing my wallet aside and gripping her hips as she rides me. My hand eventually shifts forward, slipping beneath the fabric of her skirt to gently stroke her clit. Her orgasm comes on hard, her pussy clamping down around me as she cries out. I wrap an arm around her, tugging her toward me, smothering the noise with a kiss as I continue to stroke her clit, not letting up, my movements faster, firmer. I hold her there, thrusting up into her when she stops moving her hips, fucking her as hard as I can in the position. The sound of wet skin slapping consumes the room, mixing with the jingle of my belt, her squeals and cries muted as I breathlessly whisper against her lips.

"You like that?" My voice is a low growl. "You like it when I fuck you?"

She groans loudly, incoherently, the only answer I need. She's already close to the brink again.

"You're so beautiful, Avery," I say. "*So beautiful.* I've been thinking about fucking you all day long."

Mere seconds after the first orgasm subsides, another one hits her, her body convulsing before those words are even completely from my lips. She cries out, louder than before, a growl that resonates in her chest and echoes through the room, so loud I can't smother the noise. I immediately flip her over onto the couch, her face smashed against the cushion. Her cries turn to giggles, her body shaking as she starts laughing. She sags against the couch, her ass poked up in the air.

Without hesitation, I shove her skirt up and slide into her from behind, a satisfied groan escaping my throat as I fill her deeply. My hands run over the swell of her ass before grasping her hips, holding her there as I thrust. It won't take me long, the pressure building, my body close to exploding. I thrust again, and again, and again, nearly losing myself in her, hearing nothing but bodies colliding, and Avery's moans of pleasure, when a voice calls out through the haze.

"Daddy?"

It's like a switch is flipped, shoving me off of cloud nine. I instantly slam right into the ground. The voice is distant, just down the hall, but it's still too close... *way too fucking close.* I pull out of Avery, tucking myself away and hastily buckling my pants. "Yeah, Little Miss?"

I stand, shooting Avery a quick glance as she fumbles with her clothes, when I hear the tiny footfalls. I take a few steps that way, pausing in the center of the living room when Lexie appears. She looks around in the darkness, spotting me.

"Do you need something?" I ask.

She half-shrugs, half-nods, sleepily rubbing her eyes. "I heard a noise."

Avery laughs behind me, covering it with a forced cough.

"I heard it, too." I smirk, glancing over my shoulder at Avery on the couch, her cheeks flushed pink, her hair a fucking mess.

"What was it?" Lexie asks.

"I don't know," I say, turning back to my daughter. "Something outside, I guess."

"It sounded scary."

"It's nothing to worry about," I say, stepping over to her when she starts yawning. "Come on, let's get you back in bed."

"Can I sleep in your room?" she asks as I scoop her up in my arms. "Please?"

"Uh, sure." I carry her back to my room, tucking her in on the center of my bed. Leaning over, I kiss her forehead. "I'll be in the living room if you need me."

I stop off in the bathroom after tucking Lexie in. Avery is on her feet, slipping on her shoes when I make it back to the living room where she is.

"Going somewhere?" I ask.

"Yeah, I should… I mean, it's late so I should probably, you know… go."

I eye her warily. "You don't have to. In fact, I'd rather you not, considering it's almost midnight."

"So?"

"So, it's late, and dark, and it's fucking New York, Avery. That's why. You look too damn tempting to be out on the streets alone at this hour, especially in *this* neighborhood."

She gazes at me with surprise. "I'm not sure if that's sweet or sexist."

"It's the truth," I say. "If you really want to leave, I won't stop you, but I'm just saying…"

"You're just saying?"

"I'm just saying I'd rather you stay. I *want* you to stay."

She stands there for a minute before kicking her shoes back off and leaving them lying in the middle of the floor. I grab a blanket from the hall closet and settle in on the couch with Avery snuggled up against me, tucked under my arm, her head on my chest. I grab the remote, turning the volume up on the TV enough for me to hear it, before starting to flip through channels again.

"Thank you, Reece," she whispers. "For today."

"I should be thanking *you*. You did me the favor."

"Yeah, but you kind of did me one, too," she says. "You trusted me with your daughter, and I know that couldn't have been easy."

"She likes you."

"I like her, too."

My eyes drift to Avery. "And I like you."

"I like you, too." I can hear the smile in her voice. "I feel bad, though."

"Why?"

"Because I couldn't be quiet," she whispers. "Because you never got yours."

Before I can say anything, her hand slides along my crotch,

rubbing me through my pants. Sighing, I close my eyes. "You don't have to do that."

"I want to," she says, shifting her body around to look at me. She presses light kisses along my jawline as she unbuckles my pants and wraps her hand around my cock, blindly stroking it beneath the blanket. "I always finish what I start."

Tiny jabs against my shoulder rouse me from sleep, the relentless prodding migrating the small radius around my arm.

"Daddy." Her voice is the loudest damn whisper I've ever heard. "Hey, Daddy."

I don't move… don't speak… don't even open my eyes. I'm not sure what time it is, but knowing Lexie? It's too early for even the birds.

She pecks with her fingers some more, poking my chest before ultimately jabbing me right in the cheek. I flinch, my eyes opening, my gaze instantly meeting my daughter's. She stands right in front of me, her face mere inches from mine, her eyebrows raised in question. "Daddy, you awake?"

I stare at her. "I am now."

She grins, dropping her hand. Her finger was aimed dangerously close to my eyes, like she was going to poke me in it if I hadn't acknowledged her when I did. "Breakfast!"

"Now?"

"Yes."

I sigh. "Aren't you tired?"

I sure as hell am.

"No," she says. "I'm hungry."

I shift around on the couch, managing to get up without waking Avery. She slept soundly in my arms all night, finally drifting off sometime in the early morning hours. Groggily, I pat Lexie on the head before wandering to the kitchen with her right on my heels.

I start going through the motions, dazed, as Lexie climbs up on the stool at the bar to watch. "Do you have naners?"

Bananas. "Of course."

"Do you have chocolate chips?"

"Uh." I open the cupboard and glance inside for a bag. "Yep."

"Chocolate naner pancakes!"

"No walnuts today?"

"No, I want chocolate."

Shrugging, I put together the batter, throwing the bananas and chocolate chips into it before cooking the pancakes. I've made half a dozen of them when there is a shuffling in the doorway. Glancing over, I watch as Avery staggers in, yawning, groggily rubbing her eyes.

"Morning, Sleeping Beauty," I say, plopping a stack in front of her. "Just in time for some breakfast."

Forgoing her usual small dab of butter, Avery opts to drown them in maple syrup, while Lexie piles hers high with whipped cream, spraying everything within a five-foot vicinity.

"These are *really* good," Avery says after taking a bite. "I like the chocolate chips."

"Me, too!" Lexie says excitedly.

"You know what would make them even better?" Avery says, stabbing a forkful and staring at it. "Peanut butter."

Lexie's eyes widen as she turns her attention to me. "Daddy, I want peanut butter!"

"Maybe tomorrow," I say, strolling out of the kitchen. "I'm going to shower now."

I can't hang around long this morning, as much as I want to. My first appointment is at ten o'clock on the dot, and I have some work to get done before they arrive. At nine o'clock, I begrudgingly head for the door to leave. "What are you ladies going to do today?"

"Little of this," Avery says. "Little of that."

"I'll be at the shop if she gets to be too much. Just bring her by and—"

"Reece." Avery cuts me off, her hand clapping over my mouth to silence me. "We'll be fine."

Sighing, I pull her hand away, pressing a kiss to the back of it before leaning over and softly kissing her lips. I turn to Lexie next, lying in her favorite spot in the hallway, her plastic dinosaurs scattered around her. I crouch down in front of her. "I gotta go."

She frowns, not looking at me. "Bye."

"You'll have fun with Avery." I kiss my hand and press it to her forehead as I stand back up. "I'll be home later."

No sooner I'm out the door, the desire to turn around nags me, but I ignore it and instead forge on, getting to the shop about thirty minutes before opening. I unlock the door, setting straight to work, trying to push them from my mind and focus.

Hours pass, the day a blur of faces and ink, music and chaos. I'm constantly busy, never a down minute in my schedule, as I see client after client, losing myself in work. I'm so immersed in business that I'm surprised when my last client pays me and leaves.

I glance at the clock. How was it ten o'clock already?

I clean up, sanitizing everything so it will be ready to go first thing Monday morning. I bid the others goodbye, having barely had a moment to speak with them all day, and make the trek back home. It's nearing eleven at night when I arrive, but the apartment is as alive as ever, the lights on, the television so loud I can hear the distinct roaring before I even open the door.

Shaking my head, I head inside, slipping into the apartment undetected. Quietly, I step toward the living room, spying the two of them. Lexie is twirling in the middle of the room, moving so fast watching her makes me dizzy, while Avery stands back and watches. Lexie stops abruptly, swaying a bit, before jumping up and down, her hands straight in the air as she tries to stand on her tiptoes.

My girl's trying to do ballet.

After she finishes, she bows theatrically. I push away from the doorway, clapping loudly, startling both of them. Avery grasps her chest, while Lexie lights up excitedly and runs right toward me. "Daddy!"

I scoop her up in my arms. She's a hell of a lot happier now than when I left her hours ago.

"Avery took me to do ballet!"

"No shit?" I hesitate. "I mean… really?"

Lexie gasps, clamping her hand down on my mouth. What is it with these girls telling me to shut up? Playfully, I pretend to bite her hand until she pulls it away, giggling.

"My parents own a studio here in the city," Avery chimes in, shrugging. "We stopped by and I showed her some stuff."

"Meaning you danced for her?"

"Yes."

"Before you danced for me?"

"Yes."

I shake my head, turning back to my daughter, frowning dramatically. "No fair."

Lexie playfully pushes my face away from her, squirming out of my arms. I put her down, motioning toward her bedroom down the hall. "Go put your pajamas on, Little Miss."

She doesn't need to be told twice. Her bare feet are slapping against the wooden floor instantly as I turn to Avery. She isn't looking at me anymore, instead darting around the living room, cleaning up the mess they made while I was at work.

"Don't worry about it," I tell her. "Lexie will tear it all back out in a minute."

Avery hesitantly sets down the toys before joining me on the couch.

I grab the remote, turning the television down so I don't feel like I was screaming every time I talk. I stare at the screen, watching as a T-Rex burst through some trees. "Jurassic Park."

"She wanted to watch it," Avery says. "I mean, I wasn't sure if she was allowed, since it's PG-13, and she's not even close to thirteen, and I'm not her parent… I didn't know, but then again, I don't really know anything about children. Hell, I still feel like a child myself."

"Don't we all." I peer over at her as she fidgets. Fuck, she's cute when she rambles nervously. "I can promise you're most decidedly all woman, though."

She blushes. "Thanks."

"You're welcome. And don't worry—she's seen this movie so

many times she can quote the damn thing."

Just as I say that, Lexie comes bounding back in, wearing a pair of pink princess pajamas her mother obviously picked out. She skids in her socks, stopping right in front of the television, growling, and shouts out a line before the movie even says it.

I motion toward her. "Like I said. So don't worry, you did good. The place is still standing. Nobody got arrested. You both still have all of your teeth." I pause. "You got your teeth, Little Miss?"

She turns around, grinning wildly. "Most of them still!"

"And did you brush them?" I ask, her expression the only answer I need. *Hell no.* "Go do it."

She's off again, skittering down the hallway for the bathroom.

"Daddy?" she shouts back at us. "Can Avery spend the night again?"

"Uh, yeah… if she wants to."

"Can she sleep with me this time?"

I don't know how to answer that.

I can only laugh.

Sunday—the one day out of the week where I can just relax, but there's no sleeping in with Lexie around.

I'm dragged out of bed at dawn to make peanut butter, banana, and chocolate chip pancakes, and spend the afternoon lounging in front of the TV. Avery hangs around all day, seemingly having nowhere else to be.

It's early evening, nearing dusk, when I sit on the couch, Lexie beside me, wedged between Avery and me. The girls watch whatever is on the television while I zero in on what I'm working on: the head of a wooly mammoth.

It looks more like a distorted elephant, but there isn't much I can do. The more I work on it, the more fucked up it seems.

"There," I say, giving up. It's as good as it will ever be. "One *woody* mammoth tattoo."

"It's woody," Lexie says, trying to correct me and still getting the word wrong. "*Woody* mammoth."

"My mistake." I toss the marker down and stand up, stretching as my gaze shifts toward the clock. That feeling is starting to brew in my stomach, the building anxiety as the roller coaster slowly trudges up the hill, the plunge not far off. "We should get going, or we're gonna be late getting you home."

"Do we have to?" Lexie whines, grasping at her arm and straining her neck to survey the drawing. "I wanna stay!"

"Sorry," I say, grabbing her little pink backpack from the corner, the bag untouched, as usual. "Your mother's expecting you. Besides, you have school tomorrow."

"You can take me to school."

I wish I could, and hell, I *could*, technically, but still… I can't. I'm not allowed. The custody order expressly says our visitation ends seven o'clock on Sunday, and if I'm even ten minutes late taking her home, Rebecca rails on me about responsibility and respect, two words I'm damn tired of hearing her say.

Lexie slips on her shoes, pouting, and grabs her backpack from me, dragging it along the floor for the door. Avery casts me a sympathetic smile before jogging over to the girl, offering to take the backpack from her. Lexie declines, but her expression brightens a bit. "Are you coming, too?"

"Sure." The moment she says it, she tenses and glances back at me. "I mean, if it's okay."

I shrug. If she wants to make the trek, I won't stop her.

We take the subway from my place to the Upper Westside, a journey that always makes me feel like I'm exiting into an entirely different city. So used to the day-to-day bustle of my chaotic neighborhood, the upscale streets leading to Rebecca's brownstone seem completely foreign. Rarely in the city do people give me a second look, my tattoos and piercings everyday sights around New York, but in this neighborhood I feel out of place. Maybe it's my imagination, or maybe I'm just projecting, but I feel like everyone is fucking staring at me.

I slow when I reach the brownstone, grasping ahold of Lexie before she can run up the steps. Leaning down, I kiss the top of her head. "Love you, Little Miss. See you next time."

"Bye, Daddy. Love you." As soon as I let go, she runs up the steps, pausing at the very top, her hand grasping the knob. She turns around, grinning, and waves. "Bye, Avery!"

"Bye, Lexie."

Lexie thrusts open the front door, unlocked in anticipation of her arrival, and nearly slams right into her mother. Rebecca stands in the foyer and laughs lightly, grabbing Lexie before she plows her over. "Hey, sweetheart."

"Hey, Mommy."

Rebecca surveys her, eyes sweeping along her, assessing.

"Look!" Lexie drops her backpack, holding her arm out. "Daddy gave me a woody mammoth!"

"I see that." Rebecca runs her hand along it, as if trying to rub it away. "Why don't you go pick out some pajamas? We'll get you a bath."

Lexie is gone, running upstairs inside, as Rebecca steps to the doorway and looks out. I stand along the sidewalk, my hands shoved in my pocket, as I regard her silently.

It's coming.

I can see it in her eyes.

"I asked one thing of you," Rebecca says. "*One* thing, Rhys. That's it. You couldn't give me that? Do you know how hard it is to get that marker off her skin?"

"If you use baby oil—"

"That's your response?" she hisses, cutting me off as she steps out onto the top step. "She's not one of your clients. She's a five-year-old little girl. She has no business being around those people, much less having you treat her like them!"

"She likes it," I counter. "She asks for them."

"So? She's a kid. She doesn't know any better! She asks for chocolate for breakfast and ice cream for dinner, but you don't give her that, do you?"

"Well, actually…"

Guilty as fucking charged.

Rebecca shakes her head. "You're hopeless, Rhys. Completely hopeless. It's a waste of breath even talking to you."

From the corner of my eye, I see Avery shift around a few feet away, lurking, trying to stay in the shadows. I glance at her, seeing how uncomfortable she looks, just as Rebecca seems to notice her presence. Eyes narrowed, she stares her down, judgment piercing through the air as she assesses her, visually picking her apart.

I'm not sure what do to. Am I supposed to introduce them? That seems like the polite thing to do, but knowing what I do about Rebecca? Avery is better off never exchanging words with the woman.

Rebecca's eyes shift back to me, her glare so hostile I can feel it crawling along my skin. "You have a lot of nerve."

I take a step back, pulling my hand from my pocket to salute her. My personal life is one conversation we're not going to have, especially in front of Avery. "I'll see you Friday, Rebecca."

"I don't think so," she says. "You just had her."

"Doesn't matter. It's my weekend."

"You're not getting her."

I laugh dryly. "Try to stop me."

I turn around, stepping toward Avery, and motion with my head for her to follow me. The door of the brownstone behind us slams as Rebecca disappears inside. Avery hesitates before walking with me, the two of us strolling slowly back the way we came.

"You were right," Avery says. "*Not nice* was putting it mildly."

I merely shrug, my fingers twitching. Man, I could use a cigarette, my nerves on edge. I keep walking, but Avery stops when we reach the end of the block, grabbing my arm. My footsteps falter as I turn to her, raising my eyebrows. I just want to get back home, back to familiar territory, back to where it doesn't feel like everyone is mocking and judging the lowlife.

"I, uh… I should, you know…"

No, I don't know. I eye her warily as she motions left, away from the subway and down toward Lincoln Plaza. *Ah*. Juilliard. "That's right… you live around here."

An Upper Westside girl. *Go figure.*

"Only about half a mile," she says, glancing down at herself and grimacing. "I need to shower, and change, and I really need a good night's sleep, since I have to start hitting my choreography hard tomorrow, and well… as much as I'd like to go with you…"

She's rambling.

"Don't worry," I say. "I get it."

"Do you?"

"You won't get much rest at my place."

She smiles sheepishly. "So I guess I'll see you later this week?"

I nod. "You know where to find me."

Avery reaches up on her tiptoes, pressing a soft kiss to my lips, before starting to back away. I turn around to head to the subway, only making it a few steps when she calls my name.

"Reece?"

I glance back. "Yeah?"

"You're a good father," she says. "Lexie's a really happy kid, the happiest kid I've ever seen, and all she talked about this weekend was how much she loved being with you, and I just… I thought you should know."

Giving me a last smile, she turns around.

I watch her as she walks away, quietly muttering, "thank you."

Intermission

An array of color slathered the outside of the five-story brick building on Amsterdam Avenue, coating most of the bottom floor. The paint covered the windows and the glass door, completely obscuring the view inside, making it all blend together like an unending canvas. The lines were sloppy, almost amateurish, but what else could be expected from such a big undertaking?

It popped up overnight, a mural of vibrant graffiti. It took him two hours under the cloak of darkness to finish it.

He was lucky no witnesses called the police.

Sticking around was risky. He rarely did it. But today he felt compelled to watch. Lurking across the street, his rainbow-stained hands shoved in his pants pockets, he watched as the crowd gathered to gawk at his latest work. Anger and disgust twisted most of the onlookers' expressions as they shook their heads and grumbled amongst themselves about what he imagined was the vandalizing degenerate.

Police joined them, interviewing neighbors and filling out reports. They'd have it removed right away. He could see it on their faces. None of them understood or saw it for what it was.

Except for her.

She approached the building, wearing typical dancer's clothing, heading for the studio with her backpack on her back. She was soft, and pretty, and graceful.

She was everything he wasn't.

She stalled on the outskirts of the crowd,

scanning the mural, and after a moment, he saw it.

A smile.

She smiled.

His own lips curved in response.

He didn't stick around any longer.

Keeping his head down, he quickly disappeared from the neighborhood before anybody noticed him.

It was worth the risk, he thought.

Someone saw it, and they understood it.

They knew art.

All it ever took was one person.

On to the next one.

Ten

The three-story brick building is just off Broadway, *Trouvaille Ballet* in block letters affixed along the front of it, right above the entrance.

Trouvaille. It's French. It means "a lucky find". Something awesome you stumble upon. I know, because I've looked it up.

I've looked it up because I've been lucky enough to stumble upon the place before. It was a long time ago... or what *feels* like a long time, anyway.

A lifetime has passed since then.

I stand along the curb after dark, staring up at the name. "Your parents own this place?"

Avery nods excitedly, pulling a set of keys from the duffel bag she's carrying. She showed up at the shop right at closing tonight, asking me to go somewhere with her instead of hitting the bar as usual. I agreed, asking no questions, taking the subway to the Upper Westside with her.

I should've asked where we were going.

I wasn't prepared to come here.

"They let me use it whenever I want to practice," Avery says, "so it's pretty much always open for me."

"Is that why we're here now?" I ask, glancing at her. "So you can practice?"

"Something like that."

She unlocks the front door and motions for me to go inside. I hesitate by the curb, not moving. "I don't think—"

She doesn't let me finish, rolling her eyes. "Don't *think* then. Just come on."

Taking a deep breath, I follow her inside, knowing if I don't she'll want some kind of explanation, an explanation I don't have it in me to give. The interior, like the outside, appears pristine, the long hallway in front of me dark and empty, like a vacant runway.

Avery swiftly disarms the alarm system before relocking the front door. I follow her down the hall, to a door on the right. Avery pushes it open, motioning once more for me to go in.

This time I don't hesitate.

There's no point anymore.

I'm already trespassing.

The massive studio is open and airy, despite the darkness, a mirror covering the entirety of one wall with windows spanning the opposite, making it feel twice its size. Everything is bright, the floor a light gray, the high ceiling white. It's strict and sterilized—a big ass void of space.

It isn't the kind of place that lets just anyone walk in off the street to dance. Not necessarily bland, I think, but it damn sure feels soul-sucking.

I've always thought that about this building.

It needs some color, for fuck's sake.

"It's, uh..." I glance around, not sure what to say. "It's nice."

"It is," she agrees, setting her bag down on the floor. "I've been training here since I was old enough to walk. I've probably spent more hours in this studio than in my own bedroom growing up... more time dancing here than doing anything else."

"That's, uh..." '*That's nice*' is on the tip of my tongue, but I can't say it, not when I don't mean it. "That's depressing as fuck."

She lets out a laugh. "It is."

"You agree?"

"Yeah, but I mean, it is what it is." She shrugs it off, pausing a few feet from me to look around. "My first memory is of this room, wearing a little tutu and trying to copy my mother as she danced. It's just always been my life. It's who I am. If I don't have dance, what do I have?"

I watch her for a moment, not replying. I don't have an answer to that. Without my art, I feel like nothing more than a shell, a poor excuse for a man, a miserable son of a bitch.

So what is she without dance?

She's *me*, probably.

Slowly, I stroll toward her, pausing behind her, my hands lightly grasping her arms as I lean down to kiss her neck. "So you always wanted to be a ballerina?"

"Well... I've always wanted to *dance*," she says. "My parents—they were both with the American Theater Ballet. My father was older, a principle dancer, pushing thirty. And then there was my mom... came on one season at eighteen as a *corps de ballet*. They had this forbidden love affair, and my mom left when she got pregnant with me. My father walked away not long after and opened this studio."

I hook an arm around her waist, pulling her back against me. "So they gave up their dream for you?"

That I can empathize with.

"Nope," she says, pulling from my grasp and turning to peer at me in the darkness. "They didn't give up their dream. They just went about it differently. They still dance every day, and they love it just as much as they did when they were touring. The dream lives on, Reece, and it never gives up on you, no matter what you might think. Dreams sometimes just *change*."

Before I can say anything, Avery grabs the bottom of her flowery top and pulls it up over her head, tossing it on the floor beside the duffle bag. I stare at her, eyes widening, surprised by her boldness as she reaches behind her, unclasping her black bra. It falls down her shoulders, joining the shirt on the floor, before she pushes her skirt down and steps out of it, kicking it aside.

She stands before me, wearing nothing but the tiniest black thong, barely a string of fabric covering the most intimate part of her, and a pair of pale slip on shoes. Unconsciously, I reach out toward her, but she takes a step back and holds her hand up. "A deal is a deal."

A slow smile spreads over my face as those words sink in.

She's going to dance for me.

"How did you know I wanted you to take your clothes off?"

"Because I'm not an idiot."

Laughing, my eyes drift to the windows, the city outside alive and chaotic, as cars pack the streets and people stroll by. I turn back to Avery, motioning with my head. "Can't people see you?"

Maybe she's into that voyeurism shit, after all.

She shakes her head. "Two-way tint. The outside looks like a mirror."

As if the universe wants to prove her point, someone ambling by comes to a stop to survey their reflection, checking their teeth and fixing their hair, before moving on. Huh, I hadn't noticed.

I casually lean back against the wall beside the door, my hands shoved in my pockets, as I nod for her to proceed. Avery plucks a tiny remote from her bag and presses a circular button on it, classical music instantly starting up from incognito speakers, blending into the corners and the ceiling. The music is soft and smooth, easing some of my tension.

Avery backs away from me, smiling sheepishly, her bottom lip tucked beneath her teeth. She approaches the bar that runs the length of the mirrors and starts stretching, her movements subtle and fluid as she extends her arms and legs, reaching on her tiptoes as she flexes her feet, warming her body up. It lasts only a few minutes, just long enough for the music to shift.

The notes ring louder, more dramatic, the lullaby morphing into a full-blown orchestra. She pushes away from the bar and takes off across the room with the grace of a prowling panther, spinning and turning, leaping and swaying, moving in ways I never thought it possible for a person to move.

I stand there, watching, her body a mere shadow blending into the darkness. My eyes are glued to her silhouette, drinking in every drop of her milky flesh when the dim moonlight streams in on her from outside. It bathes her skin as her body contorts, her leg kicking so high it nearly points straight up in the air, her muscles taut, emphasizing the contours of her petite body. She's strong—a hell of a lot stronger than I realize—so graceful, and flexible, and beautiful.

So goddamn beautiful.

It doesn't last long before the music comes to a stop, silence falling over the room. Avery freezes on her tiptoes, her feet slowly sinking back flat to the floor as she drops her arms to her side. She stands there, breathing heavily, her eyes closed, a look of peace settling over her face.

I've never seen her look so much at ease before. Confidence oozes from her pores. I push away from the wall and slowly stroll to her, my footsteps amplified in the quiet.

Avery's eyes open when I pause in front of her, so close I can smell the hints of perfume that still cling to her skin. She stands before me, damn near naked, a light sheen of sweat coating her body, glistening under the glow of the moonlight. She regards me cautiously, the confident mask slipping, a hint of anxiety in her deep brown eyes.

"So?" she asks, the word barely a breathy whisper.

"So," I repeat, reaching out for her. This time she doesn't move away, staying still as I caress her side, my hand drifting along her stomach and up her chest, my thumb brushing against her hardened nipple. She shivers, a gasp escaping her parted lips when I do it again.

And again.

And again.

And fuck if I don't do it *yet again.*

Her body reacts to my touch, goose bumps trailing my fingertips wherever I touch her. I watch with fascination, lost in the moment, as I play her body like a fine-tuned instrument.

"So?" Avery says again. "That's all you have to say?"

My eyes drift to hers, seeing her anxiety has increased tenfold. Once more she bites down on her lip, her already flushed body growing redder.

"Sorry," I say. "Your tits distracted me."

Rolling her eyes, Avery pushes away from me. I chuckle, grabbing her hips and pulling her back before she can walk away.

"Beautiful," I say. "Absolutely stunning."

"My tits?"

Fuck, just hearing her say that makes my cock impossibly hard. As if by instinct, my eyes drift back down to her tits. "I meant your dancing, but yeah… those, too."

Avery laughs, wrapping her arms around my neck, some of her anxiety lessening as she gazes at me. "Thank you."

"You don't have to thank me," I say. "I'm the lucky one, getting to witness it. I feel like I should've had to pay to see you do that."

"You don't pay to look at art. You pay to keep a piece of it."

"Huh." I lean down and softly kiss the corner of her mouth, my lips trailing along her cheek before drifting toward her ear. "How much is that going to cost me?"

"To keep a piece?"

"To keep *all* of it."

"Depends," she says. "What have you got to offer?"

What do I have to offer?

"Not much," I admit. "I'm a college dropout and everything I have is either rented or leased. My most prized possession is my 1990s boombox with an extensive tape collection. I really have nothing else to my name. So if you're looking to barter, I could probably offer one of my kidneys. That's about it. I work twelve hour days but some months I barely break even, so, you know… if I can't get it on credit, I probably just can't get it."

"Wow." Avery's eyes widen. "You sure know how to woo a woman."

"Yeah, well, I also come with a three-feet tall sidekick. We're sort of a package deal… and I might be rough around the edges, but I like to think she's special enough to make up for it."

"Hmmm, this is sounding better…"

"Although, her mom's sort of a bitch, so it's not *all* roses and sunshine." I smile softly, gazing at her. "But if it helps, I'll throw in a lifetime supply of orgasms."

"Sold!"

I chuckle, pulling Avery tighter against me, my hands finding their way to her ass. "How about we get started on them now?"

"Ah, I *was* right. You *do* know how to woo a woman."

"I do," I confirm, pushing against her, making her take a few steps backward. "I also know how to make one scream my name."

I pull Avery over toward the middle window and pick her up, placing her on the deep window ledge that stands nearly waist-high. Before she can say a word, I grasp the sides of her thong and pull it off, flinging it across the room toward the rest of her clothes. I settle between her thighs, stroking her skin as my hand makes its way toward her pussy. Leaning down, I capture a nipple with my mouth, my tongue swirling around it, as I carefully push two fingers inside of her.

Avery lets out a moan, morphing into a squeal of surprise when I drop to the floor in front of her. My mouth finds her flesh, the tip of my tongue encircling her clit, as I pump my fingers in and out. I work slowly, agonizingly, warming her body up for me. Once I have her writhing, her back pressed up against the cold glass, her eyes closed, hands unconsciously seeming to make their way to her breasts, I know I have her.

Curving my fingers, I feel for her g-spot, the simplest touch eliciting a loud gasp. I stroke the spot, increasing pressure, my movements faster, as my mouth finds her clit again. I suck on it, flicking my tongue with the rhythm of my fingers. It doesn't take long before she grows tense, a scream bubbling up in her chest that she tries to contain, bursting forth as a strangled cry as she convulses from orgasm.

She never has time to catch her breath. As soon as her body starts to relax again, the pleasure subsiding, I stand up and unbuckle my pants. I grasp her hips, pulling her closer to the edge, not bothering to get undressed. With one swift motion I'm inside of her, the deep thrust making her cry out. She wraps her legs around my waist, falling back against the glass as I fuck her, taking no mercy on her body, giving her everything I can. Again and again, over and over, my hips slam into hers as I fill her deeply, the wet skin slapping like frantic pounding echoing through the studio.

Avery cries out, orgasm ripping through her once... twice... three times. Her body never seems to have time to relax, never has time to recover, before I'm reaching for her clit again and rubbing in harmony to my thrusts. I stare at her, watching her come apart in front of my eyes, melting to a puddle of agonizing pleasure that only I am here to absorb. People walk by on the street, mere feet from where I fuck her, every single one of them oblivious to what's happening on the other side of the glass.

That fact gives me a thrill like never before, driving me on. I want to come—fuck, do I want to—but I can't. Not yet. I'm not done with her. I push the feeling back, ignore the pressure building in my balls, the warmth spreading across my entire body, and focus on her instead.

The fourth orgasm rips through her, the pleasure barely subsiding, her body just starting to relax, when I'm back at it again. Avery starts to speak, her lips moving, the words catching in her throat. All it takes is a few seconds and some firm strokes to drive her right back over the brink. Her mouth opens, a scream escaping, with it what I've been waiting for. "Reece! Oh fuck, *Reece!*"

The moment she says it, I lose control, my own orgasm unable to be contained. I thrust a few times, grunting, hardly able to move as the intense relief washes through me. Stilling my movements, I lean forward, snaking an arm around Avery to pull her away from the glass. "Told you I could make you scream my name."

"Oh God, no more," she says, her voice strained. Sweat coats her flushed face. "I can't come anymore."

My other hand slips between us. "Wanna bet?"

The moment my fingers graze her swollen clit, she gasps. "Oh God, you're going to kill me."

Chuckling, I pull my hand away and slowly slide out of her. "Death by orgasm."

"Sounds about right," Avery says, gazing at me. "It feels like you murdered my pussy."

I just stare at her. No woman should say the word *pussy* in such a sexy, breathless voice, unless they want that pussy pounded again. Shaking my head, I tuck myself away and fasten my pants again. "Now you're trying to kill *me*."

Grabbing her hips, I pull her down from the window ledge and set her on her feet. One arm holds onto her while my other hand cups her pussy, my fingers caressing the flesh, dipping inside. Avery gasps, pulling away from me.

She thinks I'm trying to get her off again.

I laugh, instead bringing my hand up and sticking my finger in my mouth. "I've wanted to know what you tasted like since the moment I saw you."

She gapes at me, her eyes wide, blush spreading across her cheeks. Her reaction only makes me laugh harder. She has no qualms dancing naked then being fucked silly against a window, yet the mere reminder of me tasting her brings out the blushing virgin that still, somehow, exists deep inside of her.

"Don't worry," I say, reaching over and running that same finger along her bottom lip. "You're just as sweet as I thought you'd be."

Rolling her eyes, her blush deepening as she tries to fight off a grin, Avery pushes away from me. She scampers around the studio, gathering up her clothes and getting dressed again.

"So I wanted to ask earlier, you know, before your tits distracted me," I say. "Was that the choreography you've been working so hard on?"

Avery puts on her shirt as she turns to me. "No, that was something I learned a long time ago. It was actually the dance I auditioned for Juilliard with. My mom choreographed it."

"Why didn't you show me your stuff?"

"It still needs a lot of work," she says, pulling on her skirt and twisting it around, trying to situated it.

"So?"

"So it's not ready," she says. "You can't really look at a work-in-progress and see the big picture. You have to wait until it's finished."

"Ah." I can understand that. "Maybe some other time."

"You, uh… you wouldn't want to come, would you? To the performance? I mean, I know you work, and you'll probably be too busy, but we do a few shows and I thought maybe you could come to one. If you weren't, well… too busy. And if you *wanted* to. You don't have to. I just—"

I stare at her as she rambles nervously. "Avery."

"Thought I'd ask." She pauses, eyeing me with uncertainty. "Yeah?"

"Of course I'll come. Just tell me when and where and I'll be there."

Eleven

"Where did you get all of these?"

I'm sketching out something. I don't know what it is anymore. It started out as a psychedelic dragon but is starting to look more and more like one of Lexie's damn dinosaurs. I keep getting distracted by the ruckus in the room as the goddess sits on the floor in the corner, shifting through my box of music.

Tapping my pencil against the desk, I glance at her, seeing she's eyeing me curiously, her eyebrows raised in question. Shit, what did she just ask me? "What?"

"These things," Avery says, waving her hand overtop the box full of cassettes. "Where did you get them?"

"Uh, here and there," I say. "Thrift shops, flea markets... some I've had for years, others were donated by clients who had no use for them anymore."

"Why?"

"Why what?"

She waves her hand over the box again. "Why cassettes?"

This isn't the first time I've been asked that question, and I'm sure it won't be the last, either. I don't have an answer, though. I never do. Why cassettes? *Why the hell not?*

Why does society always have to move on to something new when the old still works just as fucking good, you know?

"They're cheap," I say. "I see no reason *not* to use them."

"Because they're outdated." She shifts through the box, pulling a few out and holding them up like she's trying to prove a point. Michael Jackson's *Thriller*. AC/DC's *Back in Black*. The *Dirty Dancing* soundtrack. "Your music collection ends about the time I was born, Reece. You need something *new*."

"New music sucks."

"Does not."

"Nothing's original anymore," I say. "I can't tell Bieber from Timberlake. It all sounds the same."

She gasps, staring at me with horror. "Take it back."

"It's true."

"Blasphemy!"

I laugh at her reaction, turning back to my horrid drawing. Snatching the paper from the desk, I ball it up and throw it at the trashcan, ignoring it when it bounces off the side and rolls across the floor. Leaving it there, I move on to a fresh piece of paper and start sketching out another dragon.

Besides the sound of Avery rifling through the box of cassettes, occasionally snickering as she reads the labels, it's mostly quiet in my space. I try to focus, to work on the drawing, but my heart just isn't into it.

Sighing exasperatedly, I ball up my second attempt as Avery speaks up behind me. "So, when's your birthday?"

"It was a few months ago," I say. "Why?"

"Figured I could get you a Walkman," she says. "Maybe even do something crazy like buy you a CD player."

I turn to her when she laughs, tossing the balled up drawing at her. It lands right in her lap, and she quickly abandons her musical treasure hunt to be nosey as shit and see what I've been sketching.

She unfolds it, eyeing the crinkled paper. "This is awesome."

"Awful, you mean?"

She rolls her eyes. "No, that's not what I mean."

Her gaze flickers along the sketch for a moment before slowly, carefully, she folds the paper up and slips it into her pocket without uttering another word. Shaking my head, I turn back to my desk, a small smile tugging my lips when I snatch up another blank piece of paper, settling in for attempt number three.

"I should get going," Avery says, putting the music back away, shoving the box across the floor toward where I'm sitting. "I have rehearsals, and I know you have work to do. I just wanted to stop by and say hello."

I nod, vaguely sketching, feeling her hand on my back as she passes me on her way to the door. She said she was *just in the neighborhood* when she showed up, but the woman exists in practically a different world. There's nothing here for her... nothing, that is, except for me.

I'm glad whatever this is between us is mutual. Maybe I drive her as crazy as she's starting to drive me.

I cut my eyes her way, clearing my throat. "So what are you doing tomorrow?"

"Nothing that I can think of. You?" She doesn't give me a chance to respond before she continues. "Oh, right... never mind... it's your weekend with Lexie."

"It is," I respond. "We're going to get up early and explore the city a bit, you know... make a day of it, if you want to join us."

"Really?"

"Yeah, sure, why not?" I shrug, turning to my work. "Probably head out around eight if you wanna tag along."

"Absolutely," she says. "I'll see you then."

She casts me a shy smile before turning to skirt out the door, running straight into Ellie when the receptionist walks in. Avery mumbles a quick apology, ducking her head before disappearing as Ellie blinks a few times, watching her retreat with confusion. After Avery's gone, Ellie shakes her head, muttering, "talk about *gorgeous*."

I laugh dryly. "Tell me about it."

Ellie turns to me, raising her eyebrows curiously as she steps into my workspace, clutching the appointment book. "So the two of you...?"

"Do you need something?" I ask, cutting off her question as I avoid answering. "I'm busy here."

"Yeah, wanted to tell you your client just called."

"Don't do it," I say, shaking my head as I close my eyes, tip of the pencil still pressed to the paper. It was the only person on the books for me today. The job was scheduled to take all damn afternoon. "Don't tell me they cancelled."

"Rescheduled them for next month."

Groaning, I toss the pencil down and snatch up the paper, balling it up and throwing it over my shoulder, vaguely in the direction of the trashcan. *Fuck this.* Running my hands down my face, I take a deep breath before shoving my chair back and standing up. Ellie watches me warily as I gather my things, not bothering to clean up my mess. She follows me out of the room, lingering there as I lock up my workspace.

"Tell Kevin I'm taking the day off," I say. "No point staying here."

"You can hang out with me," she chimes in, leaning against the wall beside me. "I'm sure there will be a few walk-ins you can pick up later today."

I cut my eyes at her, seeing her amusement, and simply shake my head as I step around her, heading for the door of the lobby. "I'll catch you on Monday, El."

"Bye, Reece," she says. "Tell the little one I said hey."

I wave back at her before walking out.

There's a chill in the air outside, the ground damp as drizzle falls from the sky. Whipping my hood up over my head, I shove my hands in my pockets as I stroll down the block.

When I reach the corner to turn down the next street, I pause, waiting for the flashing sign to change to *walk*, my gaze flickering toward the construction site across from me. I haven't seen a single worker in the neighborhood, not a damn thing done to the place except boarding it up and covering it with tarps.

"About time, huh?"

The voice calls out behind me, so close it makes the hair on my arms stand on end, a chill running the length of my spine. The motherfucker snuck up on me.

I glance over my shoulder, seeing him lurking there. Previn Warren. He looks almost like a normal officer, with his dark uniform and handcuffs, a 9MM holstered at his hip, but the word 'probation' is affixed to his jacket where 'police' would otherwise be.

He's older, with graying hair and leathery skin, built like a bulldozer with the cockiest grin I've ever seen.

I turn back around, looking away from him, my gaze flickering toward the construction site again. "Are you following me, Officer Warren?"

"If I am?"

Pulling my hands from my pockets, I hold them up, raising them in the air so he can see. "My hands are clean."

"Good to know," he says, strolling over to stand beside me. "Where are you off to today?"

I really want to tell the man to fuck off, but I know I can't. Because my business is his business until the courts say otherwise. Oh, how I look forward to that day...

"Home," I say.

"Home? Not feeling well or something? You usually always work on Fridays."

It bothers me that he knows that.

It bothers me that he knows *everything*.

"No work to do," I tell him, "so I'm taking a personal day."

He nods, motioning toward the flashing sign just as it changes to *walk*. "Go on then, Hatfield. Just stay out of trouble."

I quickly walk away from him, grateful for the dismissal, knowing he could be a pain in the ass and keep me if he wanted to. I glance behind me, seeing the man disappear from sight, heading in the direction of the tattoo shop.

He's going to talk to Kevin.

I'm not surprised, but I'm not worried, either.

I have nothing to hide. Like I told him, my hands are clean.

There's something about a flea market that makes me feel at home.

Maybe it's the laid back atmosphere.

Maybe it's because everything's so cheap that even *I* can afford to buy something.

The people are nice and don't bat an eyelash when someone who looks like me browses through their shit. They don't watch me like I'm not good enough to be there, don't look at my kid like she doesn't belong, either.

It's a cool morning but the sky is clear, the sun out and shining bright as I stand in the middle of the old garage in Hell's Kitchen. Booths and tables span every inch of the space, packed full of antiques and collectables, knick-knacks and fucking paddy-whacks, everything imaginable under one roof. I stroll through the crowd, Avery right beside me, while Lexie insists on leading the way. I keep my eye on her, making sure she doesn't get too far ahead... making sure she doesn't bowl over any old ladies along the way.

Wouldn't be the first time.

"Slow down, Little Miss."

She slows down for half a second before rushing ahead again. Avery jumps in, stepping in front of me when I groan, and casts me a smile. "Don't worry, I've got her."

I start to say she doesn't have to do that, but my words fall on deaf ears, because she's already slipping through the crowd, disappearing before I can stop her. Part of me screams to follow the second I lose sight of my daughter, but I keep from hurrying after them, telling myself to chill out.

I invited Avery here with us.

Invited her around my daughter.

I trusted her enough to come into our lives.

I trust her to look after Lexie.

I make my way through the crowd, hearing Lexie's loud, excited voice above the other chatter, and follow the sound straight to a table in the corner.

Where she stands with Avery.

Where she's clutching a gigantic Godzilla toy, still in the package, the hideous, plastic action figure damn near as tall as her.

"Look, Daddy!" Lexie screeches the moment she spots me, dragging the thing along with her as she runs to me. "A dinosaur!"

"Technically, it's a lizard monster, uh... *thing*." I'm not sure what the hell it really is. It looks kind of like the shit I drew yesterday, honestly. "You need to put it back, though."

"But—"

"Put it back where you found it," I tell her again. "It's not yours."

"But—"

"You heard me, Little Miss."

She stares at me like she'd like to duct tape my mouth shut to keep me from saying some shit like that again.

"Actually, it sort of *is* hers," Avery chimes in, her voice hesitant. "I just paid for it."

My eyes dart to her. "You did what?"

"I paid for it," she says again. "It was no big deal... she liked it so I figured there was no harm getting it for her."

Sighing, I run my hands down my face before reaching for my wallet, pulling it from the back pocket of my jeans.

"How much was it?" I ask. "I'll give it back to you."

"It was fifty."

I damn near choke on thin air at that. "Fifty *what*? Cents?"

Her sheepish look tells me no, I'm not that lucky. The son of a bitch was fifty *bucks*.

"It's a collectible," she says quietly. "It's still in the package."

"You know she's going to open it, right?" As soon as I say that, Lexie starts ripping into the cardboard, just like I knew she would. "She's going to destroy it in some *Cloverfield*-esque massacre like she does all her toys."

Avery watches Lexie as she demolishes the packaging, ripping that shit to pieces to yank out her brand new *dinosaur*. After a moment, Avery shrugs, glancing back at me. "She really likes it, though."

I shift through the cash in my wallet, seeing how much I have, when Avery reaches over and snatches it all from hand. I watch her warily as she forces the bills back in before folding it up. Reaching around me, she shoves it in the back pocket of my jeans.

"It's a gift," she says. "From me."

"You shouldn't have."

"But I did."

I want to argue the matter but keep my mouth shut instead. Lexie and Avery both look really fucking happy, and I can't be the dick that takes that away simply because my pride doesn't like me to admit that my daughter wanted something and *I* couldn't afford it.

There's no time to dwell on it, though, before Lexie is off again, finally freeing Godzilla from the packaging. I clean up the cardboard mess she made as Avery slips away to keep up with her.

Whatever havoc those two are off wreaking, I probably don't want to be a part of it.

I find a few cassette tapes. Avery shows back up with some secondhand books. Lexie makes out like a fucking bandit, walking away with more stuff than she probably should. It's pushing afternoon already when we leave the flea market, strolling along the sidewalk on our way to the subway to head back to my neighborhood. Lexie skips along in front of us, Godzilla tucked under her arm, the massive tail dragging the ground.

Sighing, I reach over and wrap an arm around Avery, pulling her to me, pressing a kiss to the top of her head. "Thank you."

"For?"

"For coming with us," I say. "For buying her that."

"Not a big deal," she says again. "It's just money, right?"

I laugh dryly. "Right."

There's a commotion right in front of us then, some young guys rushing out of an alley. There's two of them, dressed in black, hoods up over their heads. Bandanas cover part of their faces. I know the look. They're up to something.

Letting go of Avery, I take a quick step, my hand coming to rest on Lexie's shoulder and yanking her to a stop before she runs into their backs, knowing damn well she's too distracted by her new toy to notice. I glance down the alley, making sure it's safe, when my eyes fall upon a massive mural covering the sides of the brick buildings. Nothing new in the city, of course. You'd be hard pressed to find a building *not* tagged in this part of town. But what stalls me is the spray painted image, dead center, surrounded by other elaborate, colorful monikers.

A shadowy figure looking down, a top hat perched on its head. It's a barely defined silhouette in black paint, like a void in the otherwise vibrant rainbow of graffiti. My chest tightens, my muscles taut, my head swimming as I stare at it in shock for seconds that feel like minutes... like hours... like *days*. The new, black-stained canister lies on the asphalt beneath it, the paint so fresh it's glistening. I can smell it above the city stench.

Those little motherfuckers.

"Watch her," I say automatically, letting go of Lexie, leaving her there with Avery as I dart away, breaking into a sprint to catch up with the guys. They're walking along like they have not a care in the world, laughing and chatting, like they're sure they got away with what they did.

They hear my approach, turning around as their conversation stalls, confusion on their faces. Before they can say anything, I grab ahold of the first one I reach, my fist clutching his jacket as I yank him toward me. I glance between the two of them, my heart racing, adrenaline pumping through my veins. They're just kids... sixteen, maybe seventeen, no older than that... but they have that look in their eyes, that look that says they've been through more shit than most guys.

"Which one of you did it? Huh?" I look between them, trying to swallow back my anger, but it makes my voice shake. "Which one of you assholes painted it?"

The kid grasps at my hand, trying to pry it off, as his friend gets between us, shoving me away. The second his hands connect with my chest, I see the black paint staining his fingertips, streaks of it on his palm. I snatch ahold of his wrist, yanking his hand up, shoving it toward his face as he yells, "What the fuck is your problem, man?"

"My problem is *this*," I growl, hitting him with his own hand before shoving him away, making him stumble a few steps. "What business do you have tagging that building that way? Huh? Who the hell do you think you are? What gave you the *right*?"

People around us are looking but I can't find it in me to care. All I care about is what they just did, wondering why the hell they would do it, what they were *thinking*. They back away, their confusion morphing with anger, before they turn around and take off running. I almost follow, I take a few steps, but something stops me. Something locks me in place. I watch as the kids cut down another alley, nearly plowing someone over as they make their escape, disappearing into the afternoon crowd.

Dropping my head, I look at my hands. My hands, so clean, with not a stitch of color on them anywhere. I can't even remember the last time they'd been stained with paint.

Clenching them into fists, I close my eyes for a moment, taking a deep breath, before I turn around and walk away.

I don't see Avery and Lexie until I reach the alley, finding them standing not far from the mural. Avery's eyes are on it, slowly scanning it, while Lexie plays beside her, still distracted by her new toy.

Avery glances at me when I approach. I see the questions in her eyes, but she restrains from letting them flow from her lips for the moment.

"Sorry," I mutter, looking away from her. I'm not sure why I'm apologizing, or if she'd even possibly understand. "I just..."

"Was it him?"

I cut my eyes back at her. "Who?"

"Hatter."

Shock freezes me in place as I stare at her, stunned to hear that name come from her lips. *Hatter.* "How do you...? How would you even...?"

She rolls her eyes. "I grew up in this city, Reece. When I was a kid, that... *thing*... was everywhere." She motions toward the fresh painting on the brick wall. "Drove people crazy... it used to pop up overnight, like out of nowhere. It was like a calling card or something, I don't know..."

"A moniker," I say.

"Yeah, that." She looks back at it. "It was the guy's signature or whatever. They called him Hatter."

I stare at the moniker, my eyes scanning the outline of the thing. It's mediocre at best, the kid who painted it an amateur, a generic imitation. It wouldn't fool an artist, not a real one, but I can see how some might think it's the real thing. It's the equivalent, though, of finding a Van Gough at a garage sale. You know that shit's got to be fake, but for a split second, just a glance, you stall and wonder if maybe... just maybe...

Maybe it's really him.

"It wasn't him," I mumble, looking away from it as my stomach twists in knots so tight I feel like I might fucking puke right here. "It was just some stupid kids."

"Why'd you chase them?"

"Somebody's gotta teach them."

"What, that vandalism is wrong?"

"No, that thievery is." I shake my head, turning away from the replication. "Nobody likes a cheap knock-off. If you're going to be an artist, you've gotta do your own thing. Be your own person. Create what's in you instead of impersonating others. They say imitation is the sincerest form of flattery, but I call bullshit. It's one thing to be inspired by something. It's another thing to fucking *copy* it."

She raises her eyebrows, like she's surprised by my outburst. "And that's what you told them?"

"That's what I *wanted* to tell them."

"So what did you tell them?"

"That they were assholes."

I don't know what to expect... maybe for her to be irritated, maybe even disturbed by my behavior... so the last thing I anticipate is for her to burst into laughter. She wraps herself around my arm, slipping one of her hands in mine as she leans her head against my shoulder, her eyes drifting to the graffiti again. "So what do you think happened to him?"

"What do I think happened to him?"

"Yeah... Hatter." My heart almost stalls when she says the name again. "I know he got caught, because my parents got a restitution check."

Just as I'm starting to relax again, those words hit me.

"They were the recipients of one of those," she continues, nodding toward the graffiti. "I was fifteen or so when it happened... he covered the front of the dance studio. I thought it was gorgeous but my father obviously disagreed. They got a check in the mail a year or so ago, a couple hundred bucks to compensate them for graffiti removal."

"Interesting."

"Yeah, I tried to talk them into keeping it, but no dice," she says with a laugh. "It's kind of sad, you know... not saying it's cool to vandalize, but it's art... it was that guy's art, and as quick as he did it, it got wiped back away, you know?"

"Yeah, I know," I say.

"So I just wonder what happened to him. He kind of just disappeared."

"I guess it's hard to say," I tell her. "Maybe he saw the error of his ways."

Or maybe he's just still paying for all those mistakes.

"You ready, Little Miss?"

Lexie sits in the hallway, toys scattered all around her on the wooden floor. The sun has set, darkness falling outside already as it pushes seven o'clock. If we don't get a move on, we're going to be late getting her home today.

She glances at me, frowning, as she continues to play. "Not yet."

"Then you need to get ready," I say. "We've gotta get going."

"Why can't I stay?"

"Because it's Sunday," I tell her. "You have to go home today, you know that."

"Why do I have to?"

Because your father's a fuck up.

Because your mother's a bitch.

Because the court said out of the two of us, you're better off with her somewhere.

"Because your mother loves you," I say, "and it's her turn to spend time with you now."

Lexie makes a face but doesn't question it anymore, leaving her toys scattered all around as she puts on her coat. I grab her pink backpack, slinging it over my shoulder, and take her hand as we head for the door.

"Wait!" She yanks away from me, disappearing to her bedroom before I can ask what's wrong. She returns after a second, dragging the massive Godzilla along with her, and takes my hand again. "Okay, now I'm ready."

We head down, and I'm distracted as Lexie chats away, paying not a bit of attention to my surroundings until I look up when we step outside of the building. I pause right in front of the entrance, spotting the man approaching.

He's here for me.

Of course he is.

You'd think I'd be used to it now, Officer Warren showing up unexpectedly wherever I am. My home, my work, my usual hang outs... he talks to my friends, he questions my coworkers, and if my family hadn't written me off, he'd probably hound the fuck out of them, too. He gets paid to babysit me, so to speak, and has for the past five years.

I can't wait to fire the son of a bitch.

It's been a long time coming.

Despite it being late on a Sunday, he's dressed in his usual work clothes, the word 'probation' mocking me in bright yellow on his black coat. The entire neighborhood can fucking read it.

Not like most of them don't already know...

"Hatfield," he says, nodding in greeting as he approaches.

"Officer."

He turns to Lexie, his usual grim expression cracking with a grin. "Hello there, sweetheart."

Lexie just stares at him.

She doesn't say a word.

He's a stranger to her.

After a moment of awkward silence, I clear my throat. "Is there something I can do for you?"

He looks away from my daughter, focusing back on me. "We found something this weekend, some graffiti..."

He doesn't have to finish his statement. I know where it's going. "It wasn't me."

"Yeah, well..."

I hold my hands out, pulling Lexie's up with mine, to show them to him. "You can check me. There's no spray paint on my hands or my clothes. You can search if you want. You'll find nothing."

"I just have to ask," he says right away. "You know that."

"I know." I step away from the apartment, still holding onto Lexie. "If you'll excuse us, we've gotta get going. She's supposed to be home soon."

He waves me away. "Do what you have to, Hatfield. Don't let me stop you."

He lingers there even after I start to walk away. It won't surprise me if he heads upstairs after I'm gone, finding a way into my apartment to look through my things. I don't have time to worry about it right now.

Can't be late.

We make it to the Upper Westside without a second to spare. Lexie grabs her backpack from me and runs up the steps just as her mother opens the front door of the brownstone. I stay on the sidewalk, waiting for her to go inside, but her mother steps in front of her, blocking her path. "Oh, God, what in the world is that hideous thing?"

I'm an asshole.

I know.

My instinct is to tell her it's just her reflection.

But I keep my mouth closed, knowing it'll do nothing but make this whole thing worse. We have a tenuous civility that's damn easy to break, and for the sake of Lexie, I try to keep it together.

I try my damnedest.

It doesn't always work.

Lexie holds up her new toy, grinning. "Daddy's friend bought me a dinosaur!"

"Daddy's *friend*?" Rebecca looks from our daughter to me before focusing on the toy. "What in the world would he do that for?"

Lexie giggles. "She's a girl, Mommy, not a *he*. And she likes dinosaurs, too! She told me so!"

The shift in Rebecca's demeanor is subtle but enough for me to catch it, her shoulders squaring and back straightening, like she's preparing for an attack. I don't have it in me to fight with her, though. She quickly shoos Lexie inside, waiting until she's gone, before turning around to face me. She takes a small step out onto her porch and pauses there, hands on her hips, eyeing me intently.

I think she's waiting on me to say something, but I owe the woman nothing, much less an explanation. My life is my life, and if she doesn't like it, tough shit. I've been through the ringer because of her, because of how she feels about my choices, and I take it in stride. I keep my head down and mouth shut, letting her berate me, taking the brunt of her anger, because maybe I deserve it. Maybe I earned the harsh punishment. But I've kept my hands clean for five goddamn years, and at some point she's going to have to cut me some slack for it.

She shakes her head after a moment and storms inside with little more than a scoff, like she's so disgusted that she can't even find any words to explain it. I walk away then, in no rush to get home, stopping at the store on the way to grab some cigarettes.

When I make it home half an hour later, the probation officer is still hanging around, sitting on the front steps of the apartment building. With a heavy sigh, I sit down beside him, reaching into my hoodie pocket for my pack of smokes.

Pulling one out, I light it, taking a deep drag before looking at it as I slowly exhale. "I stopped smoking a few weeks ago."

He raises his eyebrows. "Looks like it's going well."

Laughing dryly, I take another drag. "Yeah, well, nobody said I was perfect. But I tried... I'm *trying*. It's hard, though. I get so wound tight, so frazzled, so *frustrated*, and it makes me feel like I'm going fucking mad. So I light one, and I tell myself that's it, that after this one, I'm done with them. And I mean it... until the next time something gets under my skin."

"You need a hobby," he says.

"I had one." My eyes flit to him, a small, amused smile on my lips. "It's how we met."

He nods as he laughs under his breath. "Have you been painting lately?"

"I told you... I've kept my hands clean."

"I'm not talking about that. I'm talking about *painting*. You know, with paints and brushes and paper. Art."

"No."

"Really?" He seems genuinely surprised. "Your studio room looked like you've used it recently."

My shoulders instinctively stiffen at the words. I knew it. The fucker went upstairs when I was gone. I continue to smoke my cigarette in silence, trying to ignore the sense of invasion I feel.

"It was just some stupid kids," I say after a while, my voice low. "Some stupid kids who didn't know what they were doing. It's not the first time it has happened, you know."

He knows. He's come to me every time it has happened, but it's been a while since the last time, almost a year. It's the first time I've seen it, though. The first time I witnessed it happening somewhere.

"Do you find it weird?" he asks. "All these years later, people still paying homage to you?"

Shaking my head, I take a deep drag from the cigarette, my chest tightening. *Hatter.* That's what they used to call me back in the day. "They don't do it for me. They don't know shit about me. They do it because they think it stands for something, that it has some meaning that's bigger than all of us. They do it because they want to believe they have the power to make a difference. They turned it into this thing... this *ideal*... like they're bucking authority and sending a message that they're here, and they're not going away, because they think people are actually paying attention. They think people actually care. But they don't."

He stares at me, his expression guarded. "Why did *you* do it?"

"Because I thought I was an artist," I say, tossing my cigarette

160

down on the stone steps and tramping it out. "Really I was just another stupid kid."

He seems to have no response for that.

Standing, he stretches, before heading off the steps and pausing on the sidewalk. After regarding me for a moment, he motions toward my discarded cigarette butt.

"Littering could cost you a few hundred bucks in fines," he says. "It's also a violation of your probation, which we both know you don't want. Would hate to get this close to the end and me to have to haul you in."

Reaching down, I pick up the cigarette butt, clenching a fist around it.

"And all that you just said? About why you did it? I don't believe it for a moment. The guy I met wasn't stupid. And he *was* an artist." Officer Warren starts to back away, shaking his head. "That guy just got lost somewhere."

Twelve

It's early in the evening, dusk approaching, the sky a dark blue streaked with vibrant shades of orange and pink, like someone painted the skyline around the buildings.

The city that never sleeps is wide awake, lights flashing, horns honking, people wandering the streets, as the first warm spring weekend creeps up on everybody. I stand in front of the shop, leaning back against the bricks just beneath the colorful sign for *Wonderland Tattoos*. The windows are dark, the door locked up, the open sign unlit. The shop stays open seven days a week, someone always tattooing, except for one exception: today.

But just because we aren't at the shop doesn't mean we aren't working.

Or supposed to be, anyway.

Sighing, I glance at my watch in the dim lighting right as it turns seven o'clock. I'm officially late. I'm not sure if I even want to go, to be honest, but I hate the idea of leaving Kevin in a bind.

He's always been there for me, and he asked me for a favor.

The least I can do is give him a few hours of my time.

It's going to be a fucking disaster.

I consider leaving, maybe sticking a note on the door, or just chalking it up to a loss, when I finally see her down the street. *Avery.* She's speed walking, breaking into a jog when she spots me.

I push away from the building to meet her on the sidewalk, hands shoved in the pockets of my hoodie, the hood covering my head. Avery looks stunning, wearing a pair of skintight black legging capris and a black sports bra, a tattered oversize white shirt thrown on overtop of it, hanging off her right shoulder.

Perfect.

My gaze trails along her exposed collarbones as she comes to a stop in front of me. She's been rehearsing from the look of her… hair falling out of her ponytail, her pale skin glowing with sweat.

"Hey!" she says, smiling brightly. "I got here as soon as I could."

"You're just in time," I say.

"Are you on a break or something?" Her gaze shifts toward the shop, eyes surveying the dark florescent *open* sign, everything locked up tight. "Wait, are you guys closed?"

"Yep."

"But it's Saturday."

"I know."

Her brow furrows in confusion as she glances between the shop and me, but she doesn't press the issue. I asked her to meet me here at six-thirty, wearing as little as possible with not a stitch of makeup, and much to my surprise, she actually listened, despite the fact that I probably sounded like a fucking creep with that request.

If I could've gotten away with it, I would've told her to come naked.

"So, what are we doing?" she asks, her gaze finally settling back on me.

"We're working," I say. "Or, well, *I'm* working."

"Then what am I doing?"

I reach out and grab her hand. "You're going to a party."

Her eyes widen. "What?"

"A party, Aphrodite," I say. "You *have* heard of one, correct?"

"Yes, of course. I've had birthday parties."

"Birthday parties, huh? Did your parents throw them for you, with cake and ice cream and all your girlfriends? Did you have sleepovers where you talked about boys and braided each other's hair?"

Her eyes narrow fiercely but she doesn't refute my words. "I'm not dressed for a party, Reece."

"You're dressed perfect," I say as I eye her. "For the kind of party we're going to, anyway."

"What kind of party is that?"

"The kind without presents and bouncy houses," I say. "The kind you won't want your parents to ever know about."

She eyes me peculiarly, like she wants to refuse, but curiosity is eating away at her. I can see it in those *oh-so-innocent* eyes.

"You're, uh... you're sure I look okay?"

"I'm positive." Rocking back on my heels, I glance down at myself. "I mean, fuck... look at me."

My jeans have more holes than a block of Swiss cheese, the denim stained with ink and old paint. My sneakers are scuffed, my hoodie falling apart, and my hair?

Fuck, I don't even think I brushed it.

It's starting to get so long Lexie has actually put the shit in a tiny ponytail.

"That's different," she says. "You're, well... you're *you*."

"What's that supposed to mean?"

"It means the whole grunge thing works for you, but I look like someone chewed me up and spit me back out."

Sighing, I tug on her hand. "Just trust me. You'll fit right in."

She doesn't resist anymore, shrugging as she lets me pull her to me. Squeezing her hand, I kiss her softly before turning away.

"Now come on," I say. "No time to waste."

If I put it off any longer, I'll let her talk me out of it.

By the time we make it to the meatpacking district, I'm running damn near thirty minutes behind. We step out of the subway and head down the shabby block, Avery's hand in mine with her nervously glued to my side.

The old warehouse stands on a street corner, the massive hunk of brick and concrete crumbling on the outside. The windows are completely blacked out, and the place appears forsaken, but I can hear the subtle sound of music as we approach it.

It's fucking covered in graffiti.

I love it.

"This is it?" she asks hesitantly. "You're taking me to an abandoned warehouse?"

"Technically, yeah, but it's not abandoned."

"It looks it," she says. "I seriously think this was a scene out of one of those Friday the 13th movies."

"Nah," I say, smirking. "It's much, much freakier than that."

Around the back of the building, cut through the small dank alley, and down a set of concrete stairs to a thick metal door, rusting and aging. A familiar man lurks in the shadows there, invisible despite his hulking appearance, working security. Avery audibly gasps, squeezing my hand so tightly her nails dig into the skin, when she spots him hovering in the darkness in front of her.

Jay Brandon.

"Hatfield," he says, his eyes fixed on Avery as he regards her. "I see your recent development has stuck around."

"Jay," I say, nodding in greeting. "How's the tattoo holding up, man?"

Jay lifts his shirt up, showing off the grim reaper on his burly chest, still scabbing a bit but healing nicely. "Good as ever."

"Awesome," I say when he drops his shirt. "Call the shop and we'll set up your next session."

"Good deal." He reaches for the door, grasping the handle. "Go on in."

There's a code to get through the door, a password for permission, but I'm immune to needing an invitation.

The moment the door opens, music spills out into the night, the frantic beat of some electronica song, loud and banging, vibrating the floor and walls around us. I lead Avery down the long hallway, a maze of darkness that gradually lightens with a subtle purple glow. It seems to infuse with everything when we step into the main area of the warehouse basement, bathing the entire space in purple from the sea blacklights.

"Holy crap," Avery says, her voice barely audible over the music. It pumps above us, inside the warehouse, echoing down along the floor. I've been here a few times before for one of these underground parties, but this one is special.

Wonderland turns five years old today.

That's reason for celebration.

A few dozen people linger in the basement, in front of a long span of mirrors, covering the entire wall like at the ballet studio. A few people huddle in the stations along the wall, tables set up, women dressed in nothing but white string bikinis standing in line, awaiting their turns.

Body paint.

Squeezing Avery's hand, drawing her attention to me, I give her a small smile and lead her to the only empty station dead center of the chaos. Kevin glances up from his spot beside it, a white medical mask on his face, shielding him as he airbrushes glowing orange onto the body of a model. He catches my eye and stops what he's doing, sitting back and pulling the mask down.

He's quiet for a moment. I know what he's thinking. He's thinking my *retirement* would keep me away. "You're late."

"I know."

"I didn't think you were coming."

"Yeah, well, I'm here."

He nods. "You're here."

I see the relief in his eyes. He doesn't have to express it. I know he's grateful.

I have someone bring an extra chair for Avery to take a seat between Kevin and me as I settle in at the station, opening the array of blacklight paints scattered around. No sooner am I there and people start lining up. I wave the first girl over, her white bikini glowing under the lights, her body sparkling from the sheen of glittery gold paint. I quickly paint flames on her skin, a golden orange mix of color around her stomach and back, the inferno spreading down her legs and along her arms. Once she's covered, her body standing out under the lights like a neon statue, I send her on her way and wave over the next one.

It's methodic, and swift, a slick assembly line of living art. Martin airbrushes the models while Kevin and I add some fine detail, before shipping them down the line to Ellie, who does the final touches with makeup. There are other artists, other guys Kevin hired for this reason, working together to get everyone painted.

After the models are done and shipped upstairs, the doors are opened and others let in. A steady stream of scantily clad women and bare chested men flow through the basement, stopping by the stations for body paint. It isn't as elaborate as the models, most getting mere swirling designs of color on their exposed skin. It's steady, body after body, time slipping away. The music above us grows louder as more people flood the warehouse. Hours faded away as I work, pausing occasionally between jobs to glance at Avery, taking in her fascinated expression as she watches us.

I almost get lost in the art.

It makes my chest ache.

When the clock strikes midnight, we shut down the stations. I turn to Avery and am about to speak when she beats me to it. "And here I thought I was special."

I cock an eyebrow in question.

"What we did at your house," she explains. "I thought it was special. I didn't realize you made a habit of painting women."

Ah. "I wouldn't say I make a habit of it."

"How many have you done?"

"You were the first."

"But I'm not the only."

"Huh." I eye her peculiarly. "Is that jealousy I hear?"

"Of course not."

Her answer is quick, accompanied by a forced dismissive scoff.

Jealous.

Wordlessly, I pat the table, motioning for her to join me. Her eyes widen slightly as she hesitantly takes the space. I pull her shirt off, tossing it aside, and eyed her in her black sports bra and leggings. She isn't showing a lot of skin, but it's enough for me to work with. I take my time, creating an elaborate pattern of neon splatters on her body, a blacklight supernova of color marking her.

Maybe she isn't my only, but she was my first, and now the last, too.

When I finish, I stand up, towering over her as I stare down at her. Leaning close, I whisper, "You *are* special."

"Am I?"

The question is timid, laced with genuine curiosity, vulnerability accentuating every syllable. It surprises me, hearing her sound so insecure, her eyes regarding me with a familiar uncertainty, like she isn't sure what to make of anything.

I know this look well.

Skepticism.

This woman is a walking, talking goddess, an angel in disguise, and she looks at me like she fears I don't really see her at all.

But I see her, all right... I saw her the first time she stepped into the shop, have seen her every moment since then, and I certainly see her now. And maybe it's all in my head, but I'm sure I even saw her *then*, the day I spray-painted her father's studio.

She smiled, when she saw it.

It was beautiful.

Cupping her cheek, my thumb brushes across her bottom lip before I lean over and kiss her. I take my time, kissing her softly, sweetly, feeling her body relax against mine. I pull away eventually, a catcall from the chair beside us disrupting the moment. Smirking, I kiss her a few more times, innocent little pecks, before taking her hand and pulling her away from the station.

"I'm out, Kevin."

He salutes me as I stride by. "Catch you on the other side."

"Where are we going?" Avery asks as I lead her through the basement, past the people still lurking down here. A few people greet me, former clients, calling my name. I smile and nod, moving past them, and pull Avery in front of me when we near a set of stairs. These lead up into the warehouse, the music louder here, so intense I can feel it pulsating through my body, infusing every cell as it pumps through my veins.

"Down the rabbit hole," I whisper in her ear, pushing her hair aside when we reach the top of the stairs.

The warehouse is a dark purple abyss streaked with neon. Hundreds of bodies pack the space, glowing under the blacklights. In the front of the massive room, on a stage, the DJ spins records, the frantic electronica pouring from speakers.

The Mad Tatter

A strobe light sporadically flashes to the beat of the song, briefly washing the room in bright white light, before everything falls right back into darkness. Avery pauses at the edge of the room, her body rigid as she surveys everything.

"What are you waiting for?" I ask, urging her on. "Don't you want to dance?"

At the question, she spins around to face me, eyes wide. "What?"

"Dance," I say again, motioning out onto the dance floor. "I sort of got the impression dancing was your thing."

"It is," she says. "But not *this* kind of dancing."

"What's wrong with this kind of dancing?"

"Nothing, but I do choreography, Reece. I do ballet."

"So?"

"So I don't know how to *rave*."

I laugh at her incredulous tone. "First of all, it's not a rave... it's a blacklight party. And dancing is dancing. You feel the music and you move to it. You don't think about it. Art is art, baby. You just *feel* it."

She eyes me skeptically for a moment before turning back around and scanning the crowd. "I've only ever done ballet."

"If it helps, I'll get you something to loosen you up."

"Like *drugs?*"

"I meant a drink, but if you want something harder, I'm sure a few people have—"

"Of course not," she hisses, cutting me off. "I just... I didn't know."

Shaking my head, I grab her hand and tug her into the crowd. She doesn't resist, letting me lead her to the other side of the room, to a makeshift bar along the wall. Some of the models stand behind it, pouring shots. It's none of the fancy shit—no mixed drinks, or martinis, or fucking cosmopolitans. No cotton candy whatever-the-fuck-it-is. It's straight up liquor, whatever cheap shit is on hand, or bottled water.

After all, it's free, and beggars can't be choosers. *Drink it or don't.*

I jump past those waiting for drinks, stepping right behind the bar and weaving past the workers to grab a bottle of vodka, pouring two double shots. I slide one to Avery, clinking my shot glass with hers before throwing it back. The liquor scorches my throat, the burn settling deep into my chest, warming me from the inside. I hear Avery cough as she swallows hers, having to try three times before she gets it all down.

"Oh God," she gasps, "that tastes like rubbing alcohol."

"Might've been," I joke, setting my shot glass down on the bar. "Want another?"

"No, I'm good," she says, turning away from me to scan the crowd. "Never drinking that crap again."

I can tell the alcohol is already having an effect on her, her posture relaxing, her head subtly bobbing to the beat of the music.

"Come on," I say. "Dance with me now."

"I didn't realize you danced."

"I don't," I say. "But someone wise once told me that for the right woman, you've gotta be willing to do anything."

Her cheeks redden at my words as she concedes, nodding. She pushes away from the bar, letting me lead her through the crowd. We stop dead center of the dance floor, bodies surrounding us, light flashing above us, her skin glowing under the blacklights as I pull her back to me, my hands on her hips.

"Close your eyes," I whisper in her ear. "Feel it."

The song is catchy, vibrating the room. Avery starts out slow, subtly swaying to the beat. I can't dance, so damn uncoordinated I can hardly pass a sobriety test when stone cold sober. But I couldn't care less. I move to the rhythm, blending into the darkness like I don't even exist, a chill running down my spine as Avery presses herself against me, grinding against my cock.

The music shifts, songs blending together, the beat persistently frenzied. Avery loosens up more and more as everyone around us reacts to the melody, losing themselves in the song like they've caught the Holy Ghost of Dubstep. *Praise motherfucking Skrillex.* They flail around, moving wildly, flipping and spinning, doing splits in the middle of the crowd.

171

Her movements become more exaggerated, all pretense, all hesitation, all *modesty* going out the window, as she relaxes and just feels the music. It doesn't take long before she's joining the others, throwing her hands in the air and bouncing on her tiptoes, turning and dipping, jumping around to the beat, a mixture of ballet and whatever the fuck this kind of dancing is.

It's art.

Her art.

She was made for this shit.

The smile on her face is bright enough to light the darkest room, to warm the coldest soul.

I practically feel my heart growing three sizes just watching her.

All night long, until the wee hours of the morning, I lose myself in her as she loses herself in the music. Nothing exists to her except for the melody—I'm not sure she even notices when I slip away to get a drink, or confer with Kevin, or converse with Ellie—but it doesn't matter. I don't mind a bit.

My girl's first love is dancing.

And I love her for it.

Fuck, I *love* her.

It's a stark reality, like a slap in the face, slamming me right on my ass. She got under my skin, beat her way through my chest, and snuck right into my heart before I could even think to object to it.

It's messy.

So messy.

"You're fucked," Kevin says, leaning back against the bar as he sips a bottle of water. I stand beside him, drinking straight from the cheap ass bottle of vodka, my eyes glued to her still out on the dance floor. Despite the darkness, I know which one is Avery... my mark is all over her. It will wash off tomorrow, but tonight it's there.

"I know," I reply, because I do. I know. I'm fucked.

Kevin laughs, punching me on the arm. "Never thought it would happen, Hatter. Never thought I'd see the day."

Still laughing, he walks away. I take another swig from the bottle of vodka before discarding it on the bar and making my way back out onto the dance floor.

Avery is a sweaty, paint-covered mess by the time the party starts winding down, her body soaked, her hair all over the place. The crowd has thinned, the alcohol drying up, as night outside slowly moves toward daylight.

She turns to me, eyes bright and wild. I've seen her happy before, but this is like someone seeing sunshine for the first time. How the fuck have I ever survived the darkness before?

Maybe it's bullshit, I don't know, but they say van Gough used to eat yellow paint because he thought it would bring some happiness inside of him. They claim he was mad, that it was proof he'd gone crazy, but I don't believe it.

I think, if he did it, it was just desperation.

Because looking at her, I know she's my yellow. She's the happiness inside of me.

It's not crazy to want to eat that up, to capture that feeling forever.

"Wow," she breathes, her voice strained. "Now *this* is a party."

"Better than all those birthday parties?"

She wraps her arms around me, beaming as she stares into my eyes, her fingers running through the hair at the nape of my neck. "I don't think they even deserve to be called parties now."

I laugh lightly. "I'm glad you're enjoying yourself."

"I am," she says, her voice genuine. "I feel like I'm in an entirely different world when I'm with you, a world I never knew existed before… like I never knew it could be this way, that *I* could be this way."

"That's why they call it Wonderland, Aphrodite."

Her smile brightens. "It's more than that, though… it's *you*."

"Can I see more of your art?"

I glance down at where Avery lays on the living room floor of my apartment, right in front of the couch where I sit. Her long hair is loose, splayed out on the carpet, her knees up, arms spread wide. One is wrapped around my leg, her fingers absently toying with the bottom of my jeans, grazing my ankle, while the other clutches a half-empty bottle of cheap vodka.

Paint still covers her from the party. She lost more clothes along the way. Fuck if I know what happened to them. There one second and gone the next. She's wearing a pair of black panties and her sports bra. I see less on women walking the streets some Saturday nights, but somehow, with her, it looks damn indecent. I almost want to cover her up, but the other part of me isn't having that shit.

"My art?" I ask. "What art?"

She uses her head to nod in my direction. "Your art."

Confused, I glance behind me, freezing when I realize she's motioning toward the painting on the wall above the couch. I sometimes forget the damn thing is still there until it's pointed out to me.

"Ah." I turn back around, taking a sip of my beer. "I have no more for you to see."

"Why not?"

I shrug, hoping she'll drop the subject as I delay answering, taking my sweet time drinking the rest of my beer, but when I set the empty can down on the end table and glance at her, I see she's still waiting for an answer. "You ever have something frustrate you so much that you just wanted to rip it to pieces, throw it on a pile, and kill it with fire?"

"Bridgette."

I let out a laugh at her response. "I'm serious."

"No," she says after a moment of silence, like she was legitimately considering it. "Can't say I have."

"Well, I have, and that's exactly what I did. I destroyed it all, every bit of it, save for *that* piece of shit." I wave toward the watercolor behind my head. "That's all that's left."

"You really destroyed it all?" she asks, propping herself up on her elbows to better look at me. "Why would you do that?"

I shake my head. "You wouldn't understand."

"Try me."

174

I want to. I wish I knew how. I wish I could find the words to explain how it made me feel, to see those pieces of who I was supposed to be, the reminders of the man I could've been, knowing I'd never live up to that fantasy. It was like playing house, knowing you'd never be worthy of a home... smiling when you really want nothing more than to cry. It's the feeling of waking up in the morning and getting out of bed, when all you want to do is crawl back into the motherfucker and drift away.

Looking at it made me feel like my parents were right about me, that the person I've become isn't worthy of the air I constantly breathe.

"It was like staring my worst fear right in the face," I say quietly. "And I wasn't a strong enough man to endure that day after day."

"But you kept that one."

That isn't a question, but I hear the curiosity in her voice, like she wants to know but she's afraid to pry for an answer. Looking back at the painting once more, my eyes scan it in the relative darkness.

"I painted it the day my daughter was born," I tell her. "I painted it about her... painted it *for* her. I couldn't bring myself to destroy it. I already worry I'm destroying her."

She rolls her eyes. "You are not."

"You don't underst—"

"No, I *do*," she says loudly, her words slurring a bit as she cuts me off. "I know what it's like to wish your parents could accept you for who you are. That's all kids really want. And, you know, sometimes they want chocolate in their pancakes and dinosaurs drawn on their arms, and you know, why not? I didn't get that at first, because my parents didn't raise me that way. They said no a lot, because they thought they knew what was best for me, and maybe they did... maybe they *do*... but sometimes it just feels good to be able to say yes. And maybe you aren't perfect, but you make her happy—which, for the record, is the total opposite of destroying her."

I'm not sure what to say, or how I'm supposed to feel about

what she's saying. It twists me up inside and it's not something I want to deal with tonight… or ever. I'm twisted enough about my feelings for her. So instead of responding, I stand up and grab my empty beer can, taking a step to walk away.

She quickly clutches onto my leg, though, pinning me in place.

I try to take another step, and another, dragging her a bit across the floor, but stop and look down as she drunkenly laughs, not letting go. She tries to pull herself together, but she can't help it, another laugh coming out as she tugs on my leg, almost making me lose my balance. "Don't leave!"

"I'm just going to get another beer," I say, shaking my empty toward her.

"No, you're trying to avoid this conversation," she says, finally letting go of my leg to sit up, but she isn't finished. "You do that, you know… whenever I bring this kind of stuff up." She wags a finger at me. "I'm on to you."

I stare at her, watching as she brings the bottle of vodka to her lips and takes a swig, making a face and spewing half of it back out on herself, like she didn't realize what the hell she was even drinking. Shaking my head, I reach down and grab the bottle from her, putting it aside, before taking her hand and pulling her to her feet. She stumbles, laughing even more, and wraps her arms around my neck before I can move away. She smells like sweat and liquor, with the hint of something else…

Paint.

It's intoxicating.

"I want you to draw me like one of your French girls," she whispers playfully, her lips just a touch away from mine.

I laugh, my hands settling on her hips. "I've already painted you… twice."

"You painted *on* me," she says. "And I saw it then, you know. I saw it tonight and I saw it last time."

"Saw what?"

"You. Your passion. You looked so alive, like there was a spark in you, a spark you got from doing art."

"You're imagining things."

"No, I'm not," she says. "I know what I saw. There was no mistaking it. You looked like a man in love, Reece."

That word makes my heart do those things I didn't think my heart was capable of doing again. *Love*. You could say that I love art. I definitely love my daughter. If you catch me on an off day, I might even declare my love for a much needed cigarette. I've often thought I loved pussy, and sometimes beer makes me feel like I love it, too, but loving a woman? Fuck that. Never thought it would happen.

But it did.

When I wasn't paying attention, it snuck up on me.

I went from slipping out of bedrooms in the middle of the night to inviting her right into mine, and I can't even pinpoint when it happened or why. It started with wanting to draw on her skin but now... now she's starting to become everything.

"Maybe I am," I whisper, leaning down, lightly kissing her mouth, tasting the vodka lingering on her lips.

"Maybe you are what?" she murmurs.

In love, I think.

She kisses me back, her fingers running through my hair.

She doesn't press me for an answer.

I think she's already forgotten she had a question in the first place.

Thirteen

Buzzing fills the back room of the shop, mixing with the sound of some new local indie band. Once again, like every other day, I don't get to choose the music.

This time, Kevin does.

It hums from his iPhone, docked into a speaker, streaming live from some underground show in the city. It's a Saturday, and I technically have the day off. I should be with Lexie, I was supposed to be with Lexie, but she's home sick for the weekend.

Or *supposedly* sick.

Rebecca called me, cancelling my weekend due to her not feeling well. I argued, saying I'm just as equipped as her to take care of a sick kid, but her argument about my selfishness eventually made me concede.

What kind of father drags their sick kid out so late at night?

What kind of man does that make you, Rhys?

Why are you always thinking of yourself and not her?

Why can't you just let her stay home and sleep?

Needless to say, I'm irritated as shit, and bored to boot without my daughter for the weekend. Downtime is unheard of for me. And to top it off, I've hardly seen Avery all week. After our stint out dancing at the party to celebrate Wonderland, she has only shown up once, too busy working on her choreography to visit with me.

She said she finally figured it out, that she knew what she wanted to do for the production.

I understand, of course... when inspiration strikes, you run with it... but fuck if part of me doesn't hate it anyway. I've gotten used to having her around.

Sighing, I close my eyes, feeling the vibration spread through my chest. Numbness long ago crept in, dulling the tiny cat-scratch pain to mere irritating jabs. I've felt worse. Hell, Lexie inflicts worse trying to wake me up in the mornings. Thankfully, Kevin has a light hand, so I barely feel the needle most places.

After a moment, the humming dies down as Kevin switches off the tattoo machine. "Have a look, man."

I open my eyes and glance down at my chest, surveying the cartoon T-Rex. It completely clashes with the rest of my tattoos, but it makes me smile. I had Kevin trace it off the wall in my workspace. Lexie drew it. "Looks great."

"You don't want to check it out in the mirror?"

"Do I need to?"

"Of course not."

I stand up and grab my shirt as Kevin jokingly spouts off facts about aftercare, treating me like any other client. He has done the majority of my tattoos, starting with my very first one the day the shop opened.

I was the first client in his chair.

He gave me my start in this business, taking a chance on a little roughneck delinquent. He could've made my life hell, but instead he appreciated me for who I was. He gave me the respect I hadn't given him.

I had no idea what this building was going to be when I first saw it, the place still vacant, the only thing written outside being the lone word *Wonderland*. It called to me, though, sparking inspiration.

In the middle of the night, I vandalized the place.

When the sun rose the next morning, he showed up at his shop to find the outside covered in a *Through the Looking Glass* mural and me right beside it, in handcuffs.

I got busted.

I took too long.

I got lost in the art and forgot my surroundings until the cops showed up.

I help myself to a bandage from Kevin's supplies and cover the fresh wound. I sling my shirt over my shoulder, not bothering to put it on.

Kevin was the only one to not press charges against me. His only request was that I clean the graffiti off. So I did, as my first assignment for community service. I removed my own art.

Ever since then, he's been trying to get me to put it back up.

"So how much do I owe you?" I ask.

"You know better than that shit, Hatter. Your money's no good with me."

Hatter. He's also the only one who still calls me that name. *Hatter, the Mad Tatter.* I roll my eyes every time he says that shit.

I turn to walk out, stalling when I see Ellie lurking in the doorway, holding the appointment book. "Kev, your next client called to ask if we could push their session back an hour. You have a gap in your schedule later so I worked it in."

"Cool with me," Kevin says, shrugging.

Ellie's gaze turns to me. "We've got a walk-in."

"So?" Reece asked. "Why are you telling me?"

"Figured you might want to do it."

I shake my head. "I'm not working today."

"I can do it," Kevin chimes in, shrugging as he starts sanitizing his station. "I got an hour to burn."

Good, I think. I slip past Ellie and stroll toward the lobby, seeing a group of girls gathered around the hanging display, shifting through the pre-drawn tattoos. They huddle together, whispering, giggling. I look away from them and start for my room, figuring I can knock out some paperwork while I'm here, when one of their voices cuts through, louder. "Oh, there's the one I got!"

That voice is vaguely familiar. I look back that way, surveying the girls, my eyes falling on the blonde. The blonde... I know her. It takes me a moment to remember from where.

Bridgette.

I don't know the other two girls, but Bridgette is recognizable, her tattoo partly visible on her chest above her low cut shirt.

Without even pausing, I head back toward Kevin's room, where Ellie still lurks in the doorway. "Ellie, what's the walk-in's name?"

"Uh..." Ellie surveys the appointment book. "Michelle. She's the pale blonde that looks kind of like a stern librarian."

"Sounds hot," Kevin chimes in.

"See," Ellie says, punching me in the arm after closing the appointment book. "I knew you guys dug those nerdy chicks."

I glance across the lobby at them, seeing the petite blonde with her hair in a tight bun. Librarian? Nah. Dancer? *Most definitely.*

I turn back to Ellie briefly before looking past her, into Kevin's room. "You mind if I take the walk-in, after all?"

"Be my guest," Kevin says. "It'll give me time to grab something to eat."

Go with the flow.

I love that about Kevin.

Ellie eyes me suspiciously but I ignore her, slipping on my shirt before strolling through the lobby toward the three waiting girls. "Ladies."

They all glance up at the same time, their whispers and giggles silencing as they cast me equally sheepish looks. Bridgette steps forward, clearly the bold one of their group. "Hey! Remember me?"

"Sure do," I say. "Johnny's girl."

Her expression lights up. "You do remember me! I feel special."

Don't, I think. *I only remember you because of Avery.* "So which of you lovely ladies would be Michelle?"

"Me!" the blonde with the bun declares.

"And what can I do for you?"

"I want a small anchor," she says. "With the words 'never sink' written around it."

Nothing off the wall. *Thank God.* But I'm not much impressed with her choice of tattoo. "You know that's actually what anchors do, right? Sink?"

She giggles. "Of course. It's a metaphor."

I don't press the matter. She isn't the first one to ask for something like that, and she won't be the last. It's beginning to be a fad tattoo, like Chinese characters and tribal bands and infinity symbols. *To each their own.* "Have a seat and I'll draw it up for you."

It takes me less than ten minutes. I stroll out into the lobby, spotting the three squeezed together on the couch, flipping through the outdated shop magazines. I show Michelle the drawing, and set off to make a stencil when she murmurs her approval.

Afterward I lead them back to my room, pulling up an extra chair to the doorway for their other friend to sit.

"Pick your music," I tell Michelle.

She picks something out of Lexie's repertoire, some obnoxiously cheery pop star addicted to auto-tune.

Michelle settles on the table and places her arm on the armrest, since she wants it on her wrist. I place the design, once more asking her approval, before flipping on the machine to set to work.

"So what do you do?" I ask casually, a question I often ask clients to distract them, but this time I have ulterior motives.

When the fuck did I become a gossipy high school chick?

"I'm a dancer," Michelle says. "Mandy is, too."

I meet her eyes briefly, brow furrowing. "Who?"

"Mandy," she repeats, motioning toward their other friend—the quiet girl in the doorway.

"Ah." I focus back on the tattoo. "You a dancer, too, Johnny's girl?"

Bridgette giggles. "No, I'm in theater."

"Huh, that's great."

"Yeah," she says. "You'll see my name in lights someday. Just as soon as I graduate, I'm heading straight for Broadway."

"Juilliard, right?"

"Yes," she says, sounding stunned. "How'd you know?"

I shrug a shoulder. "Where else do actors and dancers hang together?"

Probably a hundred other places in this city. How the hell would I know? But it's clear to me, from her response alone, that she has no idea about me and Avery, or she'd know how I know where she goes to school.

"We've been friends since first year," Michelle chimes in. "Hard to believe we're almost at the end."

183

"And what about Johnny?" I ask. "What does he do?"

"He's in a band."

"Huh, what instrument does he play? Piano? Oboe? Trumpet?"

Bridgette laughs. "Guitar."

"Juilliard has guitar lessons?"

"No. He's in a band, not *the* band. He plays bass guitar for the *Black Derringers*."

I have no idea who that is, and honestly couldn't care less. I'm just trying to make conversation. So I smile and nod when she declares she's going to find a way to get me their latest single on tape, just waiting for the first chance to change the subject again.

"So where's your other friend?" I ask.

"Who?"

"The one that came with you last time."

"Oh, you mean A!"

Michelle laughs, interrupting. "A? Whoa, you brought *Avery* with you?"

"Yes," Bridgette says. "Can you believe it? She actually came along."

I glance up, my senses tingling, the hair at the nape of my neck stirring from a combination of defensiveness and sheer curiosity on what the fuck *that* means. "What's wrong with Avery?"

Yep, I need to check and make sure my balls are still attached after this…

"Nothing… I'm just surprised she'd come *here*." Michelle's eyes dart to me. "No offense or anything, but Avery, well… this isn't really her kind of thing. Her father would have a coronary just knowing she stepped foot in here."

Those words aren't spiteful, but they still manage to sting as they sink in.

"Oh, God, could you imagine him coming here?" Bridgette asks, laughing. "The great Laurence Moore slumming it in the Lower Eastside."

"He'd use an entire bottle of hand sanitizer before he even made it through the door." Michelle turns to me once more. "Not saying it's germy here or anything…"

184

"He's just a bit of a tight-ass," the third girl chimes in. Monica? Mary? I can't remember her name already. "Real snob. Serious germaphobe."

"Seriously," Bridgette says. "But anyway, yeah… I don't know where Avery is."

"She's at *Trouvaille*," Michelle says. "She's practicing with some others. I was supposed to be there, but… well, here I am."

"I haven't seen much of her lately," Bridgette says. "I think it's because Mr. Moore doesn't want her hanging around me. I'm on his shit list, apparently."

"I'm about to be, too," Michelle says. "When he sees this tattoo, he's probably going to ban me from the studio."

"Not a fan of body art?" I ask.

"Not at all," Michelle says. "He takes any kind of modification seriously, like we're violating our bodies. He wouldn't even let Avery get her ears pierced, said if God wanted her to have more holes, He would've given them to her."

I unconsciously flick my tongue out, running it along the piercing at the corner of my lip.

I say nothing else, grateful when they change the subject. My attention focuses on my work, only vaguely listening to their conversation, nodding and humming, chiming in only when one of them speaks to me directly. When the session is up, I flip the machine off and push my stool back. "What do you think?"

"It's perfect!" She lets out an excited squeal as she stares at it. "Thank you!"

She tips me well, the girls once more giggling and chatting as they pay and depart the shop. I sit on my stool for a moment, the music still playing, but I hardly hear it, too lost in my thoughts.

I strike the lighter, igniting the flame, and light the cigarette between my lips as I step out the front door of Wonderland. It's nearing dark, and I just finished up, ducking out before Ellie could try to give me any more walk-ins.

It's the warmest night we've had in a while, the air humid. I shove the sleeves of my hoodie up to my elbows as I stroll along. People rush past me but I'm in no hurry to get anywhere, considering I have nowhere to be.

I reach the end of the block and pause on the corner, glancing around. The sun is starting to set, casting dark shadows along the streets.

I inhale deeply, my chest burning as I welcome the smoke into my lungs. My eyes drift across the street, to the construction site. It still looks as if they've done nothing to it, and curiosity gets the best of me, curiosity that I've tried to ignore since the first tarp went up on the side of the place weeks ago.

I wonder...

Turning, I cross the street, right toward the place, walking slowly as I assess it closer. A chain-link fence surrounds it, but it's easy to slip right through, some of the chains broken and peeled away, like I wasn't the first person to have this idea.

The wooden front door of the building is needlessly locked, the glass covering the top of it shattered and missing. I reach inside, angling my arm around, and shift the lock out of place, nudging the door open with my shoulder.

I slip inside, making sure to shut the door again behind me.

The air is stuffy, and musty, and rank. It smells like rat shit, and I can hear the critters scurrying around in the darkness, but it doesn't bother me, not like it should. I guess I expect it in this place. It's always been a pit. I carefully walk through the building in the darkness as I puff on my cigarette, letting the nicotine soothe my nerves.

When I reach the back of the building, I take one last, long drag, before tossing the cigarette down and tramping it out, just leaving it there.

Reaching into my pocket, I pull out my lighter again, igniting it, illuminating a bit of the darkness around me. I hold the flame out toward the wall, letting the light wash over the crumbling cement, bathing part of it in a soft glow.

I stare at it as I hold my breath, feeling a burn in my chest that runs deeper than cigarettes have ever scorched me. It attacks my very soul, splintering a part of me that I worry will never again be whole.

It's still there.

It's worse for wear, but it's there.

It's fucking there.

Five-year old graffiti covers the wall, an elaborate mass of peeling color and fading images, the black mass dead center the easiest to make out: a silhouette of a figure in a top hat.

A moniker.

My moniker.

Reaching out with my free hand, I run my fingers lightly across it, the wall crumbling beneath my fingertips, some of the color flaking off on my skin. I look down at my hand as I let go of the lighter, the flame extinguishing. Even in the darkness, I can see the black flakes of paint on my palm.

My chest tightens even more.

I feel like I'm suffocating, but at the same time, it feels almost like I'm just now remembering what it's like to breathe. Despite the stench, as I inhale, I can almost sense the aroma of the spray paint, and I know it's just my imagination, but I welcome it anyway.

I was a different person back then, the kind that made the fucked up choices that turned me into the man I am today. The world had been streaked with vibrant color everywhere I looked, until the day I turned around and it all caught up to me.

The color crashed together, swirling and mixing, until all I was left with was utter blackness, blacker than the paint that covered my hands that day. This blackness was a void, a trap I fell into, one that seemed bottomless with no way of escape.

Five years ago, I tagged over a hundred buildings. Two hundred, maybe. I never bothered to keep count. I vandalized and trespassed and left buildings in ruins, all in the name of art. The police spent months trying to unmask the mysterious street artist, and this right here?

This is the last of my graffiti.

It's all that's left of the notorious Hatter.

It was the only one they never found, the only one they didn't remove.

Extensive probation, hundreds of hours of community service, and tens of thousands of dollars in fines and restitution has a way of breaking a man, but nothing hurt me more than the final punishment delivered to me in court that fateful day:

Defendant is not to own or possess any graffiti tools during the duration of probation.

They took my art away, my real art, the one that called to me most.

For five years, I've struggled to try to recapture that feeling, to find that thrill again, and a few times I've gotten close. But nothing has ever matched the high of this right here. The thrill of turning a mundane city, lost in the hustle of nine-to-five, into a massive work of art.

Sure, not everyone appreciated it.

Some were downright furious.

But every now and then, I'd find someone who understood, and for me, that always made it worth it in the end.

I give the old mural one last look, barely able to make it out in the growing darkness, before I turn around and leave. I head back out of the building, shutting the door behind me, and slip out through the broken fence.

Nobody notices.

Nobody looks at me.

It's like I'm invisible to all of them.

I blend in here.

I should go home, but instead I take the subway to the last place I feel like I belong: the Upper Westside. Shoving my hands in my pockets, I stroll through the neighborhood, toward the brick dance studio not far from Broadway.

I can't see inside, can't see through the mirrored glass that wraps around the building, but I know Avery's here, inside somewhere, doing what it is she does, what it is she *loves*, and that's enough to placate me for the moment.

Leaning against the building across the street, I pull out the cigarettes and light the last one. After crumbling up the pack, I toss it in the nearby trash, watching as it bounces around on the lid before falling right in. I smoke it in silence, my eyes drifting along the neighborhood. People rush past, casting me peculiar looks, probably wondering what I'm doing prowling around this place. I'm not invisible here. Here I stick out like a sore thumb.

I'm not sure how much time passes until I see people coming out of the dance studio. Glancing over toward the door, I watch as a few women stream out, chatting animatedly, Avery dead center of the pack. She's smiling, talking, but I can't hear her the whole way over here.

She doesn't see me. She doesn't have a chance. I duck my head and walk away before she can notice I'm even around.

Passing a trashcan, I toss my lighter in, finally getting rid of the thing. I'm done. That's it.

Fourteen

"Daddy… hey, daddy!"

It's late afternoon on Friday. I cancelled my appointments at the last minute when Rebecca called, asking if I wanted Lexie for the weekend. I need the money, yeah, and I know I shouldn't have done it, but I couldn't pass up the chance to spend time with my girl.

I glance down at her as we stroll away from her mother's house, pink backpack on her back and hair chaotic, like it hasn't been brushed all day. "Yeah?"

"Can we get fro-yo?"

"Fro-yo?" I reach out and take her hand. "Is that like yolo?"

"I have a yolo!" she exclaims. "I can do walks my dog with it and go 'round the world!"

Brow furrowing, I stare at her. "What?"

"My yolo," she says. "I got it for Christmas."

I laugh when it dawns on me what she's saying. "That's a yo-yo, not a yolo."

"What's a yolo?"

"Uh, it's a saying… you only live once."

"What's that mean?"

"It means you only live once," I say, shrugging. "So you want to stop by the store and grab a Popsicle or something?"

"I want fro-yo!" she says, tugging my hand and motioning across the street. "Can we go to the place Mommy takes me sometimes? The place with the pink berries?"

Pinkberry. I sigh, shrugging. What the hell? "Sure, why not?"

There's one right on Broadway, just about a block away. We make the trip there, and I open the door, motioning for Lexie to go ahead. She slips around me, excitedly running inside and joining the line. I wait right behind her, my hands shoved in my pockets, my long sleeves covering my tattoos for the most part.

It only takes a few minutes for the line to move along and our turn to come. Lexie waltzes straight up to the counter and stares in the man's eyes, waiting for acknowledgement. The worker glances between her and me, contemplating, before ultimately settling on Lexie.

Good choice.

"What can I get for you, sweetheart?"

"Yolo," she says, giggling before correcting herself. "Fro-yo!"

"What flavor?"

"White."

I chime in when the worker casts me a questioning look for clarification. "Just the regular kind… a small."

"Large," Lexie says.

"Large," I correct myself.

"With toppings!" Lexie says.

"One original," the worker says, nodding. "Anything else?"

"Nope, that's it," I say.

I pay, shoving my change back in my wallet, and grasp Lexie's shoulder to pull her along to the side. The second worker gets to us quickly, the woman smiling down at Lexie. "What toppings do you want?"

Her eyes greedily scan the various compartments. "I want the gummy bears and Captain Crunch and chocolate candies and—"

"And I think that's enough," I say, cutting her off.

"And the pink berries!" Lexie turns to me, grasping my shirt and tugging on it. "I want the pink berries, too, Daddy!"

I concede, motioning toward the worker. "Raspberries."

Lexie hugs my waist, grinning, knowing she got her way yet again. I'm such a sucker for her. I ruffle her hair, shaking my head as she pulls away. She steps around me, to pause behind me, a loud gasp escaping her that echoes through the place like a squeal. "Avery!"

The sound of that name sends a chill through me, followed by another when I hear the voice to match. I haven't seen Avery all week long. Lexie races away, dodging around people. I quickly grab her frozen yogurt, not wanting to hold up the line, and turn around to go after my daughter.

After taking a few steps, I freeze. Avery stands there, waiting in line, her eyes wide with alarm. Her gaze darts between Lexie and me, my stomach dropping at the look on her face.

It's the deer in headlights, '*oh fuck, I'm screwed*' expression.

I notice them then, the others... the man and woman standing with her, middle-aged and stern and looking downright fucking confused. I've never met them before, but enough of Avery resides in their features for me to take a guess that they are her parents. They regard my daughter with apprehension as Lexie wraps her arms around Avery, no hesitation.

"Uh, hey," Avery says, her smile strained as she pats Lexie on the back.

"You know this child, Avery?" the man asks. Laurence Moore, I gather. He looks like the tight-ass he's been described as, tall with broad shoulders, muscular but not bulky. He does nothing but stand there, his arms crossed over his chest, but his stance carries a confidence that borders on downright conceit. And his wife isn't much better, poised and tall, thin as a rail, but her face is softer, kinder, as she stares down at Lexie.

She must like kids.

Before Avery can respond, half-words stammering from her lips, Lexie chimes in. "She's my daddy's friend that's a girl. Right, Avery?" Lexie turns around, giving no time for a response, her gaze seeking out me. "Right, Daddy? But not a girlfriend?"

I smile tersely, walking the rest of the way over to them, and nod. I don't know what to say. Instead of speaking, I hand Lexie the cup of frozen yogurt, hoping she will shovel it in her mouth to stop any further flow of words.

"Yeah, Reece is a, uh... friend," Avery says, motioning toward me. "This is his daughter, Lexie."

"Nice to meet you, Lexie," Avery's mother says, a soft smile touching her lips.

"Nice to meet you!" Lexie says, mumbling as she shoves a spoonful of yogurt in her mouth. "Are you a ballerina, too?"

I know I should remind her not to talk with food in her mouth, but I keep my lips sealed as Laurence's gaze burns through me, uncomfortable, unwelcoming. There's suspicion there, but it's deeper, I think. I can see it in his eyes. Part of him recognizes me somehow.

"I used to be a ballerina," her mother answers. "What about you?"

"No, but Avery took me to dance with her at her studio once!"

"Is that right?" The woman's eyes widen with interest. "My husband and I own that place."

"It's really nice," Lexie said. "Can I come back?"

Laurence clears his throat then, drawing attention to him. "Name's Rhys, you said?"

I haven't said shit, technically, but I nod anyway.

"Do you have a last name?"

I nod again. "Hatfield."

I didn't have to say it. His expression gave him away. He figured out how he knows me. He already knew my last name.

Lying about it is senseless. I've spent five years trying to avoid this, even going so far as to change the spelling of my name. You search 'Reece Hatfield' online and you find nothing. But Rhys has a rap sheet to rival every rapper in the game.

Over a hundred charges, pled down to just three felonies.

I blow out a deep breath, reaching for my daughter as she continues to chat the ears off of Avery's mother. My gaze briefly catches Avery's as she fidgets nervously, clearly uncomfortable with us being here.

"Come on, Little Miss," I say quietly. "We need to get going."

"Can we go to the shop?" Lexie asks, chewing on a gummy bear. "Can I have a tattoo?"

"No, we're heading home."

194

"Can Avery come?" she asks. "She can spend the night!"

"Not tonight," I mutter, not missing the fact that Avery cringes, her eyes nervously darting to her father, as she seems to slink away, yielding to his presence.

Lexie pouts, but her frown doesn't last long when Avery's mother pats her on top of the head. "Well, it was nice to meet you, Miss Lexie."

"You, too, Miss Lady," Lexie says. "Bye, Avery."

"Bye, Lexie," Avery says quietly.

I glance between them, nodding politely at Avery's mother, before my gaze settles on her father.

I hold my hand out. "Sir."

Laurence stares at my extended hand for a moment, his lips a hard, thin line of contempt. Seconds pass—strained seconds of silence that seem to drag. Just when I'm about to drop my hand, Laurence takes it, shaking it, squeezing tightly. He says nothing, letting go quickly.

I turn away, not even looking at Avery as I usher Lexie right out the door. As soon as we're outside, the glass door closing behind me, I glance back, watching as the man wipes his hand on his pants, rubbing his palm against the material, as if he can erase my touch.

A feeling sweeps through me, settling as heaviness in the pit of my stomach. Avery glances over then, as if she can still sense my presence. She frowns, the sadness shining in her eyes, as she mouths a simple word. *Sorry.*

Shaking my head, I turn away, my hand clamping down on Lexie's shoulder. "Let's get out of here."

Lexie shovels the frozen yogurt in her mouth, chomping on the cereal and candy covering the top of it, completely content. She walks along, skipping, like she's six feet tall and untouchable, whereas I've never felt so small in my goddamn life.

Night has fallen, the apartment dark except for the glow of the television. I lounge on the couch, my arm stretched out along the back of it. A small penguin-shaped pillow rests on my lap as Lexie lays on me, snuggled up with it. She's half-asleep, staring at the television blankly, trying to stay awake to watch *The Land Before Time*, but each blink is exaggerated and lasts just a little bit longer every time.

A light tapping registers with my ears, so faint it isn't until the third time I hear it that I realize someone's at the door. Sighing, I carefully move Lexie down the couch and slip away. I stroll toward it and glance out the peephole.

I see her then, standing in the hallway, illuminated by the soft yellow glow of the light. She fidgets, frowning as she quietly taps again.

I turn around, glancing at Lexie. Her eyes are closed now, her mouth open as she sleeps soundly. Contemplating, I reach for the door, quietly turning the locks and opening it.

Avery's fist is raised as she prepares to knock again, her hand dropping quickly with surprise when I appear in front of her. Before she can say anything, I step outside into the hallway, so close our bodies brush together, as I pull the door shut behind me.

Startled by my sudden proximity, Avery takes an automatic step back.

"Yeah?" My voice is harsher than I intend, based on how Avery seems to balk, momentarily speechless.

She blinks a few times, pulling herself together. "I, uh… I just wanted to come by."

"Why?"

"To see you."

"You saw me earlier."

I don't mean to sound so cold, but I can't seem to warm my tone. Just the sight of her brings back those feelings I've tried to drown out, the feelings of inadequacy… the feelings of downright failure. The way her father looked at me? The way she slunk away? I deal with that enough in my life and don't need it with her on top of everyone else.

"Yeah, but… I mean… we didn't get the chance to talk…"

"We had the chance," I say. "You could've said something… anything… but you said *nothing*. So you had the chance, Avery, you just didn't take it."

Before she can respond, I walk away, heading downstairs and outside onto the top step of the building.

Avery follows behind me, hesitating when I sit down on the top step. It takes her a moment to sit down beside me.

"Look, I'm sorry," she says. "I just…"

"Don't be sorry." I glance at her, reaching over to grasp her chin, tilting her face so she'll look at me when she tries to duck her head. Regret runs deep in her eyes. I don't like it. It doesn't look good on her. "You have nothing to be sorry for. You owe me nothing. You're not my girlfriend."

"But I want to be." She stares at me imploringly. "I want to be your girlfriend."

My thumb brushes softly across her bottom lip, my voice quiet as I mumble, "I wanted you to be, too."

Her eyes flutter closed, her lips parting, like she expects me to kiss her. I want to—fuck, do I want to—but I can't. It isn't right. None of this is right. Instead, I drop my hand and pull away.

At the loss of contact, she reopens her eyes, hurt twisting her expression. Unspoken questions shine from her eyes, but I don't have the answers she wants to hear. All I have is the truth, the *why*, and it's ugly. She might've thought she liked it dirty, but she doesn't know dirty. She can't know it, unless she has lived it. Unless she *is* it.

"You're fooling yourself if you think you want to be with a guy like me," I tell her. "Our lives are too different. You might like dabbing your feet in my lake and running around naked on my shores, but you aren't ready to swim in my waters, Avery, because you'll fucking drown."

"I don't understand," she says, shifting her body my direction, the scent of her perfume washing over me, making me wish I didn't have to say this shit to her. "Where is this coming from?"

"You know where it's coming from," I say. "You and me? We don't go together. I saw the way your father looked at me today,

197

disgusted that his little girl would sink so low… and then the way he looked at my daughter—*my* little girl. And it's fine… I'm used to it. I'm used to people looking at me and seeing a fuck-up. But they don't look at my little girl that way. She's done not a goddamn thing wrong in this world to be looked at that way, yet they do it. Because of me."

"But I don't," she says, shaking her head. "I don't think that about her *or* you. And I don't care what other people think."

She reaches out toward me but I snatch ahold of her wrist, clutching it before she can touch me. It would be a mistake, because if I let her touch me, those gentle hands might trick me into believing that all of this is actually okay.

"You're lying to yourself again if you think you don't care. I saw the look on your face when you saw us, like we invaded your pretty little picture... like we interrupted your perfect little life. I'm sure you've had a blast, slumming it with me, but it's over now. Shit is getting messy, and I don't do messy, so it's best we both just move on."

I don't give her a chance to respond. I let go of her wrist and stand up, opening the door to head back inside. I pause in the doorway, my back to her, and close my eyes. Fuck, I'm pretty sure those words hurt me more than they could ever hurt her. "Take a cab. You shouldn't walk alone in this neighborhood. Do you understand?"

Her voice is barely a whisper. "Sure."

"Good."

I step inside and close the door behind me. My footsteps are heavy as I make my way back up to the apartment, matching the feeling in my gut. Once inside, I step over to the window in the living room, shifting the curtain aside, seeing her still standing there on the top step, staring at the door in shock.

After a moment, she finally turns to walk away.

I watch her as she listens, hailing a cab, and stare as it until it disappears into the darkness. Taking a deep breath, I try to steel myself to the fact that it might very well be the last time I ever see her, but it's hard.

It hurts like a son of a bitch.

"Will I come to your house next weekend, Daddy?"

I glance down at my daughter as we stroll down the block toward her mother's house. She clutches onto me, her hand wrapped around two of my fingers. "I don't know, Little Miss. You're supposed to, but I don't know. Guess it depends on your mother."

"If I do, can we go to the museum?"

"Whatever you want."

"Can Avery come, too?"

"I'm not sure about that."

"Can you ask her?"

"I don't think that's a good idea."

"But she likes my dinosaurs."

"Yeah, she does, but Avery's busy."

"With what?"

"I don't know."

"Then how do you know she's busy?"

It's a damn good question. She's much too smart for her own good. "Because she has school, and dancing, and her family, and friends…"

"I'm her friend, too."

"I know, but it's complicated.

"Doesn't she like us anymore?"

These questions have come non-stop all weekend long, but that's a new one. And I don't like the sound of it. *At all.*

I freeze in my tracks, pulling Lexie to a stop. She looks up at me, eyes wide, as I stare down at her. My expression is stern, hardening, as her question washes through me. It's precisely why I've never brought anyone into her life before, but she's gotten used to her, I realize. Avery's become a fixture in her weekends, and she's not understanding why she's suddenly gone.

Messy.

"How could somebody not like you?"

She shrugs.

"They'd have to be crazy not to *love* you, Lexie. I mean that. You're the smartest, prettiest, bravest, most badass little girl to walk this earth, and if anyone ever tells you differently, you tell me and I'll set them straight. Got it?"

She nods.

"But Avery has a life. That doesn't mean she doesn't like us. It just means that she has other people she likes, other people who want her time. She's smart, and pretty, and badass herself... we can't monopolize her time."

"Like with Monopoly?"

"Monopolize... means we can't keep her for ourselves. We have to share."

Her nose scrunches up, a look of pure disgust on her face.

"I know how you feel, but it's just a fact of life. The sky is blue, dinosaurs are big, boy bands are terrible, and Avery doesn't belong to us. She never did."

Lexie giggles, not resisting as I start walking again. "Boy bands aren't terrible, Daddy."

"We'll agree to disagree there."

"And dinosaurs aren't all big! Some are little like lizards! And the sky's black at night, but sometimes it looks like bubble gum, too."

"Can't argue with that logic," I say, "but it still doesn't change what I said about Avery."

She doesn't question me anymore on the walk. I pause on the sidewalk in front of Rebecca's brownstone, leaning down to kiss Lexie's forehead before motioning for her to go inside. I watch as she runs up the steps, the front door opening and Rebecca appearing, her phone clutched to her ear. She dramatically lets out a breath, clutching her chest. "Never mind, Officer, they're here now. Thank you so much."

I glare at her. *Officer?*

Rebecca hangs up the phone and greets our daughter warmly, telling her to get ready for a bath as usual. Lexie runs up the stairs inside as Rebecca turns back to me, eyes narrowed. "You can't tell time, Rhys? It's half past seven!"

I glance at my watch. 7:22 pm. *Shit*. "Lexie was watching a movie and wanted to see the end."

"Of course," Rebecca grumbles. "Knowing you, it was probably some R-rated trash she shouldn't have been watching in the first place!"

"It wasn't."

"Yeah, right. Like I can believe a word you say. I'm just grateful you got her home in one piece. Your probation officer was about to start a search! He couldn't believe it when I told him you were violating the court order."

Officer.

Probation officer.

The bitch called my probation officer?

Those words ignite the fuse of the bomb that has been building all weekend long, the pressure inside of me, the anger and hurt and loathing reaching the point where I just can't bottle it up anymore. The moment they're out of her mouth, my vision hazes over with red.

"You know what, Rebecca? Fuck you."

She blanches. "What did you say?"

"I said fuck you," I repeat before emphasizing each word. "*Fuck. You.* I put up with a lot of shit from you. I roll over and take it, let you fuck me again and again, to keep peace for our kid, but I'm sick of it. So, you don't like me? You hate me? Wish you didn't have to look at me? Well, news flash, Rebecca—I feel the same fucking way about you. But I keep it to myself, I keep my mouth shut and smile and deal with it on my own, because that's what an adult does."

"What the hell do *you* know about being an adult?"

"I know plenty. Maybe I'm not perfect. Hell, I *know* I'm not perfect. But I give what I got, even if what I got isn't good enough for you, or her, or them, or *anyone*. I still give it. If you don't like it? If my best isn't good enough for you? If I'm not good enough for you? Get over it. Get over *yourself*. Because I don't give a fuck anymore." I back up a few steps, shaking my head as I glare at her.

"I'll be back for Lexie on Friday."

Rebecca doesn't argue, turning around and storming inside, slamming the door behind her.

Fifteen

The metal chair shifts, scratching against the floor when Kevin plops down in it. I cast him a quick glance before going back to cleaning up my station. Ten o'clock on Monday, and I'm just as agitated as I was over the weekend.

"Man, what a day," Kevin says, clasping his hands together at the back of his head. "I could use a smoke... and a drink. *Something.*"

"Tell me about it." I finish what I'm doing before turning around, leaning back against my table. "I'm heading to the bar across the street for a drink if you want to join me."

"Now you're talking!"

We lock up before heading to The Spare Room. The bar is quiet, as always, only a few patrons hanging out at this hour. I take my usual stool at the bar, needing not say a word, the can of Genesee sliding down the bar to me. I pick it up, nodding my thanks at the bartender, and take a drink.

Kevin slides onto the stool beside me, ordering whatever is cheap and on tap. We drink and chat, comparing notes on clients, just unwinding from a long day.

"You're not meeting your girl, are you?" Kevin asks after a while. "I don't want to be in the way."

I laugh dryly. "What girl?"

"The cute brunette that's been hanging around lately."

"Nah." I take a long pull from my drink, the mention of Avery putting me on edge. "She came and went."

"Literally?" Kevin asks. "*Hit it and quit it* is your usual M.O., isn't it?"

I smile sadly. "She's not the kind you can fuck and forget."

"I could tell. You actually brought her around everyone."

"Lapse in judgment."

"I don't know, man. She seemed like a keeper. Housewife material, verses your usual whorehouse type."

"Yeah, well, I think I ought to just stick with what I know."

"Speaking of which..." Kevin smacks me on the arm and motions toward the door when two women walk in. "Barflies are my favorite."

Always were mine, too.

Kevin motions for the bartender as the women settle into a booth off to the side. "Send them over a round of shots for me, will you? You can put them on my friend here's tab."

The bartender looks to me curiously, for confirmation, but I just shrug.

Whatever.

That's all it takes—two shots of cheap tequila, ten measly dollars, for us to get an invitation to join the ladies at their table. Kevin choses the busty brunette, leaving me to entertain her blonde friend. I slide into the booth beside her, casting her a peculiar look. She's vaguely familiar, but I can't really place her face.

The moment I settle in beside her, she smiles widely. "Reece!"

Fuck. She knows me, which means I'm supposed to know her.

"Hey, uh..." I hesitate. I can't even fake it. "Sorry, what's your name again?"

"It's Amy," she says. "You tattooed me a few weeks ago, the quote on my side?"

It clicks in my head the moment she says it, before she stands up and brazenly pulls up her shirt, barely keeping her tits covered as she shows me her tattoo. I unconsciously reach over, running my fingers lightly along the inked text, feeling the texture. It's healing nicely. "I recognize you now."

Smiling, she pulls her shirt back down. "Guess I'm easier to remember with my clothes askew, huh?"

"Guess so."

I pick up my beer and sip on it, lounging back in the booth. Kevin and the other girl end up wandering off, journeying to the bar for shot after shot, while I just sit there, vaguely listening as whatshername—*Aaron... Annie... Amy?*—babbles on and on.

I drink a few beers, politely nodding and humming, acting like I know what the hell she's talking about. The drunker she grows, the more touchy-feely she becomes, her hand eventually slipping onto my lap.

I wish I had it in me to enjoy it. The easiest way to erase Avery from my mind, to purge her from my thoughts, to rid myself of those goddamn inadequate feelings, would be to lose myself in another woman, one without expectations, without hopes for me, but there's nothing.

Not a stirring, not a tingle, nothing.

That's a first. Seems painting isn't the only thing that left me feeling impotent anymore. My dick has finally given out. One step closer to that breakdown, after all.

"I should get home," I mutter, shifting away from her.

"Do you want some company?"

Do I want company?

Yeah, I do, but not her.

"Thanks, but not tonight," I say, standing up, barely offering her a look as I walk away. I stride by Kevin, slapping him on the back as I go. "See you in the morning, Kev."

"You leaving?"

"Yeah."

"Alone?"

"Yeah." I motion toward the booth, where the woman still sits. "All yours."

Kevin laughs and says something in response, but I'm heading out the door before I can hear it.

My steps are leisurely as I stroll down the street, in no hurry. Nobody is home, nobody waiting on me, nobody wondering where I am or when I'll be there. I could stay out until dawn, go missing overnight, and nobody would notice. Nobody would worry. Nobody would care.

Nobody.

It's a sad reality.

I don't like to admit it, but I was starting to get used to having somebody.

The apartment seems darker than ever when I make it there. Sighing, I open the door and step inside, kicking something. I glance down, seeing a white envelope on the floor, shoved through the crack at the bottom of the door. Picking it all up, I head to the kitchen and flick on the light. It has no postmark, the only marking the pre-stamped return address:

The Juilliard School.

I stroll toward the refrigerator and grab the only beer in it, opening it and taking a swig. I set it down beside me as I lean back against the counter and tear the envelope open, glancing inside.

Two tickets to the senior dance production.

I stare at them for a moment before shoving them back inside and tossing the envelope on the small table. Grabbing my beer, I walk back out of the kitchen, shutting off the light as I go. I'm wound tight—too edgy to sleep, too preoccupied to watch television, or read, or do anything except *think*.

Frustrated, I make my way down the hallway, straight to the back room.

My studio.

I keep the light off, only the moonlight streaming through, faintly illuminating the mess that had been left behind last time. Paint is smudged on the walls and floors, the futon stained, streaks of a murky gray covering everything. On the wall to my left is a partial handprint in paint, slapped there by Avery when we lost ourselves in passion. I stare at it, my stomach in knots, everything building inside of me that I need to release.

My eyes drift from it to my easel. I don't give it much thought, don't hesitate. Squirting fresh paint onto the discarded ruined palette, I grab a tattered paintbrush, and for the first time in what feels like forever, wet bristles meet a fresh canvas as I paint once again.

It's ugly, and angry, dark paint blending together in a frantic abyss of nothingness. It looks like I feel—worthless and pointless, chaotic and filthy, an all around fucked up mess.

Damn if I don't feel better when I'm finished.

"You should go."

"And you should mind your own business."

I can practically hear Ellie rolling her eyes at my response. I sit in the chair in front of her, my feet propped up on her desk, as I wait for my first appointment of the day. I'm already kicking myself for even bringing up the tickets I found on my floor. I offered them to her, thinking she'd like that kind of thing. She's all the time taking off to catch shows on Broadway, but the moment I mentioned a show at Juilliard, her expression lit up, but not in the way I expected.

"You should wear a tie, too," she says.

"And you should kiss my ass."

"Oh, and don't forget to take her flowers."

"Yeah, well, don't forget to suck my dick."

Ellie laughs that time, reaching over and shoving my feet off her desk. They hit the floor with a thud. "If you wear a damn tie and take her flowers, *she* might suck your dick."

"Drop it," I say, standing up and stretching. I didn't sleep much last night. My body aches from exhaustion. I was up until almost dawn, painting for hours, purging it out of me. "That ship has sailed."

"Then swim the fuck over to it and climb on board. It's not that difficult."

I flip her off as I walk away, making my way to my room. I have a full day—appointment after appointment, client after client. I drown myself in tattoos until nightfall, and then pack up at closing.

The same old routine.

I'm out the door at ten on the dot, hearing Ellie shout after me, "remember what I said!" I shake my head, my eyes drifting to the bar across the street, contemplating, but I shrug it off and start the trek home instead.

I stroll along, hands in my pockets, hat cocked backward on my head. I'm not paying much attention to my surroundings, losing myself in the chaos of the Manhattan streets. There's new graffiti in my neighborhood, covering the side of an old office building, stenciled warheads and a flag with some line about bombing for peace.

Everyone seems to have a message.

Sometimes I still wonder what mine used to be.

When I approach my building, I glance up, my footsteps faltering when I see the person sitting alone on the top step.

Avery.

I stare at her, pausing on the sidewalk. My presence garners her attention, and she jumps up, wringing her hands together as she looks at me. "Hey!"

I'm quiet for a moment before responding. "Hello."

"I, uh... just wanted to make sure you got the tickets I dropped off yesterday."

"I did."

"Are you going to…? I mean… would you still come?"

Slowly, I shrug.

"The tickets are good for any night," she continues. "Thursday until Sunday. You can come any day you want and they'll let you in."

"Okay."

"And you can bring Lexie… or anyone you want, really… but I think she'd really like it."

"She would."

She stares at me, vulnerability shining from her. "So you'll come?"

There's that hope, the hope she has for me. She shouldn't have it, though. I'll only disappoint her like I do everybody.

"I don't know," I say quietly. "I'll think about it."

My answer seems to be enough for her. Nodding, she heads

down the steps and hesitates beside me, offering me a small smile before slipping past. Her arm brushes against mine, her perfume tickling my nostrils as I inhale deeply. I just stand there as she walks away, hearing her soft voice after a few seconds. "Reece?"

Slowly, I turn my head, regarding her warily. I don't speak, merely look at her, eyebrow raised. She stares back, but after a moment shakes her head, muttering, "forget about it."

I'm trying, I think. *I'm trying like hell to forget all about it.*

I watch as she walks away, shoulders slumped, gazed fixed on the sidewalk. Her name is on the tip of my tongue, and I almost call out to her, wondering what she would've said. Wondering what she *wanted* to say.

But I do nothing.

I merely watch until she rounds the corner, disappearing into the night.

I don't sleep much again.

The next morning, I show up at the shop early, having everything set up and ready before anyone else arrives for the day. I'm sitting in the chair in front of Ellie's desk, my feet propped up on the front of it just like yesterday. She eyes me suspiciously as she settles in for the day, dropping her bag on the floor and setting her cup of coffee on the desk.

"You pick out that tie yet?" she asks.

I just glare at her, too tired to even think of a snappy comeback. Anything beyond "fuck you" seems out of my range today.

"I think a dark color would look best on you," she continues, ignoring the look on my face. "Black, gray, maybe blue… solid, not stripes. You're not a stripes kind of guy."

I'm not a *tie* kind of guy.

"Maybe a skinny tie," she suggests. "But not a bowtie. Unless you're getting married or your name is Matt Smith, you have no business wearing a bowtie."

My brow furrows. "Who's Matt Smith?"

"The Doctor."

"Whose doctor?"

Ellie stare at me. "More like *Doctor Who*, dumbass. Seriously, do you know nothing?"

"I know I'm not wearing a tie," I reply, shrugging. "And I know you have work to do that doesn't involve meddling in my love life. Pretty sure we don't pay you for your advice."

"You ought to," she says, sitting down and grabbing the appointment book. "I'm serious, Reece. You should go. You won't regret it."

Sixteen

Cheery pop music echoes through the downstairs of the house, some One Directional Bieber bullshit with too much treble and not nearly enough bass, whining from the small speaker on my phone. Lexie screeches along to the words in the living room, making up her own lyrics along the way.

They're probably better than the real ones.

I stand in the bathroom, staring at my reflection as I fiddle with the plain black tie around my neck, trying to fasten the knot and terribly failing. I've been at it for nearly ten minutes and practically have myself in a noose. Cross, pull, loop, over, under, crisscross fucking applesauce… I feel like I'm teaching Lexie to tie her shoes all over again.

Just make the goddamn bunny ears, loop and pull. How hard can the shit be?

Sighing, frustrated, I unknot it and let it hang loose around my neck as I walk out of the bathroom, slapping the switch to turn off the light on my way out. I head toward the living room, cringing at the obnoxious clatter of music. Lexie is jumping on the couch, clutching the phone tightly in her hand as she dances around, falling on her ass on the cushion before jumping right back up.

"I should've bought a damn clip-on," I mutter. "I can't tie this tie to save my life."

"Oh, oh, me, me!" Lexie jumps up and down excitedly, tossing my phone down on the cushion beside her as she frantically waves me over. "I can do it, Daddy!"

I cock an eyebrow at her but shrug it off, stepping over toward her. She probably has a better chance of getting it than me. Lexie grabs both ends of the tie and loops them together, pulling with all her might. I gasp, the tie nearly cutting off my airflow, as she studiously ties it like she would her shoelaces, her expression stone cold serious. After she's finished, she smiles and snatches up my phone again, going right back to jumping. "There, Daddy."

I look down at myself. I look like I'm wearing a goddamn clown's bowtie. Shaking my head, I unknot the thing and pull it off, tossing it on the couch. I fix my collar, the plain white button down enough to make me feel suffocated. I haven't worn one in a while... not since the last time I stood in court.

Unbuttoning the top two buttons, I turn to my daughter. "Go brush your hair."

"I already did!"

Her hair is wild, as usual, the curls frizzy and unkempt. If not for the fact that she's wearing a pink dress, people might mistake her for a tiny George of the Jungle, one of those feral kids they talk about on TV. "Do it again, Mowgli."

She stops jumping on the couch, plopping down on her ass before standing up. Walking by me, she flings my phone my way as she heads for the bathroom, breathing heavily from exertion.

"Brush your teeth while you're in there," I call.

I stand there, fidgeting with my watch. We have some time before the show starts, but if I don't get out the door soon, I have a sneaking suspicion I won't make it at all.

I'm already starting to sweat.

"There," Lexie says, stomping back in. "Better?"

She looks exactly as she had a few minutes ago. Sighing, I shrug it off. I'd try to fix it for her, but that would end up about as well as the tie had.

I really need to learn how to braid.

"You look perfect, Little Miss," I say, shutting off the music and slipping my phone in my pocket before offering her my hand. "You ready?"

212

We head out, stopping by the store on the way to the subway. *Flowers,* Ellie stressed. *You always bring them flowers.* I failed the tie part, but maybe I can get this right. I don't know shit about flowers, so I let Lexie pick out a bunch.

Pink carnations. Good enough for me.

Lexie carries them, skipping along. I stroll beside her, my hands nervously in my pockets, grasping hold of the tickets. We take the subway to the Upper Westside, my anxiety escalating as we head toward Juilliard. I pause in front of the building, tugging Lexie to a stop, and stare up at the massive triangular structure, the glass framed with an orange glow at night. It looks like a piece of art itself.

My stomach twists in knots.

If I hadn't already promised Lexie, I'd turn around right now and head home.

"Come on," I mumble, leading her toward the entrance. "The show awaits."

The theater is small, tucked in on the third floor of the building. I wait in the line, handing my reserved tickets over for admission. The lady smiles warmly at me, almost setting my nerves at ease.

Almost.

Lexie stands beside me, leaning against my leg as she looks around. She nearly falls when I take a step away, giggling as she snatches ahold of me. "Wait for me."

The theater holds about a hundred people, over half of the seats already filled. I find a fairly vacant row right near the door and sit down, putting Lexie in the seat at the aisle. I settle into my seat, warily glancing around. People are dressed impeccably, sitting quietly, waiting patiently, the women in dresses and the men in three-piece suits.

I should've worn the fucking tie.

Lexie, on the other hand, can't sit still. She bounces in her seat, swinging her legs, her voice loud as she asks, "how much longer?"

"Just a few minutes," I say, glancing at my watch, wishing time would speed up. It doesn't escape my notice that Lexie seems to be the only kid present.

Despite it being as cold as an icebox in the theater, my skin feels flushed, like I'm sitting beneath a spotlight.

"Look, Daddy. Look!"

I glance at Lexie as she tugs on my arm. "Huh?"

She motions toward the door. "It's the ballerina lady! Remember?"

My eyes follow my daughter's gaze, watching as Avery's parents step in, pausing to greet some people nearby. Before I can respond to her, to say I saw them, her shrill little voice calls out. "Hey, Miss Lady! Hey!"

I start to shush her, to ask her to keep her voice down, but it's too late. Avery's mother turns, catching Lexie's eye, and smiles warmly, offering a small wave. Tickled by the acknowledgement, Lexie jumps up, squealing as she runs across the aisle.

Fuck. I'm on my feet instantly, muttering apologies to the people I nearly plow over as I dart after her. As soon as I approach, I hear her excited voice. "Are you going to dance, too?"

Avery's mother shakes her head. "I'm afraid not. I don't dance here."

"Why not?"

"Because I'm much too old to go to Juilliard."

"Why?"

That question sparks a genuine laugh. "I guess I just grew up."

Lexie starts rambling—about school, and dancing, and Peter fucking Pan, never growing up and goddamn Neverland. I interject, my hands clamping down on my daughter's shoulder before she can start acting the story out for everybody.

"Sorry," I say. "She's just excited."

"No need to apologize," she responds. "I love her enthusiasm. You ever think about signing her up for dance?"

"Oh, can I, Daddy?" Lexie turns to me, eyes wide. "Please? Can I?"

"I, uh..." I want to say yes, but I know I can't. "That's something you have to ask your mother. I don't have you enough to commit you to something like that."

A voice theatrically clears. "Divorced?"

My eyes drift to Avery's father. He looks not at all amused by our presence. "Never married."

"Yet you have a kid."

"We were in college and…" *And why the fuck am I explaining myself to this man?* "Anyway, I'm sorry for the interruption."

I pull Lexie back to our seats. I can feel Laurence's eyes piercing through me from across the aisle, jabbing like little cat-scratch pricks from a tattoo needle. I ignore it the best I can, the hair on the nape of my neck standing on end. Slouching down in my seat, I unbutton the cuffs of my shirt and shove up my sleeves.

Fuck it.

There's no fooling these people.

The theater fills up quickly, the lights going down as the production starts. Dancers are introduced, choreography announced. I vaguely pay attention to the stage, trying to keep my daughter in her seat, but her excitement can't be contained.

A few dances go by before the announcer comes on. "For the last performance of the night, Avery Moore, accompanied by the rest of the forth years, will be doing an original contemporary piece choreographed by Miss Moore, entitled *Extinction.*"

My eyes are fixed on the stage then. Instead of the usual classic music, instead of the sweet, smooth melodies of the others, the frantic thumping of bass drums echoes through the theater. A spotlight follows Avery as she steps out on the stage, each step dramatic and exaggerated, as she moves to the beat. She wears a short dress, dark green with splashes of black, tattered like rags around the edges.

The music shifts, louder, faster, growing downright angry. Avery takes off along the stage, turning and swaying, leaping and bending, her kicks high and dips low. I'm transfixed, nothing existing that moment but her, as I watch Avery command the stage alone. All eyes are on her, all attention hers. She has the audience in her hands, owning them all, body and soul.

The other dancers join her, a dozen bodies following her moves in the background, as she remains in the spotlight. She dances on her tiptoes effortlessly, gracefully, and never once does she waver.

Never once does she falter.

If I thought she was beautiful in the studio, this is breathtaking. This is gritty, and emotional, full of rage and heartache, every footfall and bang of the drum striking like lightning, thunder vibrating the room. This isn't a pretty little princess in a soft pink tutu… this is a beast, a monster, breaking through. It's gut wrenching and soul shaking.

It's fucking *dirty*.

And messy.

The music eventually shifts again, every few beats a thunderous boom vibrating the room, the lights flashing as a dancer in the background falls and disappears from the stage. One by one they fade away, leaving her all alone again.

The bass subsides to mere small drumbeats as it morphs into a solemn melody. Avery turns and turns and turns on stage, moving at a dizzying pace, before finally slowing along with the beat. Eventually she comes to a stop on her tiptoes, her gaze on the stage, as silence takes over the room briefly.

It feels like an eternity as I stare at her, stunned.

With a thunderous bang, she drops flat to the floor, the spotlight going out, everything ending in darkness.

The crowd applauds. Lexie shrieks and jumps up and down. I just stare straight ahead, speechless.

I've got chills.

The lights come on as the dancers came out to take their bows, the show over. People start filtering out while others approach the stage, showering the performers with roses. I look at Lexie as she anxiously clutches the pink carnations.

"Go ahead, Little Miss," I say quietly. "You take them up there."

She shoots away before I even finish. I stand up and step out into the aisle, keeping my eyes on my daughter as she weaves through the crowd. People move past me out the door, eyeing me warily when I don't move.

Lexie forces her way to the front, refusing to be overlooked, and shoves her flowers up toward the stage. Avery spots them, her smile lighting up. She jumps off the front of the stage and takes them, laughing when Lexie wraps her arms around her.

A soft smile touches my lips, but it doesn't last long, a low voice breaking my fleeting moment of peace.

"I know who you are."

Expression falling, I turn my head, catching a glimpse of Laurence lurking just behind me, glaring my way.

"Rhys Hatfield," he says. "I pressed charges against you almost six years ago. Of course, I didn't know your name then. I only knew what they called you. Hatter. But I know now."

I stare at the man. I don't know what to say. *You figured me out. Congratulations. Do you want a cookie? I'm fresh out of fucks to give.*

There's no hostility in his voice, no threat... he merely speaks matter-of-fact, like he's so sure about his opinion that anything I say will be chalked up to bullshit.

"I know your kind," he continues. "I know the things you do, the things you want, and you won't get them from my daughter. She has a bright future, but not if you drag her down. You're a convicted felon. A criminal. And I don't mean to be rude, but I'm just looking out for my daughter. You have to understand that, being a father yourself. Would you want *your* little girl with somebody like you?"

The words 'you don't even fucking know me' bounce around in my mind, and I nearly speak them, but instead I turn away from the man, my gaze drifting to Lexie. Laurence may not know me, but I'm not blind to what kind of man I am... a man whose relationships consist of a string of one-night-stands that rarely survive sunrise.

Would I want my daughter with a man like me? *Fuck no.*

Laurence walks away, saying nothing else, and heads up toward the stage to his daughter. He wraps his arms around her, lifting her up in the air and swinging her around in a circle. I take Avery's distraction as a chance to slip away, motioning for Lexie to come to me. She runs down the aisle, joining me.

"Let's get out of here, Little Miss," I mutter, taking her hand.

"But—"

"Not right now." I cut her off before she can verbalize whatever objection she has to leaving. "It's getting late."

Frowning, she doesn't argue as I pull her out of the theater and onto the third floor of the building. She drags her feet a bit, clearly not wanting to leave. We make it down the hall, toward the elevators, when the voice shouts out behind us. "Reece!"

Avery.

My feet seem to want to stall automatically, but I force them to keep moving, not looking back.

"Daddy," Lexie says, tugging my hand. "Stop, Daddy."

"Reece!" she yells again, her feet pounding against the floor behind me as she jogs to catch up. "Wait!"

"Please, Daddy," Lexie growls, yanking my hand hard as she freezes in place just in front of the elevator. Someone holds it open for us, and I try to pull my daughter inside, but she narrows her eyes and refuses to budge, her expression clear as day: If I yank her into the elevator now, there will be hell to pay.

Sighing, I motion for the elevator to go ahead, and stare at the shiny silver door as it closes before me. The footsteps descend upon me quickly, stopping just behind us. Her breaths come out in quick pants as she exhales my name. "Reece."

Slowly, I turn to face her. Her skin is flushed, makeup smudged from sweating, hints of glitter sparkling under the lights. And she glows… fuck, she beams, brighter than the sun, confidence and happiness radiating from her.

I don't know shit about auras, but something tells me if I could see them, hers would be bright yellow.

My hand itches to reach out and touch her warm skin, to run my fingertips along her bottom lip as she smiles at me, but I keep it locked in place at my side.

"You were just going to leave?" she asks incredulously. "You weren't even going to say hey… or goodbye? Nothing?"

"Hey," I say quietly, looking away from her as I mutter, "goodbye."

"Daddy," Lexie says, tugging my arm. "Hey, Daddy."

I ignore her, not wanting her to get involved, and glance back

218

at the elevator, wishing it would open again and end this awkward moment.

"I don't understand," Avery says, a tinge of hurt in her voice. "I mean, what did I do that was so terrible? What did I do to deserve this? I'm sorry about that day, I really am. I told you that."

"Daddy," Lexie calls out again, her free hand beating against my leg to get my attention. "Daddy!"

"Not now," I mutter, turning to Avery. "This isn't the place for this."

"Then where?" she asks. "When?"

"Daddy!"

Groaning, I look down at my daughter as she punches me hard in the side to get my attention. I wince. "What?"

"I gots to pee," she says, staring up at me as she dances around.

"Oh." Fuck. "Uh..."

"There's a bathroom this way," Avery says, taking a step back, her arms crossed over her chest. "I'll show you."

I glance back at the elevator, frowning when it opens again. Guess we *still* can't leave yet. We follow Avery down the hall to a bathroom. Lexie runs inside as I wait, leaning back against the wall in the hall, my hands shoved in my pockets, my gaze on the floor by my feet. I can sense Avery staring at me as she stands there, right in front of the bathroom door.

"I just... I don't get it," she says. "What's wrong with you?"

Everything, I think.

"What we had was great," she continues. "At least *I* thought it was great. Wasn't it?"

"It was a lie, Avery," I say. "Sure, it was nice, but you've got this life, this life I don't belong in, and it's everything to you. You eat, breathe, and *live* this world, while I can't even tie a fucking tie to try to fit in for one night. You... you're special. You have something to offer. But nobody wants to see the prima ballerina with the likes of me... it's a waste. You belong on a stage somewhere, not slumming it in the streets."

She gapes at me. "How can you say that?"

"Easily," I say, pushing away from the wall to stand up straight.

"It's the truth."

Noise draws my attention as Lexie bounds out into the hall.

"You wash your hands?" I ask.

Rolling her eyes, she shoves her way right back into the bathroom.

I turn to Avery again, stepping closer. I pause mere inches from her, smelling the sweet scent of her perfume wafting from her skin. "People still judge a book by its cover, Avery. And your story? It's beautiful. *You're* beautiful. But I'm nothing but a ripped out page, graffiti where some should never be. Don't taint your story with me."

I cup her cheek, tilting her head up, unable to help myself. My thumb brushes the corner of her mouth as I lean down, pressing a chaste kiss to her lips.

Lexie rushes back out of the bathroom just as I pull away. She shakes her hands, flinging drops of water everywhere as if to prove to me she's washed them this time. Wordlessly, I grab her damp hand and pull her away, heading right back to the elevators.

This time, Avery doesn't follow.

Seventeen

A crowd packs the lobby of the probation building in Tribeca, people sitting around, anxiously awaiting their scheduled appointments. The receptionist barely looks at me when I walk in, doesn't acknowledge me when I step up to her desk. She doesn't want to be here.

Can't say I blame her.

I'll be a happy man when I never have to step in this motherfucker again.

"I need to speak to my probation officer."

"Name?"

I hesitate as I clear my throat, speaking low. "Rhys Hatfield."

She glances at her computer before looking away again. "You're not on the list."

"I don't have an appointment."

"Then you need to make one."

"Look, if you'll just call up to him, I'm sure he'll see me," I say. "His name is Previn Warren."

The lady cuts her eyes at me like I'm inconveniencing her. Hell, maybe I am. But I've spent five years being inconvenienced and I'm ready to have it over with, no matter how she feels about it.

Huffing, she reaches over and snatches up the phone from her desk, jabbing at some numbers before bringing it to her ear. "Mr. Warren, one of your guys is here... yeah, he's down here in the lobby... he's insisting he see you... I told him he needed an appointment, but he doesn't seem to know how to listen."

I ignore that swipe as I stand there, tapping my foot, waiting.

"Yeah, uh, it started with an 'R'... sounded like 'rice' or something." She cuts her eyes at me with annoyance. "What was your last name again?"

"Hatfield."

She focuses right back on her call. "Says it's Hatfield."

The woman says nothing else, nodding to herself, before she hangs up the phone. Waving her hand, she motions toward the set of elevators. "Third floor."

I turn around to walk away. "Thanks."

"Make an appointment next time," she hollers after me.

"There won't be a next time," I call back.

"Yeah, yeah," she mutters. "That's what they all say."

I take the elevator up to the third floor, heading to Officer Warren's office toward the back of the building. His door is open a crack as he sits behind his desk, wearing his usual uniform, surrounded by mounds of paperwork. He glances up when I step into the doorway, leaning back in his chair to regard me. "To what do I owe the honor, Hatfield? You aren't one to just drop by."

Reaching into my pocket, I pull out the folded up slip of paper and hold it up as I step closer to his desk. "Wanted to bring this by."

He eyes me peculiarly as he takes it from me, carefully unfolding it. His eyes drift along the paper with confusion. It's a money order for exactly six hundred twenty-three dollars and nineteen cents.

"Restitution?" he asks, waving it at me. "These get mailed in."

"I wanted to drop this one off to you in person."

He stares at me for a second as he riddles out my reasoning. "Last payment, I'm guessing?"

I nod.

Warren's eyes shift back to the money order as he sets it down on his desk and smoothes it out. After a moment, he shifts his chair back to stand, reaching across his desk to hold his hand out to me. I take it, shaking it, as a small smile touches his lips. He says nothing, but it doesn't escape my notice when his eyes flicker to my hand in his. He's spent five years looking at my hands, watching for any sign of spray paint, any sign I might've broken my probation.

Old habits die hard.

I know.

"Congratulations," he says finally, letting go to sit back down.

"Thank you, sir."

"I'll make sure it gets where it's supposed to be," he says, referring to the restitution payment. "You just keep yourself out of trouble until I can get the court to sign off on your probation dismissal. Don't make me ever have to look at you again."

He doesn't have to tell me that again.

Turning around, I walk out, taking the elevator back down and heading out of the probation building for what I hope like hell is the last time. I haven't a penny left in my pocket, not enough to even grab a beer after work today, but it's worth it, I think.

Worth it to be done with the bullshit, to close that chapter of my life and move on to something else, something better... to write a different ending in the story of 'me'.

The back room is quiet, except for the soft buzzing and thumping coming from the other spaces in the shop. I sit on my stool at my desk, sketching out a design on a piece of paper. A client came in for a consultation earlier this week, wanting a tribal tattoo on their shoulder. I've already sketched it out three times but promptly discarded it to start over. I've done so many of them over the years that they feel redundant, like I'm doing nothing but repeating designs and not giving them anything unique anymore.

But how many ways can I draw it?

I glance at the clock—half past noon. My twelve o'clock consultation hasn't shown up. It's the end of May already, a Friday afternoon. Just a few more hours and I pick Lexie up for a long weekend—Memorial Day. I'm looking forward to taking a few days off, having done nothing for the past month except live in the shop, picking up as many extra clients as I can to make enough money to get that burden off of me.

A new beginning.

There's a light tap on the open door behind me. I glance over my shoulder, watching as Ellie leans against the doorframe, scribbling in the appointment book. "Another cancellation."

Same shit, different day.

"Your one o'clock is down with a nasty cold," she explains. "I rescheduled the appointment for two weeks from now and thanked them for keeping their germs out of the shop, because we sure as shit don't want them."

I nod, turning back to the design on my desk. "Thanks."

"Also, we have a walk-in."

I shake my head. "Not today."

"But I figured since you were free now—"

"Give it to Kevin."

"They requested you."

"Bullshit."

"I'm serious."

"Well, give them to Kevin anyway."

"That's not going to work," she says. "They're requesting a Hatfield original."

I freeze, tip of my pencil stalling on the paper. "What kind of *original?*"

"Don't know."

"You didn't ask?"

"Yeah, and they don't know," Ellie says. "Said it was up to you… that's what makes it an original, I guess."

I sit there for a moment before dropping my pencil and spinning around on my stool. I eye Ellie curiously as I stand up, brushing by her out of the room without a word. I stroll toward the lobby, freezing when I see the lone woman standing there, facing away from me, and admiring the latest shop graffiti. It's so fresh the stench of spray paint still lingers in the lobby.

I can't see her face, but I know that body, recall every inch of it in breathtaking detail, a memory that I can't escape no matter how much I try to wipe it away.

Avery.

I haven't seen her in weeks, not since the night of her performance, but here she stands, wearing a black dress, loose-fitting and backless, showing off the curve of her spine. Her legs look impossibly long, her calf muscles well defined in a pair of tall heels, accentuating the swell of her ass.

As if she can sense my sudden presence, she turns around, our eyes meeting. Slowly, I step toward her. "Avery—"

She holds her hand up to stop me from talking and interjects before I can tell her she shouldn't be here. "Just... can I have a minute? I'll leave if you want me to. Just let me get out what I came to say first."

I glance around the shop, my eyes trailing Ellie as she makes her way back to her desk, making a point not to acknowledge us, but I'm not an idiot. I know she'll strain her ears to hear every word.

Turning back to Avery, I step a bit closer, nodding for her to continue.

She stands there quietly, as if not sure what to say for a moment, before letting out a deep sigh. "I graduated this morning. Well, more like an hour ago. I'm officially a Julliard graduate."

I sit down on the arm of the couch near her. "Congratulations."

"Thank you," she whispers, smiling. "My parents are throwing me a party to celebrate... or well, what they call a party, anyway. It's happening right now, actually, at the dance studio. I'm supposed to be there, but I came here instead."

"They're probably worried."

"My mom knows I'm not coming, and my father... well, he'll be pissed, but it doesn't matter. He wouldn't understand. I don't think he *can*. He doesn't know what it's like. His entire life was always ballet, and he made my entire life ballet, too. I never chose my own art; I never picked my own path.

"And you know, he was right... I was born to dance. Dancing to me is like breathing—I don't think I could survive without it. But just because he was right about that, doesn't mean he's right about everything. It doesn't mean he's right about *you*. Because I love dancing, Reece, but that's not the only thing I love. I love *you*, too."

I blink a few times, my brow furrowing when those words strike me. I think for sure I must have heard her wrong until a squeal echoes from the receptionist's desk, followed by a forced cough.

"Sorry," Ellie calls out. "Something caught in my throat."

I shoot her a glare before turning back to Avery, unsure of how to respond. "Look, I—"

Once more, she holds up her hand to stop me from talking. "I do, okay? I know you think you're all wrong for me, but I don't care, because there's so much about you that's right. I love how serious you take art, even when it's something stupid, like tattooing Johnny's name in a banner over a damn heart. And I love how much being a good father means to you, how much you love your daughter. Hell, *I* love your daughter, too."

I stare at her, dumbfounded. "You love her?"

"How can I not?" she says. "She's a miniature you. Everything I love about you is in her. And I love that me loving her had more of an impact on you than me loving *you*. You said I was special, Reece, but you are, too, even if you don't see it. There's so much about you… the look you get on your face when you're concentrating; how you get all weirdly poetic when you get upset; how you always cook pancakes when it's so much easier just to pour cereal in a bowl, but you do it out of love, and I love it. I love it all."

Those words wash through me as I slump against the arm of the couch, crossing my arms over my chest. "You love me."

"I do," she says.

"That's what you came here to say?"

"Yes." She pauses. "Well, no. I also came here to tell you that I know."

"You know."

It's not a question.

Maybe it's the look in her eyes, but somehow I know exactly what she knows. She knows me. All of me.

"Hatter," she says quietly. "Guess it's short for Hatfield. I thought it was because of the, uh... the moniker."

"It was a bit of both," I say.

She stares at me, frowning. "Why didn't you tell me? Didn't you think I'd understand?"

"There was no point," I say. "I'm not that person anymore."

"But you are. You're *him*. Looking at you, I can see it."

"See what? That I'm a convicted felon? That I live in one of the worst neighborhoods in Manhattan? I can't drive, or vote, or even leave the fucking state. You put me down on paper, Avery, and you'll see I have nothing to offer. My pages do nothing but ruin your book."

"You're wrong," she says. "Maybe people judge books by their covers, like you said, but I don't care, because I happen to *like* graffiti. It's art... real art... the kind that comes from the soul. And if they miss out on the story because of that, because they can't see it, then that's *their* loss and not mine. And besides, books are nothing more than paper and ink, anyway. They're like, dead trees all covered in tattoos, and I happen to think that's beautiful."

I laugh at that as I stand up straight. "So *that's* why you came here? To tell me you know who I am?"

"Yes." Her voice is suddenly small. "And to get a tattoo, if you'll still do it."

I contemplate that. "Why?"

"Why what?"

"Why do you want a tattoo?"

She pauses, and I stare at her, awaiting her answer. She never wanted one before, and I'm not going to ink her if she's only doing this for a reason to be here.

"Because," she says quietly, "I want something that's me, and I know where to find it now."

"Where?"

"With you." She looks at me, expression guarded. "You said you'd help me find it, and you did. I want what's in you."

I'm not sure exactly what to make of those words. The cynical part of me wants to call bullshit, to send her out the door, back to the Upper Westside where she belongs with her family, but there's still that other part of me that wonders... does she *really* belong there?

She fit into my life with such ease. She's never been like the others. The only person standing here who has judged, and ridiculed, and condemned me, is... well... *me*. I did it to myself.

A few seconds pass before I nod down the hall, toward my workspace. "After you, I guess."

Avery hesitates, like she expected me to reject her, and ducks her head shyly as she marches past me. A small smile flickers upon my lips, drowned out quickly by a noise from the receptionist's desk. "Psst! Reece! Psst!"

I don't look that way, turning to leave the lobby as I mutter, "Mind your own business, Eleanor."

Avery stands just inside the room, wringing her hands together. She looks nervous, just as most other first timers do when they find themselves here with me, ready to face the needle.

I stride past her, plopping down on my stool as I motion toward the tattoo chair. "Have a seat."

It's positioned down as far as it will go, spread out flat like a cushioned table. Avery slides up on it, her feet still touching the floor. I wheel my stool close to her, our knees brushing together. "What do you want?"

"Whatever you give me."

A chill rolls through me at those words. The pleasure of creative freedom, of being able to do anything I dream, to possess and alter any way I see fit, is second only to the thrill of *her* being my canvas. Her body is her art, her skin and bones and muscles from head-to-toe the way she expresses herself, and here she is, offering it all to me, offering to let me mark her in a way nobody has ever marked her before.

That's what I wanted the very first time I saw her... to be the one to leave the permanent mark. I just didn't realize the mark she left on me would run even deeper. She's offering me her body, when she has already altered my soul.

"Are you sure about that?" I ask quietly, seriously. "I need you to be certain."

"I am."

"Because tattoos are forever," I continue. "You can try to remove them, but they'll always leave some kind of mark behind. You don't want to wake up tomorrow with regrets."

"I'm sure," she says. "I want you to leave your mark on me."

I slowly scan her. "Where do you want it?"

"Anywhere you want to stick it."

My eyes meet hers, curious if she realizes how that sounds, and see the small smirk lifting the corner of her lips. Shaking my head, I chuckle and stand up. "You're a brave soul, Aphrodite, putting your faith in a man like me. I could tattoo a penis on your left ass cheek, for all you know."

"I trust you," she says. "You'll only give me what you truly think I need."

Smart woman.

Brave as fuck, almost to the point of stupidity. *Almost*. But she makes up for it in confidence, because she knows I wouldn't do anything to harm her.

"What the lady wants, the lady gets," I say, motioning toward my box of cassette tapes. "Pick your music and we'll get started."

"Oh no," she says, shaking her head. "It's your art, remember? You pick it."

Huh. I pull the box of cassettes out and shift through them, snatching one toward the bottom—one nobody, in all my years of tattooing, has ever picked. It has no case, the words worn off the clear plastic cassette. Nobody has ever even asked me what's on the seemingly blank tape, no one curious enough to take a chance on it.

Music tells me a lot about people, and the fact that nobody ever inquired about it told me none of them were willing to take a blind risk. They follow logic, choosing rationally. But where is the curiosity? Where is the intuition? Where is following your heart instead of your head?

I put the tape in the boombox and press play. The methodic sound of electronica music echoes through the room, drums merging with synthesizers and keyboards, the occasional orchestra instrument mixing in. I walk over and quietly close the door, giving the two of us some privacy, before setting to work. I prepare my station, pulling out a wide array of ink, just in case I need it.

I walk around behind her, my hand slowly reaching for her, but I pause when my fingertips just graze the skin of her back.

She shivers at the sensation.

"Do you mind?" I ask, running my fingers beneath the fabric of her dress as it dips along her side, exposing her back.

"Go ahead," she says. "I don't think you can tattoo without touching me."

True, but I still feel the need to ask permission. I slip my hands beneath the fabric, pushing the dress forward and down her arms. She helps, slipping her arms out of the holes, exposing the top half of her as the fabric falls to her lap.

"Lay down on your stomach," I say softly. "This way maybe your tits won't distract me."

Avery laughs, blushing, and lays down on the table, situating herself. The dress barely covers any of her body, riding up along her thighs. I finish getting her ready and retake my seat on my stool, shifting it closer as I raise it up some, and grab a pair of black gloves to slip them on.

"This is going to hurt," I warn her. "It'll feel like little scratches at first, and there might be some burning and sharp stings, but I'll be as gentle as possible."

"It'll be worth it," she says, resting her head on her arms as she gazes at me. "Besides, I have a pretty high pain tolerance."

Despite her words, I see her body tense when I turn on the tattoo machine, the monotonous buzzing filling the air, mixing with the music. Reaching over, I slowly rub her back to get her to relax. I stare at her, letting the music wash through me, trying to conjure up some inspiration and imagine something good enough to eternally be inked onto her perfect skin.

Once she seems at ease, I dab the needle in the black ink and press it to the center of her back. She inhales sharply, gritting her teeth as the needle penetrates the top layer of skin. I glance at her, making sure she's okay, before focusing all of my attention on my work.

I lose myself easily, slipping into a trance as the beat of the music burrows beneath my armored skin. It pumps through my bloodstream, fueling me on and setting my rhythm. I freehand the curved black lines on her back, along her spine, just between her sculpted shoulder blades. I ink randomly, erratically, the collective jumble of strokes and marks coming together to form a sleek abstract figure.

I switch the needles out, giving her a brief reprieve as I flip the tape over and start the music again. My eyes drift to hers as I smile softly. "You okay?"

"Yes," she whispers. "Are you done now?"

I chuckle. "Not even close."

She returns my smile as I settle back on my stool to delve into the colors. I work fluidly then, shadowing and shading, the pink, green, blue, white, and purple bleeding together. The colors blur around the edges, coming together as they run past the pre-marked lines. Her skin is irritated, screaming at me angrily by the time I finish, but I've never been so damn proud of a piece of art before.

It reminds me of a time, a time long ago, when I stood across the street from a certain dance studio, watching as they discovered the art I spray-painted from the door to the windows.

I wipe the tattoo, washing the excess ink away and soothing her skin the best I can right now as I admire it. A tinge of nervousness bubbles up inside of me.

If she hates it, we're both fucked.

I flip off the machine, the buzzing dying. Pushing my stool back, I motion toward the mirror. "Tell me what you think... honestly."

Avery climbs to her feet, her dress falling to her ankles when she lets go of it, propriety be damn. She steps right out of it, discarding it on the floor, and heads straight for the mirror. I hold my breath as she turns around, peering over her shoulder at her reflection.

An abstract ballerina, swaddled in color, messy but graceful, like a watercolor portrait of *her*.

Seconds pass, strained seconds of silence as she stares at the tattoo, before she whispers the words, "it's beautiful."

I stand up, pulling my gloves off and discarding them as I approach her. "You think so?"

"I do." Her eyes bore into the mirror, studying her image. "I love it, Reece."

Pausing in front of her, I gently place my hand on her hip before leaning down and lightly kissing the crook of her neck. "And I love you."

Avery turns to me quickly. "What?"

"You heard me," I say. "I didn't set out to, but along the way it happened. I fell in love with you, and I don't know what to do about it."

"What do you *want* to do about it?" she asks, trying to contain the grin that threatens to split her face.

"Considering the fact that you're standing in front of me, damn near naked? I'd say what I want to do about it puts that night in the dance studio to shame." I lean closer, my lips near her ear. "I'd throw you down on that table right now and fuck you so hard the bartender across the street would hear you scream."

Her breath hitches. "What's stopping you?"

"It would be *slightly* unprofessional to fuck up your brand new tattoo."

She laughs as she grabs her dress to cover herself, the mention of her tattoo once more drawing her attention to it in the mirror. I have to give her some credit—she most certainly has a high pain tolerance. She shows little discomfort at the moment, despite the fact that it has to feel raw, tight and sore like sunburn.

"How do I take care of it?" she asks. "I don't want ruin it."

"Keep it moisturized but let it breathe," I say. "I recommend something like A&D ointment the first forty-eight hours, then switch to a fragrance-free plain lotion after that."

She reaches her arm behind her, flinching for the first time this afternoon, her fingertips skimming the edges of it. "I can't reach all of it."

"Huh, and here I remember you being quite bendy."

"I'm flexible, yeah, but I'm not a contortionist."

"I can help, uh… rub you down," I say as I lean back against the tattoo table. "What are you doing this weekend?"

"Uh, I don't know," she says, her brow furrowing as she redresses. "It's weird, but for the first time in my life, I have nothing to do. I have nothing scheduled. I have no plan... and not just for the weekend. *Forever.* I always assumed I would join a ballet company, but I just... I don't know. I have a B.F.A. from Juilliard, and I have no idea what to do with it."

"What do you want to do?"

"I'm not sure," she says, contemplating that for a moment as she laughs. "Nobody's ever asked me that before. I've never even had to think about it. What now?"

What now? It's a damn good question; one I remember asking myself long ago. I still haven't quite figured it out so many years later.

"Well, I can't answer that," I say, "but I might be able to help you with the more immediate future. Lexie and I are heading to Jersey this weekend to the dinosaur park for a sleepover, if you're interested."

"A sleepover? At a dinosaur park?"

"Yep. A whole night of sleeping under the stars, Jurassic Park style. Tents, sleeping bags, campfires, robotic dinosaurs... it doesn't get much better than that."

"Sounds fun," she says. "I'm in... that is, if Lexie's okay with it. It's been a while since I saw her. She might not want me there."

"Are you kidding me?" I say. "You like her dinosaurs. That kind of friendship transcends time, Aphrodite. That's the shit that makes best friends forever."

She smiles widely. "I'll pack a bag."

"Sounds great."

"So, uh, how much for the Hatfield original?"

I shake my head. "No charge."

"But—"

"Don't worry about it," I say. "It was my pleasure."

"You're sure? It's beautiful, Reece. It's worth a lot."

"Positive," I say, reaching over and cupping her chin. "Besides, I did nothing but add some character. You were already a masterpiece."

She smiles, sheepishly, as I lean down and lightly kiss her lips, again and again.

"So what are you doing now?" she whispers between pecks.

"Kissing you."

"Well, I know it won't be nearly as much fun as this, but how would you like to go to a party with me?"

I kiss her once more before pulling back completely. "A party?"

She nods. "You don't have to. I just thought—"

"Are you kidding me?" I cut her off, putting my arm around her. "It's a Moore party. There will probably be cupcakes and ice cream and bouncy houses galore. I wouldn't miss that shit for the world."

Eighteen

I lounge back on the couch, haphazardly flipping through channels on the television, not paying much attention to any of it. It's the middle of the afternoon, and the bright summer sunshine streams through the living room windows, splashing the wooden floor with patches of golden glow that dance around as Lexie pulls on the curtain. Her attention is focused outside, so fixated on the busy Manhattan street that she hasn't even noticed I've turned off her cartoons.

"What time is it, Daddy?"

I don't even look at the clock. "About two minutes later than the last time you asked."

She twirls around the curtain, not paying attention to it, and wounds it so tight around her she nearly bows the rod. "What about now?"

"Same," I answer. "Just add another thirty seconds."

She's quiet for a few minutes, moving from the window to the next one. "What time is it now, Daddy?"

"About five minutes later, give or take."

"Give or take what?"

"A minute or so."

"How much does that make?"

"Uh, about a quarter after."

She stomps her foot, glaring at me. "That's too much math!"

I laugh, glancing at the clock. "It's one-seventeen."

"Thank you." She emphasizes the words, like she's had to pull teeth to get the answer out of me. Turning back to the window, she hits the curtain, twirling it around her arm, as she surveys the neighborhood. "Oh, she's here! Daddy! Daddy! She's here!"

Lexie bats the curtain out of her way and sprints for the door, excitedly jumping up and down. Within a minute, it's shoved open, Avery stepping through, carrying her black duffel bag, still wearing her dance clothes. The black leotard clings tightly to her form, while the oversized gray sweat pants are rolled down at the waist and shoved up to her knees. I scan her quickly, seeing her skin is sweaty, her cheeks flushed, hair falling out of the bun on top of her head. She looks stunning, even a sweaty mess, but the look on her face distracts me from my admiration.

She looks upset.

My stomach drops.

It has been a hard road the past few months, full of nothing but roadblocks and disappointments for Avery. Audition after audition have led to nowhere, shot down and turned away over and over again. Too short, too curvy, too old, too young... *too damn everything and not enough of what they want.* The traditional ballet companies turned her away, saying she's too contemporary, judging her when they see the hint of her tattoo along her spine, while more modern dancers snub her as being just too classically trained.

She's spent the past few weeks working on a new start-up choreography project for a measly few hundred bucks a week. Chump-change in Manhattan, barely enough for her to survive, although it's doable. I know. I've done it. Today is do-or-die, though, the last day of the project, where the dancers are either dismissed or given offers. She's been gone since sunrise, giving me hope, but the look on her face hints the other way.

"Bad news," she whispers, looking right at me.

I can barely find my voice. "What?"

"Bridgette and Johnny broke up."

It takes a moment for me to make sense of what the hell she's saying. I shake my head dramatically. "Tragic."

"Avery!" Lexie grabs her pant leg and tugs, nearly pulling them down to try to get her attention. "Did you get it? Huh?"

Avery glances down at Lexie and stares at her in stone cold silence for a moment before the biggest, brightest smile cracks her expression, lighting up her face. "Yep."

Lexie squeals loudly, jumping and clapping. "We did it!"

"We did it."

Avery drops her duffel bag to the floor, not even bothering to close the front door as she jumps around with Lexie, the two of them chanting those words. I toss the remote down and stand up, strolling over to them. I push the door closed before grasping a hold of Avery's hips and pulling her to me. Laughing, she wraps her arms around my neck, gazing at me as Lexie runs around us.

"Congratulations," I say. "You did it."

"*We* did it," she corrects me as Lexie continues to chant those words. "If it weren't for you, it never would've happened. You've been so supportive. And I know it's not the best job out there... it's just a dancing gig, but it's on Broadway, and it's making triple what I am now, so I can help more."

"It's wonderful," I say, leaning down and kissing her softly. "*You're* wonderful."

Lexie makes an exaggerated gagging noise, forcing herself between the two of us when I kiss Avery again. She pushes Avery's legs, separating her and me, protectively standing in front of Avery as if to keep her all to herself. "Daddy, can we get ice cream to celebrate?"

"Yeah, Daddy," Avery says playfully, reaching down and running her hands through Lexie's hair, brushing the wayward locks back from her forehead. "Can we have some ice cream?"

"After dinner," I say. "We have plans tonight, remember?"

Both girls make faces at me at the reminder. I laugh, holding my hands up defensively. "Hey, don't blame me. I'll gladly cancel."

Lexie cheers, but Avery dashes her excitement quickly. "Ugh, yeah, we can't cancel. We cancelled last time."

"And the time before that," I point out. "And basically every other time they've invited us."

Dinner with the Moores. Avery used to meet her parents at

least once a week, but since moving in with me after graduation, the visits have become few and far in between. They haven't completely cut her off, not like mine did, but I wouldn't exactly call them *proud parents.*

Sighing, Avery glances down at Lexie and theatrically frowns. "Guess ice cream has to wait."

The girls run off to start getting ready as I plop back down on the couch and pick up the remote again. Once more I flip through channels, wasting time, until the bathroom clears out and I can slip in the room and sneak in a quick shower. I wash up and dress, putting about as much effort into it as I usually do. I learned long ago that I will never win Avery's father's approval and have stopped trying to impress him. Or anyone. If who I am isn't good enough for them, then that's their problem.

I am who I am.

Slipping on a clean pair of jeans and a long-sleeved black shirt, I grab my black and white Adidas sneakers and stroll back to the living room. Avery stands there, wearing a simple black top, slightly low cut in both the front and back, showing off a hint of cleavage and the top of her tattoo. I smile, my eyes surveying her as I walk past, my gaze lingering on the swell of her ass in a pair of skin-tight hot pink pants. "Your father's going to have a coronary."

"If he hasn't had one yet, I think we'll be okay," she says. "No shock is ever going to top me moving in with you."

"That sounds kind of like a challenge," I say, taking a seat on the couch. "I accept."

Avery laughs, slipping on a pair of black flat shoes. Lexie comes bounding into the room, slightly more dressed up than the two of us, having picked out her own outfit—the frilliest pink tutu skirt, a gift from Avery's mother, paired with black leggings and a black-and-white polka dotted shirt, topped off with a pair of tan cowboy boots. *Everyone needs cowboy boots,* she told me, *in case they need to ride a horse someday.*

Who am I to argue with that logic?

"Looking snazzy," Avery says, holding her hand up for Lexie to high-five it. "Want me to braid your hair?"

"Yes, please."

They sit beside me as Avery quickly puts Lexie's hair in French braided pigtails. When she finishes, Lexie runs off to look in the mirror as Avery turns to me. Laughing, she reaches over and runs her hand along the side of my neck. "You must've been painting today."

"This morning."

"You missed some paint." She gently scratches at it with her nails, flaking it from my skin. "There."

"Let's go!" Lexie says, running out of the bathroom and heading straight for the front door. "I'm hungry!"

Dinner is at a French restaurant in the theater district. We arrive a few minutes past seven, after Avery's parents are already seated. The restaurant is upscale, with elaborate gold-toned walls and a high ceiling, the carpet trimmed with gold and matching the soft burgundy booths. Vibrant white tablecloths cover the long tables, fine china and crystal wine glasses at each place setting, along with an array of silverware. I eye it as we follow the hostess through the place, clutching my daughter's hand tightly, keeping her at my side.

I cast Avery a wary look when we reach the booth, motioning for her to slip in first.

This is a disaster waiting to happen.

After Avery is situated, I motion for Lexie to climb in next. I sit on the end, the booth so long the three of us fit comfortably.

Before anyone can even speak, I snatch the wine glass and knives from in front of Lexie and hold it all out just as a waiter arrives. "You'll want to do something with this, unless you want your stuff broken or someone stabbed."

He takes it all, nodding stiffly, and promptly disappears again.

Greetings are polite, albeit a little forced, except for the one Avery's mother offers Lexie. I don't mind getting the cold shoulder so much anymore... this is for Avery, and I tolerate it for her, knowing Laurence only tolerates me for the same reason.

The waiter returns once more, this time to distribute menus and offer complementary wine. Avery declines unsurprisingly... her parents have no idea she drinks, another aspect of her life she's kept secret.

Heaven forbid she be a normal young woman.

I happily take some, knowing the alcohol will soothe my nerves, while Laurence scoffs at the very offer. His wife, however, indulges in a bit, despite her husband's look of distress at the very idea.

It's not like he has to fucking pay for it. The shit is *free.*

"My wife and I will have water," Laurence says.

"Me, too," Avery chimes in. "Reece?"

"Yeah, water's fine for us, too."

As soon as the words are out of my mouth, Lexie grabs my sleeve and tugs. "Can I have a Coke, Daddy? Please?"

"Make that a Coke for her."

Who am I to deny her when she asked so nicely? So, okay, whatever... maybe it's not *good* for her. Maybe I shouldn't give her soda, or put chocolate in her pancakes, or give the girl fake tattoos. But I do. That's me. That's the kind of father I am. And yeah, I have flaws, but whatever I lack, I make up in love.

And with as much love as I have?

I'm hoping it's impossible for me to fuck her up too bad.

Avery chats with her parents as I pick up my menu and relax back in the booth, staring at it. Half of it is in French, very little explanation about what it is, while the rest is about as appetizing to me as shit pulled straight from a garbage bin.

This is going to be a long dinner.

Lexie follows my lead, mimicking me, her expression dead serious as she studies her menu. I smirk, cutting my eyes at her, speaking quietly so not to interrupt the others' conversation. "See anything you like, Little Miss?"

"I dunno," she whispers back. "What's it say?"

"Your guess is as good as mine, kid."

She points at the menu as she props it against the table in her lap, her finger scanning the words. "What's that?"

"Bigeye tuna tartare," I read. "It's raw tuna."

"Can they cook it without the big eyes?"

I chuckle. "They don't cook it... it's served raw." I point out the entire sushi section. "That's all raw, too."

She scrunches up her nose and moves onto something else.

"What's this?"

"Haricots verts."

"Does that mean it's gots hair?"

"Uh, I don't know what it means. It's French."

"Why's it French?"

"Because this is a French restaurant."

"Oh." She scans the menu some more, pausing when she comes to a word she knows. "Oh, cheese! I like cheese! Daddy, what's that other word?"

I glance at it. *Selection of Artisanal Cheeses.* "Artisanal."

"What kind of cheese is that?"

"The kind for anal artists," I mutter.

A bark of laughter echoes from where Avery sits. She covers her mouth with her hand, cutting her eyes at the two of us, before looking back at her father. He's rattling on and on about something, words that sound to me like they could've come straight off the menu, but I gather from the context they're ballet terms. The waiter returns with our drinks, setting the thick heavy glass filled with ice and soda on the table in front of Lexie.

"You don't have any cups with lids?" I ask. "Straws, maybe?"

"I can get you a straw."

"Thank you."

The waiter walks off, returning swiftly with a small red straw, the kind used to stir a drink. I sigh, taking it. It would cause even more problems than it solved.

The second the waiter asks if we're ready to order, Lexie drops her menu and shouts out, "chicken nuggets!"

The women at the table laugh, while I shake my head and skim through the menu. "Bring her the lobster mac 'n cheese."

"What's lobster?" Lexie asks, gaze going right back to her menu as she seeks it out.

"It's, uh… it's seafood, like crab."

"What's crab?"

I was about to say 'it's like shrimp' when the waiter interjects. "Like Sebastian, from *The Little Mermaid*. He's a crab."

Lexie's eyes widen. I groan. The waiter looks pretty proud of himself for dumbing it down to a kid's level, while I want to punch him in the throat for those words.

"I can't eat Sebastian!" Lexie shouts. "Daddy, I don't want that!"

Avery chimes in quickly. "Can we get the mac 'n cheese plain? No lobster? No, uh... *Sebastian?*"

"Absolutely," the waiter says, clearing his throat as he mutters, "Sorry."

Avery orders a grilled chicken salad with extra chicken, while her father orders the same thing minus the chicken. Avery's mother asks for the bigeye tuna tartare, laughing when Lexie asks her if she'll eat the eyes with it.

When it's my turn, I hand the menu over to the waiter and order salmon with the haricot verts for the hell of it. I planned on getting a crab cake, but I won't dare order that in front of my daughter now.

"So, I have some news," Avery says, folding her hands in her lap. "I had an audition today and got the part."

Laurence's question is immediate. "What's the part?"

"It's just a small dancing gig, in a musical," she says. "It's a swing part, and I have a shot at being dance captain someday."

"A swing part?" Laurence says. "We sent you to Juilliard so you could come out and be someone's backup in a musical?"

Avery blanches, and I start to interject, to point out that she's worked her ass off for the part, when Lexie snatches up her glass to take a drink. I see it happening seconds before it tilts, unbalancing, and slips through her small fingers. I stall, mid-word, and quickly snatch up the glass the second she tips it over. Soda splashes out, an ice cube landing on her leg. Setting the glass back down on the table, I snatch up the cloth napkin and wipe her lap.

The commotion stalls the conversation. By the time Laurence focuses back on his daughter, her mother is chiming in, smiling sweetly. "That's wonderful, honey. We'll have to get tickets."

Avery returns her smile, nodding, and says nothing else.

"Sorry, Daddy," Lexie says, picking up the ice cube and shrugging as she pops it in her mouth, chomping loudly on it.

"It's okay, Little Miss," I say, leaving the napkin in her lap. Knowing her, she'll do it again. "Accidents happen."

Dinner is one of the longest hours of my life. When our food finally arrives, Lexie refuses to eat her mac 'n cheese, just in case any *Sebastian* just happens to be in it, and we're both less than thrilled to discover *haricot verts* is French for green beans. I ignore my food while she steals chicken right out of Avery's salad, ignorant to the tension that seems to be mounting as time goes on.

I breathe a sigh of relief when dinner is over. I clutch Lexie's hand again, leading her straight for the exit, and wait out on the curb for the others to join us. Avery bids her parents goodnight, kissing her father's cheeks and hugging her mother before they climb into a waiting town car.

"Well, that was about as painful as I expected," Avery says, turning to me. "Next time, we cancel, instead of coming to *Château de stuck up food.*"

"Now you're speaking my language," I say playfully, nudging her. "But it wasn't so bad."

"Not so bad?"

"Nah, we learned a lot, at least. Isn't that right, Little Miss?"

Lexie stands in front of me, holding the napkin she—for some godforsaken reason—decided to steal. "I learned French people give you little blankets with dinner!" She waves the napkin at us. "And *hairy words* are really green beans, and artists have their own cheeses, even though Daddy's an artist and he doesn't eat that kind of cheese. Oh! And I learned not to eat mac 'n cheese no more."

I stare at my daughter, shaking my head as she swings the napkin around, twirling it like a scarf. I turn to Avery, cocking an eyebrow at her. "Having regrets yet, Aphrodite?"

"Nope." She wraps her arm around me, slipping her hand into mine as she leans her head against my shoulder. "Never."

"Ice cream now?" Lexie asks, turning to them. "It's after dinner."

"Sounds good to me." I wave her on. "Lead the way."

We head to a small ice cream parlor on Broadway, a little shop tucked in on a block corner. Just down the street, people are lined up at Pinkberry, waiting outside the door.

Never going to that place again.

Lexie runs straight to the counter, pressing her hands to the plastic and peering down at the various flavors of ice cream. "Three scoops!"

"One scoop," I say, strolling over to pause behind her, still holding Avery's hand.

"Two?" she negotiates. "Please?"

"Fine. Two. But I get to eat some of yours."

Lexie makes a face at me. Her negotiations didn't go as planned this time. "Fine! Cookies 'n cream and bubblegum! With whipped cream and nuts and hot fudge and—"

"That's plenty."

"And a cherry!" Lexie grins at the boy working. "Thank you."

"You want anything?" I ask Avery.

"Hmmm…" Her eyes trail over the tubs of ice cream. "Vanilla. In a cone."

A second worker rings up the order while the teenage boy fixes the ice cream. I pay, stuffing most of the change in the tip jar. I hold a quarter out to Lexie. "Here."

She grabs it excitedly and scurries over toward the door, dropping to her knees in front of the little red quarter machines. She sticks the coin in the slot and tries to turn it, but it won't budge.

I pull away from Avery and walk over to help her. I twist the handle, the pink sparkly bouncy ball sliding right out. Lexie snatches it, bouncing it before I can warn her, and sets off chasing after it through the shop. She'll lose it in less than five minutes.

Please don't fucking throw it and break something.

Shaking my head, I scan the other machines, hesitating before slipping a second quarter into another slot. I turn it, the small plastic egg popping out.

"Ice cream," Avery calls out, holding up the little cup piled high with everything Lexie asked for… including the cherry. Lexie runs that way, grabbing her ice cream, as I slide the plastic egg into my pocket.

"You want some, Daddy?" Lexie asks, holding a clump of it out on her spoon. It's all mixed together already. It looks like bad art.

"Yeah, no, I'll pass on that monstrosity, thanks."

We stroll along Broadway in no hurry after that, taking in the bright lights and chaos of the city, as they happily eat their ice cream. Someday I'll see Avery's name here, I think. Someday she'll be more than just somebody's backup.

I know it.

I believe it.

I believe in *her*.

Reaching into my pocket, I pull out the plastic egg and hold it out to Avery. "Here, this is for you…"

"Aw, you shouldn't have." She grins, snatching it from me. She pops it open, pulling out the little ring, the adjustable winding band colorfully woven like a rainbow. "It's beautiful!"

"It's not much, but it's all I have right now. It's all I can afford. Literally. I just used my last quarter."

Avery laughs.

"But someday I'll have more," I continue, "and when I do, I promise you… it's yours, Avery."

She stares at me in silence, her eyes drifting to the little plastic ring. She nods subtly as she slips it on her ring finger, holding it up to look at it in the moonlight. "I don't need more, Reece."

"Maybe not, but you deserve more, and I'm going to give it to you." I smirk, leaning down to kiss her. "Even if I *seriously* have to pawn my boombox and sell a kidney to do it."

Finale

The metal ball rattled inside the canister as he shook it, stirring up the fresh black paint. His hand was wrapped around it, his pointer finger pressed against the cap as he stared at the wall of the shop in front of him, at the mediocre mural his friend once painted.

Almost a year had passed since that day, and he still hadn't figured out what the white blob in the mural was supposed to be. All that his friend would say was 'it is what it is'.

And what it was, he thought, was something that needed fixed. Maybe it was a cloud, a sheep, or a marshmallow... but at that moment all he saw was a blank canvas.

Maybe that had really been his friend's intention.

Aiming the nozzle, he pressed down, hearing the distinct hiss as the paint came out. It was instinct, as his hand followed a pattern it would never forget, drawing the outline of the shape he knew as well as his own signature. It *had* been his signature, once upon a time, the way he signed his art while still remaining anonymous.

Until he wasn't anonymous anymore.

Hatter.

He used to think the life he wanted was impossible, that he'd fallen too far, done too much to ever make right what had somehow gone terribly wrong. But like the real Hatter would tell you, the one from the storybooks: it's only impossible if you believe it so.

He didn't believe that anymore.

He got everything he dreamed of: a blank canvas,

a clean slate to start over.

His hand moved swiftly, expertly, filling in the white space in the center, completing the black silhouette of the figure in the top hat. He lowered the spray can when it was finished and stared at it, the intoxicating scent of paint fumes heavy in the air around him.

It felt a bit like déjà vu, but he knew it wasn't. This was nothing like before.

He wouldn't fuck up again.

He had too much to live for.

He couldn't make those same mistakes anymore.

Acknowledgements

This story is unlike any story I've ever written, so if you've stuck with it this far without throwing it against the wall and shouting 'what is this shit,' thank you. Thank you for taking a chance on the tortured artist and his crazy little miss.

Thanks to Sarah Anderson, who read this story from the very beginning and assured me that it's okay if nobody gets kidnapped… or dies… or is seriously maimed. You assured me that not every story needs violence or tragedy or even seriously heavy angst. So thank you, from the bottom of my heart, for looking at this story and seeing the worth in it, worth my self-doubt made it hard to see. I couldn't ask for a better writing buddy.

To Nicki Bullard, my best friend, the greatest book signing assistant imaginable. So many of our adventures end up in my stories… none of this would be what it is without your friendship. I love you.

To my family, for their unending support, and to my friends, all like three of you. You are absolutely amazing. You make me who I am.

To Charlie Keller, who graces this gorgeous cover. The moment I saw you, I knew you'd make a perfect Reece. I just had no idea how much so. You're an amazing human being. To Tyler Seielstad, who took the photo that graces this gorgeous cover. You're extremely talented and I'm lucky to have gotten the chance to use some of your work.

I should also thank Brandon, my tattoo artist at Skin Prick City in Fayetteville, NC. It's hard, putting trust in someone to mark you permanently. I'm so very grateful I stumbled upon you.

Special thanks to Michelle Harper Collins for the reading this bad boy for me at crunch time. You're awesome.

Made in the USA
Middletown, DE
26 June 2015